Cowboy True

Cowboy True

A Tangled Up in Texas Romance

Michelle Beattie

TULE
PUBLISHING

Chapter One

WHEN FAITH STONE made up her mind, she stuck with it. So, despite her galloping heartbeat and sweaty palms, she kept her foot on the gas pedal. Well, she did slow down when her car crested the hill, but who could blame her? The Texas Hill Country was gorgeous.

Acres of tidy, clipped grapevines marched on both sides of the highway. Wine tasting attracted tourists from not only all over the state but also the country. But the region had more to offer than award-winning wines.

Rolling hills of fields that, even with the bluebonnets done for the year, burst with wildflowers. From the red, orange, and yellow Indian blanket that, at a distance, resembled the kind of woven fabric people paid to buy, to the pink evening primroses and brown-eyed susans. Color abounded.

Fields and pastures from the numerous farms and ranches took advantage of the area's rich soil. Faith loved seeing the red barns that dotted the countryside and the horses and cattle that seemed content to soak up the sunshine of a warm spring day.

Unfortunately, even the postcard-worthy scenery wasn't enough to distract her from what was coming. From the inevitable conversation she was driving from San Antonio to have.

With a man she hadn't been able to stop thinking about in months. Or, truth be told, a man she hadn't been able to stop thinking about since high school. Which, given they'd graduated six years ago, was kinda pathetic.

Although, in her defense, she'd managed to tuck away her memories of him for the most part. Until that night three months ago, she'd only thought of Gage Granger when she was really tired or lonely, or the odd times when she had a little too much to drink. And, okay, maybe every time she kissed a guy, but she'd managed to move on—mostly.

She'd made a life for herself in San Antonio. Maybe it wasn't the exciting life she'd lain awake at night envisioning as a child, but it was a good life. She had a full-time job at a nice restaurant on the river walk. She'd worked her way up from waitress to supervisor. She had a little savings and good friends.

And she wasn't anyone's damn burden.

Faith shook her head. She'd moved out of her grand-mother's house six years ago. One would think that would be long enough to get over the past. But that baggage just kept hanging around. Like a recurring dream she had where she wanted to go swimming, but no matter how many times she took her clothes off to put on her bathing suit, the clothes just reappeared. Yeah, that was her past with her grandma. No matter how much she tried to shed it, it just kept sticking to her.

Of course, with having to go home for the obligatory holidays and birthdays, it wasn't surprising she couldn't let go the past. And it wasn't surprising it was on her mind today, given that she'd be staying at her grandma's tonight—

and possibly tomorrow night if she chickened out before telling Gage.

"Not going to happen," Faith said aloud, her voice filling the inside of her car.

And, to prove to herself she was going to go through with it, she pushed the gas pedal a little harder, despite the fact her belly felt like a Rubik's Cube in the hands of an expert trying to solve the puzzle within seconds. It kept twisting this way and that, up, down, and sideways.

If she'd been smart, she wouldn't have veered off Interstate 10 onto Highway 87. She'd have gone straight to Last Stand before she made herself nauseous. But it was slower going off the interstate, and though she'd made the decision to do this, she was suddenly desperate for more time.

A decade ought to do it.

She sagged against her seat. She'd get through this, just like she'd gotten through the years living with her grandmother. Then she'd go back to her life in San Antonio.

Hoping that mantra stuck with her once she reached Last Stand, Faith reached into the console and grabbed a random CD. Since her old Camry didn't have Bluetooth, and she didn't want to kill her cell battery by running through her playlist, she kept a selection of her favorites in her car.

Pulling out a case, she flipped it open. She fumbled with getting the disc out. It slid from her fingers when it popped free. Glancing over, she caught it before it fell to the floor.

It didn't take more than a second or two to grasp the disc and slide it into the player, but when she shifted her gaze back to the road, her heart leapt in her throat as a blur of yellow fur dashed out of the ditch.

"Shit!"

Faith slammed on the brakes, yanking the wheel to the right. Her car shuddered. The rest was whirling colors and distorted images as her vehicle skidded sideways into the ditch. Dirt and grass scraped her undercarriage. Faith clung to the wheel as she bumped and jerked like she was on some amusement park ride. An ominous thud filled her ears. Then, with one last hard knock against the driver's door, she lurched to a stop.

For a moment, she didn't move. She remained still, her eyes pinched closed, while her breathing echoed loudly within the confines of the car. Holy crap. What just happened?

She wasn't sure how long she sat there, her head leaning against the driver's window. But when she finally dared open her eyes, her breathing sounded as though she were hyperventilating. Aware the engine was still running, Faith pried her stiff fingers off the steering wheel and turned the key.

The good news was the car hadn't rolled. And the air bags hadn't deployed. So the front end, at least, was fine. And, she realized with a shuddering breath, so was she.

Faith released the seat belt and pushed open the door. She took it as another good sign that it opened without protest.

Unfortunately, when she stepped out of the car and put her weight on her left leg, her knee wasn't as agreeable. A hot stab of pain had her gasping and clasping the top of the door to keep upright.

Balancing on one leg, Faith glanced down at the other. Since she'd dressed in shorts, her knee was easy enough to examine. There wasn't any blood. No bones sticking out where there shouldn't be. It must have just gotten a good banging. Kinda like her head. It was throbbing, too.

She had acetaminophen in her purse and a half-full bottle of water in her cup holder. But it suddenly felt like too much effort to reach onto the floor—her handbag had gotten knocked off the seat—and grasp it. Of course, the fact that she suddenly felt light-headed didn't help any.

"I'll just sit a minute."

Instead of inside the car, Faith dropped to the grass. Sitting between her vehicle and the open door, she bent her right leg and pressed her forehead to her thigh. She smelled the vanilla bean body butter she'd rubbed on after her shower that morning. She concentrated on that to keep her stomach from pitching out the candy bar she'd eaten after she'd stopped for gas.

The odds of keeping it down were swinging in her favor when she heard the sound of an approaching vehicle.

"Please keep going," she muttered. While she was starting to feel better, she was still shaky and she'd prefer not to deal with anyone, even a well-meaning Good Samaritan, until she felt stronger.

But as luck would have it, the vehicle slowed then stopped. Two doors closed. She heard hurried footsteps rush through the long grass. Realizing they couldn't see her since the car had ended up parallel to the road with the passenger side facing the highway, Faith lifted her head and called out, "I'm okay."

She was bracing herself to stand when someone knelt at her side.

Her insides clutched. She knew that cologne. Oh, man, did she know it. Twelve weeks ago, she'd rolled around a bed with a man wearing nothing but that cologne.

Ever since, she'd had vivid dreams—awake and asleep— of how that scent had wrapped around her. How *he'd* wrapped around her. Faith clutched fistfuls of grass. It couldn't be him. It was a popular brand. Loads of men wore it.

Please don't be him.

Besides, he'd have no reason to be there. It wasn't as though she'd called 911—or anyone else had since theirs was the first vehicle she'd heard. So, good. Whew. She still had some time before she faced him.

A warm hand settled lightly on her shoulder. "Faith?"

There'd been many times in her life when Faith had wished she could disappear. Just close her eyes and reappear somewhere else, anywhere else. As anyone else.

She'd never wished for it more than she did right then. Dammit. What was he even doing there?

But as much as she wanted to, she had no means of teleporting, and the longer she avoided looking at him, the more of a coward she'd seem.

Taking a deep breath, Faith turned her head and looked into Gage Granger's green eyes. "Hi."

"Hi yourself." His gaze skimmed her face. "Are you hurt?"

That was when she noticed he was dressed in his navy EMT uniform. And he wasn't alone. There was a woman behind him, also in full uniform. Tall, with her long, dark hair pulled back in a ponytail.

Faith didn't recognize her. As she appeared a little older than her and Gage, either she'd been far enough ahead of Faith in school for their circles not to cross, or she wasn't from Last Stand.

Regardless, the woman wasn't the one looking at her expectantly.

"What are you doing here? Aren't you out of your jurisdiction, county, or whatever?" Faith asked.

"Normally, yes. But we had a patient that needed transporting to San Antonio. We were just on our way back when we spotted your car."

Wasn't that just her luck?

While she had no way of knowing if he wanted to talk about that night at all—not that she had any intention of discussing it in a ditch with his partner right there—he was at least gentleman enough not to bring it up when they didn't have privacy. A knot eased in her stomach.

He settled his arms on his bent knees as though he had all the time in the world. "What happened?"

"I took my eyes off the road for like a second, and when I looked up, this yellow blur came running out of the ditch. I swerved to avoid it, and the next thing I knew, here I was."

He looked from the open door of her car to her. "You didn't get tossed out, did you?"

Even before she answered, his gaze roamed over her. While her head knew he was only looking for injuries, other parts of her remembered how he'd once touched her from head to toe. With more than just his eyes. Or his hands. And damn her treacherous body for wanting him to do it again.

Like, right now.

She swallowed hard. Unfortunately, there was nothing she could do about her beaded nipples.

"No. I was wearing a seat belt. I stepped out once everything stopped spinning. But my knee gave out and I felt nauseous, so I sat down."

"Most likely shock. It's not uncommon after a traumatic event."

Like having sex with the one man she never should have? Yeah, she'd felt sick after that, too. Not because she hadn't enjoyed it or hadn't wanted it. Because she'd wanted it for years, and the reality of being with him like that had surpassed her every fantasy.

But there'd still been regrets. Because time hadn't changed the fact his life was in Last Stand and hers wasn't. Worse, though—much worse—was that by having a one-night stand, she'd done the one thing she'd vowed never to do.

Be anything like her mother.

Although she was fairly certain feelings had never come into play when Linda Stone took a man to her bed. With Faith, the opposite was true. There'd been nothing *but* feelings.

Being close to him now, smelling him and hearing his voice, was twisting her up again. And the longer he was there, the harder it was to breathe. None of which had a damn thing to do with the stress of hitting the ditch.

"Well, it's better now, so I'll just call my grandma and—"

"You're not going anywhere until we're sure you're okay."

Her gaze whipped to his partner. Gage dug in his heels

when he was serious. Or he used to. Other than that night three months ago, she hadn't seen him since high school. But in case he was still that stubborn guy, she'd appeal to his partner. Maybe she'd be easier to convince.

Flashing her brightest smile, Faith said, "I'm fine, really. You don't need to waste your time."

"We have a duty to act on every accident we come across. We can lose our jobs otherwise."

Though it was Gage who'd spoken, Faith kept her eyes on his partner. "Is that true?" she asked.

"Yes, ma'am. It is."

Faith frowned, ruminating on that and trying to find a way out. She'd snuck out of the hotel room that night for a reason. Once the lust had burnt out, she'd once again been the insecure girl she'd been in high school. The one that didn't think she was good enough.

Watching Gage sleep, knowing what they'd done, how she wasn't as different from her mother as she'd always prided herself to be, she'd choked on her own failing.

It had been cowardly to slink off without a saying word. But she'd worked hard to try to build herself up, something she still had to work at on a daily basis, and what she'd done with Gage hadn't just been a step back. It'd felt like a slide down a mountain. And the sooner she got up and started the climb back up, the better. Which was hard to do when he was sitting right there, staring at her.

"You said you have to stop at an accident scene, but do you have to do anything else?"

"Because you didn't call us and we just happened upon you, you can refuse treatment," his partner said.

Gage stared at her. "But we're here. Why don't you let us make sure you're really okay?"

She shifted her gaze to Gage. "I don't need an ambulance."

"Well, while it'd be easier and more comfortable to assess you in it, I can do it right here, too, if it makes you feel better."

Nothing would make her feel better at this point. Not unless she could go back twelve weeks and change the past. Unfortunately, that wasn't possible. And he was being kind, like he'd been in high school, and really, she had no good reason to decline.

Her shoulders drooped. "I suppose that would be okay."

She didn't miss the hurt that passed through his eyes. Yet his tone was gentle when he said, "It'll be painless, I promise."

He pulled a small light from his pocket, leaning forward. "I just want to check your pupils. Look at the light."

His warm breath brushed across his cheeks. Orange Tic Tacs. They'd always been his favorite.

He shifted the light from one eye to the other before lowering it. "Pupils are responsive, that's good."

He circled her wrist with one hand while his eyes focused on the sports watch he wore on the other. His fingers were warm and strong, but neither helped slow her heartbeat, which was thumping faster than a group of Irish dancers.

"It's a bit fast," he said, shifting his gaze to hers. "Might be leftover adrenaline."

The green of his eyes darkened. He didn't believe that any more than she did.

"Yeah, must be," she managed before shifting her eyes away.

Then Gage slid his hand around her neck and whispered, "Lie down."

Her gaze whipped back to his and her heart slammed against her breastbone.

"I need to check the rest of you," he said.

"Right." She gave a jerky nod. "Yeah."

They continued to look at each other as he laid her onto the grass. Her mind flashed back to a hotel room lit only by the streetlights casting a glow through the sheer curtains. She'd watched him then, too, as she'd lain back. As he'd followed her down. Until he'd kissed her eyes closed.

Her tank top and shorts were more than she'd been wearing by the end of that night but somehow, she felt just as naked as she'd been then. Just as exposed.

There was nothing inappropriate about his pat down. He didn't linger unnecessarily, didn't touch inappropriately. It didn't stop goose bumps from breaking out over her skin. Didn't stop the heat from pooling between her thighs.

She jerked when he probed her left knee.

"Ouch!"

He peered down to have a better look. "It's swelling," he said as his fingers swept gently over her flesh. "And there's bruising starting on your kneecap. You must have smacked it against the door or the dash."

"I'm not sure," she answered. "I just know my head hit the window."

He finished examining the knee first. "You'll want a doctor to look at it," he said. "I don't think it's anything more serious than a bruise, but you should get it checked out. Make sure."

"I'll go tomorrow, if it still hurts."

"Or you could go to emergency today," he suggested.

"I could but it's not an emergency. Tomorrow is soon enough to go to the clinic."

He studied her as though he doubted she'd go.

She rolled her eyes. "I promise."

"Okay."

Then, crawling on his knees, Gage moved alongside her body. Kneeling at her shoulder, he slid his fingers into her hair. It brought to mind how he'd buried his face into it when he'd—

She hissed as his fingers found a sensitive spot on her head.

"You've got quite the bump there," he said as he removed his hands from her hair.

"That explains the headache."

"I'll get something for it," the other EMT said.

Faith nearly startled at hearing the woman's voice. She'd been so wrapped up in Gage, she'd forgotten they weren't alone.

She shook her head. Both at herself for being ridiculous and to stop the woman from going to get the medicine.

"Don't bother," she answered. "I've got some in my bag. I just hadn't gotten around to getting it yet. I also have a water bottle in the cup holder."

"I'll get it," Gage said. "If you want to grab an ice pack," he added to his partner.

While the woman went for the pack, Gage fished inside

her car for her handbag and water bottle.

Once he had them, he helped Faith into a sitting position. The other EMT came back with the pack.

Faith looked at the woman's nametag. *Marcella Russo. Paramedic.* Nope, the name didn't ring a bell.

Marcella handed the pack to Gage, who set it on her sore knee.

Faith rummaged through her bag until her fingers closed over the travel-sized container of acetaminophen.

Behind them, a car slowed. No doubt, the driver had seen the ambulance on the side of the road and the car in the ditch and was rubbernecking, as most do when they come upon an accident scene. Although it hadn't been much of an accident.

But it did turn her thoughts to her vehicle. She was almost scared to ask.

Frowning, she looked at her car. "Did I do any damage?"

"I can have a quick peek," Gage said. He walked around the car, the long grass swishing around his legs.

"Your right front tire popped off its rim." Then he bent and his voice drifted from under the car.

"I smell oil. But there's too much grass stuck in your undercarriage to see anything." He stood up, then came around.

Faith grimaced. Smelling oil couldn't be a good thing.

"You should probably get it towed," Gage suggested. "Even if you got the tire fixed, it's probably best to have a mechanic look at it before you drive it."

She'd gotten lucky when she'd found that car. A little old lady was looking to sell it for no reason other than she wanted a newer one in red. With its low mileage and how well it had been taken care of, Faith had felt as though she'd won the car lottery. So what if it didn't have Bluetooth? It had air conditioning, no rust, and would be reliable for years to come.

Plus, it was heads above the rust bucket she'd driven before. A definite step up from the beater she'd worked to buy in high school. Although she had to give that little car credit. It had gotten her out of Last Stand.

Though her Camry might not be the Camaro she'd once dreamed of—she hadn't given up hope of one day owning one—at least she wasn't embarrassed to be seen driving around in it. She no longer felt the need to slouch in the seat when she passed someone she knew.

This was the first trip she'd made back home since buying it. She'd looked forward to showing it off. As a status symbol, it might not be much, but it nonetheless showed she was making progress.

See? Faith Stone could amount to something.

She bowed her head. Having her vehicle dragged on the back of a tow truck was hardly the statement she'd hoped to make. Although in the scheme of things, given her life of late, that was the least of her worries.

Still, she wasn't going to risk causing more damage by being a fool.

"Know of any—"

"Ryker," Gage said immediately. "You won't find anyone better."

Of all Gage's brothers, Faith really only knew Ryker and Cam. She hadn't started spending time with Gage until high school, and by then, his oldest brother Dallas had moved to San Antonio, and the second oldest, Hudson, had left to serve in the Middle East. Though Cam had joined the rodeo and was on the road by her and Gage's sophomore year, he'd been around enough for Faith to have met him.

What she remembered about Cam was a guy who'd always been happy and fun and, even back then, had a swagger and a grin that turned more than one girl's head. Despite being popular and good-looking, he'd never been mean to her. He hadn't gone out of his way to be kind the way Gage had, but Cam had been two years older, and most seniors didn't pay attention to those two years younger.

Ryker had graduated by the time she and Gage were in high school. But even taking his apprenticeship for mechanics, he'd been around the Diamond G enough for Faith get a sense of him. She didn't remember him as having a swagger. Come to think of it, she didn't remember Ryker smiling much, either. Not that he'd ever been mean or rude, just serious.

"If you give me his number, I'll call him."

Gage pulled his phone out of his pocket. "I've got it."

"While you're doing that, I'll let dispatch know what's going on and start the paperwork," Marcella said. She looked at Faith. "You take care."

"I'll be right there," Gage called as his partner trudged up the ditch.

It wasn't a long conversation. Gage gave his brother their location and told him the car wasn't drivable. He also mentioned that Faith would need a ride to her grandmother's before ending the call.

"I could take you in the ambulance, but then you'd get stuck with a bill for medical transport and as you're mostly fine, there's no sense in that."

No, there wasn't. And she appreciated his thoughtfulness.

"Thanks."

He looked into her eyes. "I wasn't sure I'd ever see you again."

Well, if she'd had her way, he wouldn't have. But when had life ever played nice?

"This wasn't something I'd planned."

Again, hurt clouded his eyes. "So, if you hadn't hit the ditch, this would've been like all your other visits to Last Stand? In and out before I even realized you were ever here?"

She wasn't proud of the fact she'd indeed done that in the past. But it had seemed simpler. Easier. Trying to get over Gage Granger was hard enough without running into him. And then, despite everything she'd done to ensure that didn't happen, it had.

Of all the bars in San Antonio…

"Right," he said as she was still searching for a way to answer without lying. "Well, with your car at the Diamond G, it won't be so easy to slip out unnoticed."

"Gage—"

He shook his head. "Not now. Not here."

She nodded. "Agreed."

His eyes widened in surprise. "Well, that was unexpected."

He had no idea.

"All right. Let's get you up."

He held out his hand, and she grasped it, keeping her weight off her left leg as he helped her stand. He continued to hold her as she balanced on her right leg.

Studying her, he asked, "How's the head?"

"It's getting better. The pain pills kicked in." She looked to the open driver's door. "I'll just sit while I wait for Ryker."

Gage helped her into the driver's seat. He took her purse and water bottle off the ground, then passed them to her.

"Thanks."

"And you'll see a doctor?"

"Tomorrow."

"Okay," he said.

He stood there a moment, looking at her. The longer he did, the more the unspoken words between them rose like heat waves off pavement. The more the reason for her being in town weighed on her. She'd have sworn the world went silent, but the vehicle crawling by confirmed it hadn't. As did the voice coming from the radio attached to his shirt.

Gage tilted his head to better hear it. "I have to go," he said.

"Another emergency?"

"No. That wasn't for us. But we need to get back. Our shift is almost over, and we still have to clean the ambulance before we're done."

"Gotcha."

"Ryker will be right over, so you won't be out here for long."

"I'll be fine." Her lips stretched into a thin smile. "Thanks for the help."

He opened his mouth then shut it. With a small nod, he

turned and left.

Gage's departure should have eased her troubled thoughts, but it didn't. Because while he didn't know it yet, he was the reason she was there to begin with. And before she headed back to San Antonio, she needed to tell him what she'd come to say.

That she was having his baby.

Chapter Two

F AITH WASN'T GAGE'S first hookup, though he could count them on one hand. However, she'd been the first one to haunt him after. Because she'd been the only one that had mattered. The only one he'd had feelings for before sleeping with.

Feelings that had gone back almost seven years.

Feelings he'd hoped she reciprocated since she'd gone back with him to his hotel room. Instead, he'd woken up alone with no means of contacting her. With hardly anyone having a landline anymore, he couldn't simply look her up.

He could've stopped in at her grandmother's and asked how to reach Faith. However, he knew by how rarely she came to town—thanks to the town's grapevine—her relationship with Alice Stone hadn't improved over the years. Knocking on the woman's door asking for her granddaughter's contact information would lead to questions as to why he was looking for her.

He had no intention of sharing those answers with anyone, let alone Alice. They weren't anyone's business but his and Faith's.

So, without asking her grandma and with only knowing Faith lived in San Antonio, he'd had no way to reach her.

At least now he could stop driving by her grandma's

house to see if Faith happened to be there visiting. Although, lucky for him, her grandma also lived on Yellow Rose Road, which happened to be on the same street as the fire hall where he worked.

It was why he hadn't felt like a lovesick fool driving past all the time. If anyone asked, though it was shorter to take Wisteria Lane as it led to the highway he needed to take to get to the ranch, it still made sense for him to go past her grandma's, and he could easily claim work as his excuse for going that way.

At least on the days he worked. The times he had to come in for the odd errand, he'd have no such excuse. But luckily, especially since he'd been driving that street an extra tenfold in the last three months, nobody had ever commented. And he'd know if they had as there weren't many secrets in a town the size of Last Stand.

For now, at least, he knew until her vehicle was fixed, she was in town. He wanted to talk to her before she drove back to San Antonio. He'd arrange something with Ryker so his brother wouldn't give her the keys until Gage had a chance to talk about that night in San Antonio.

"That woman back there? How'd you know her?"

Marcella buckled her seat belt then started the ambulance.

"We went to school together from grade eight on. Her name's Faith Stone."

"Stone?" She pulled the ambulance off the shoulder back onto the highway. "I don't remember any Stones in high school."

Gage's lip curled.

Marcella scowled. "Don't say it."

Gage feigned innocence. "Say what?"

"That it's because I'm so much older than you. I'm not even thirty yet."

Gage grinned. "You will be within the month."

"Bite me," Marcella muttered.

Gage laughed. He'd been paired up with Marcella Russo since he was hired. Like police officers, EMT's had partners. Each ambulance consisted of a troop of two people, an EMT and a paramedic. As a paramedic, Marcella had a broader scope of medical training and was able to administer meds that Gage couldn't.

Unless someone was sick or on vacation, Gage always worked with Marcella and, over time, they'd become more than coworkers. They'd become friends. In the four years they'd worked together, Gage had gotten to know Marcella well enough to know the fact his partner was turning thirty was a touchy subject.

Not that it stopped Gage from mentioning it on occasion.

Or two.

"Got any plans for your days off?"

As a rule, they worked 24/48-hour rotations. Twenty-four hours on, forty-eight off, which meant they had the next two days free. But since his work as an EMT wasn't his only responsibility, Gage didn't have the luxury of doing nothing for the next forty-eight hours.

"There's still some haying to be finished, on top of regular chores. I'm sure Ryker will find something for me to do."

Ryker not only helped their dad run the Diamond G, he

also ran Granger Automotive out of the yard. Although, since Joe had had his heart attack almost two weeks ago and remained in a coma, it fell to Ryker, as the only Granger son to be there full-time, to keep the Diamond G operating.

It was easy enough for Gage to help when he wasn't on duty. Cam, who usually only lent a hand between rodeos, planned on sticking around until their dad's condition improved. Dallas managed one night a week and Sundays as he owned his own business in San Antonio and couldn't spare more time.

Although Dallas's new girlfriend, Ashley—on top of taking over the ranch books until Joe recovered—loved the horses, so maybe that would bring Dallas by a little more often.

If not, they'd manage. Though they were a ranch hand short with Brian recuperating from a hernia operation, Dallas had found a replacement their dad's age that was proving to be a huge help. Roy had once owned his own farm, so he was used to doing chores and running equipment, and he was damn good at both. So good, in fact, Gage just might be able to get in a little fishing this weekend.

"Does Ryker ever do anything *but* work?" Marcella asked.

"Sure he does." Gage jumped to his brother's defense. "He fishes, hunts. Likes to go to the nearby rodeos."

He also played music, which had been a revelation to Gage when he'd gone in Ryker's garage once, looking for grease for a squeaky door hinge on his Jeep, and spotted a guitar case tucked in the corner. Since he'd never heard Ryker play, and his brother had never taken lessons far as he knew and certainly had never spoken about music other than to bitch about how loud Cam liked to listen to it, Gage suspected it was a secret Ryker wanted kept.

Gage had never mentioned he'd seen it.

"I'll take your word for it," Marcella said.

Back at the fire hall, Gage wiped down the inside of the ambulance. Though the only thing that needed to be restocked was the ice pack they'd given Faith, Gage nonetheless went through the ritual of double-checking they were stocked and ready to go.

In the office, he helped Marcella finish the paperwork. With everything in order, he said goodbye to the rest of the crew and clocked out. Since it was his night to cook, Gage swung by The Hut, the best barbecue place within three counties thanks to the post oak they used in their pits. Though they only served lunch, Gage had called ahead of time and, thanks to a family event they were having privately, was able to pick up his order despite the fact they'd been closed for hours.

Then, because Ryker had done him the favor of fetching Faith's car, and the pie shop was just two doors down, he set the food into his Jeep before making a last pit stop at Char-Pie for the peach pie Ryker favored.

He wasn't the only one who'd had the idea of pie for dessert. He held the door open for Police Chief Shane Highwater, who carried out two boxes in his hands, and smiled when he recognized Macon Draeger standing at the counter. As a volunteer firefighter, it wasn't uncommon for Gage and Macon's paths to cross.

Macon had his arms crossed. His brow was furrowed.

Definitely more serious than choosing pie warranted.

Stepping up beside him and seeing only one peach pie in the display case, Gage nudged Macon's ribs with his elbow.

"You can't have the peach one," Gage said.

Macon turned and smiled. "You don't have to worry about that. I get enough of those during the peach festival."

"Me, too, but this is for Ryker because he did me a favor today. Unlike the rest of us, *he* can never get enough."

When the owner, Charlie Stockton, approached the counter, Macon said, "Go ahead. I'm still deciding."

Gage bought the pie, said goodbye to Macon and Charlie, and walked out the shop. With the smells of sweet pie and BBQ filling his Jeep, Gage headed out of town.

Once he was past the town's limits, the countryside opened up to farms and ranches. Settled comfortably behind the wheel, his thoughts turned to Faith.

She should be home by now, hopefully with her leg up and another ice pack on her knee. A picture of her grandmother's little two-story house flashed through his mind. Though he'd never been invited inside, thanks to Alice, he imagined it was set out as most homes that age and size were. Living room, kitchen, bathroom, and maybe one-bedroom downstairs, the other bedrooms upstairs.

Well, shit. Why hadn't he thought of that before?

He hadn't been able to offer her crutches because the ambulance didn't carry any, and Ryker would help her to get into the tow truck and then the house. But he hadn't thought past that. *Idiot.* He should have considered how she'd get around between now and tomorrow. She'd need help moving around the house, never mind walking into a doctor's office.

Gage took his foot off the gas as he checked his rearview mirror. With nothing to see but the long grey ribbon of highway and the fields on both sides, he pushed on the brake and made a U-turn. His phone pinged with an incoming text. He pulled over, looked at the screen. It was from Cam.

We're starving. Haul ass.

Gage fired back a quick text.

Something came up. Won't take long. Be there ASAP.

Ignoring the dots that indicated Cam was replying, Gage tossed his phone on the passenger seat and drove back to town.

FAITH, LEANING HEAVILY on Ryker for support, hobbled into the kitchen.

Judging by the spicy smell filling the room, she figured they were having chili for supper. Her grandmother looked up as they entered. Her mouth pursed. She finished stirring then set the wooden spoon on a small saucer and replaced the lid on the crockpot.

"What did you do?" Alice asked.

"I'm fine, thanks," Faith muttered. Then louder, she said, "I hit the ditch and banged up my knee. Since I also popped a tire, Ryker was nice enough to give my car a tow and bring me here."

Faith sat in the closest chair and plopped the now luke-warm ice pack and her purse onto the table. She offered Ryker a smile. "Thanks for the help. Not just with the car, but with getting in and out of your truck and into the house."

He shrugged. "That was no trouble. But you might want to get some crutches. Be easier to move around."

She supposed she could ask her grandmother to drive her to emergency given that the regular clinics would be closing for the day, but right then, it seemed like too much hassle. Faith could already hear the woman's griping if she were to suggest such a thing. She so wasn't going there.

Besides, despite what she'd told Gage, her headache hadn't stopped throbbing, and the only thing she wanted to do was take another acetaminophen and sit somewhere quiet.

"I will tomorrow."

"Then I'll let you get to your meal." He tipped his hat. "Nice seeing you again, Mrs. Stone."

Her grandmother gave a stiff nod.

Undeterred by the lack of warmth, he looked to Faith. "I'll let you know what I find as soon I get a chance to look at it."

"Sounds good. Thanks again."

The minute he was gone, her grandmother turned to her. "You weren't drinking, were you?"

"What? No! Something—a dog, I think—suddenly jumped onto the road. I swerved to miss it and ended up in the ditch."

"So you weren't paying attention," Alice scoffed. Eying Faith, she stated, "I hope you aren't looking to me to help pay for damages."

Faith pressed her fingers to her temples. "I haven't asked you for money since I left, have I? Whatever it costs, I'll pay for myself."

She might not have the best-paying job, but she was frugal with her money. It was why she'd insisted on having a roommate to share the rent. It allowed her to keep a savings account, which, in turn, kept her from ever having to ask her grandmother for anything. Because, Lord knew if she had to, she'd never live it down.

"Do you need help with supper?" Faith asked.

Her grandma, wearing a pink-and-white plaid waist apron, folded her hands over her middle. "No. But don't think a sore knee will get you out of helping do the dishes after. I don't run a restaurant."

"I know." *You made it clear every day I lived here and every time I come back to visit.* "Well, unless you need me for anything else, I think I'll go sit outside until then."

Though it was the last thing she wanted, she *had* just gotten there, and because she hadn't been back since Easter, she felt obligated to ask her grandmother to join her.

"My program is on."

And as though her only grandchild hadn't come back for the first time in weeks, wasn't sitting there in pain, Alice walked stiffly into the living room, leaving Faith alone. Which, in this case, was actually a blessing.

Though it did leave her with the problem of getting herself to the porch.

Gritting her teeth and using first the counter, then the wall, then hopping the rest of the way, which just added to the throbbing in her head, Faith finally made it outside.

She hobbled to one of the lawn chairs her grandma kept outside. Then she took the pot of African violets off the small table sitting between the two chairs and set it on the porch. Glad the table was made of plastic and not wood, Faith set it before her chair and, with a sigh, rested her foot on it.

Hopefully, her grandma would be too wrapped up in her program to harp on Faith's choice of footstool.

One could hope.

Sitting back, Faith tried to relax. It should've been easy given the tree-lined street was quiet, except for the occasional bark of a dog and odd car creeping by as someone made their way home from work.

Plumes of smoke from backyard grills filled the air with delicious aromas. American flags hung sleepily from front porch railings. All in all, it couldn't be more picturesque. But, instead of enjoying it, Faith's thoughts turned to Gage.

She buried her face in her hands. She shouldn't have accepted his invitation to go to his room. She shouldn't have made out with him in the elevator until, when it reached his floor, his shirt had been ripped from his jeans and her hands had been exploring his washboard abdomen.

Sure, she could, and did, blame some of it on the alcohol they'd consumed that night, but for her, at least, there'd been more to it.

If there was such a thing as "the girl next door" then Gage was the "boy next door". Easygoing, good-looking, and friends with everyone. Though he'd participated in school sports, he hadn't been the all-star player, but he was competent enough that the guys always wanted him on the team. And while he hadn't been top of the class academically, he certainly had never been at the bottom.

Most importantly, he was kind. Even though he'd fit in with the popular crowd, he'd had a smile for everyone. If someone needed help when he was around, he'd been the first to offer. She'd witnessed him stand up to more than one bully. Equally surprising was the fact that—despite not taking sides, despite standing up for the little guy, which sometimes meant putting a popular kid in their place—he never made enemies. There was just a way about him that people liked.

It was no surprise he'd become an EMT. Although he'd have made a good doctor. Or even a vet. Any job where he cared for things, really.

Because that was what Gage did. He took care. And if she hadn't had him as a friend in high school, she didn't know where she'd be.

Faith lowered her hands and stared at one of the pots of pink petunias that marched along the base of the porch railing. Actually, she did know where she'd be. Or at least what she'd be. A high school dropout.

After a particularly horrid night with her grandmother, Faith had gone to school the next day determined to get out of Last Stand. It hadn't mattered that she was only fifteen and had no money and no way to leave. She'd been prepared to walk anywhere by then.

Anything had seemed better than living with Alice at that point. She'd emptied her locker of her personal possessions and left that afternoon with no plans to return.

Gage, catching up with her as she'd left the school grounds, had changed her mind. Though he'd always been friendly toward her, they hadn't been close and really didn't know each other. Though, she hadn't known much about anyone.

Her grandma had never let anyone come over, and Faith hadn't been allowed to go anywhere but school, home, and work. It was hard to make friends when she only ever had the chance to talk to them at lunch or during gym class.

But he'd befriended her that day. He must have seen her clean out her locker. Or perhaps he'd caught the tears she hadn't been able to completely hold back. Either way, he'd caught up with her. He hadn't asked her anything personal. Just made small talk.

Looking back, she realized what he'd done. He'd eased her into conversation. He'd let it be her choice, rather than demanding to know what was going on.

He'd told her about the ranch. Then he'd started telling her some story about how they had to inseminate a cow that wasn't taking the usual way, and that she wouldn't believe what had happened. Then he'd left it at that.

Dumbfounded, she'd asked what had happened, and he'd just smiled, given her a friendly wink, and told her she'd have to come back the next day to find out.

"Guess I'll have to live in suspense," she'd answered.

But that night, as she sat on the bed waiting for her grandma to fall asleep so she could sneak out, she'd thought of his story. More, she'd thought of his smile. How he'd cared enough to come after her and gently tried to get her to stay.

What was one more day? She'd survived that long. So she'd gone to sleep and gone to school the next day. Instead of looking smug she was back, he'd looked relieved. And happy. He'd told her he'd finish the story at lunch, which he had. But then he'd started another and, no surprise, had left that one unfinished. To be continued.

Eventually, he'd come to finish his stories on the same day he told them. By then, they'd become friends and he hadn't seemed bothered he was never allowed over. But he had taken exception to her not being allowed at the ranch. And, more than once, had managed to sneak her there when her grandma was at one function or another.

It was because of Gage and his friendship that she'd graduated. And it was because of the kind of boy he'd been that she'd started to fall for him. Had attempted to kiss him the night of graduation. And, when he'd backed away from her, breaking her heart, the reason she'd never kept in touch. Not only because she'd been hurt, but because she'd been embarrassed. She'd wanted to distance herself from both.

"You should have thought of that before you went to his hotel room," she muttered.

Which immediately turned her thoughts from high school to a night that, despite wishing it had never happened, she couldn't forget.

After years of wondering what it would have been like to be with Gage, she still hadn't been prepared for the reality of it. His hard body. His attention to detail.

Cheeks burning, Faith cleared her throat. It'd be best if she forgot just how much he'd pleased her. Especially when the sex was the reason she'd had to come back.

She was distracted from her thoughts as a blue Jeep slowed, then stopped at the curb in front of her grandma's house. It wasn't a vehicle she recognized, but she had been living in San Antonio for almost seven years. With the angle it had parked, she couldn't see the driver until he stepped out of the vehicle.

Shit. Shit. Shit!

What was Gage doing here? Though she knew she had to talk to him, this place wasn't any better than the ditch had been earlier. In fact, it was worse. So much worse.

He stepped out and looked over the roof of the Jeep. He took off his sunglasses, hung them from the open collar of his uniform shirt. Their gazes locked. He braced his arms on the black hard top of his vehicle. A smile curved his lips.

"Bet you didn't expect to see me again so soon."

IT WAS CLEAR by her wide eyes she hadn't. Just as it was clear by the way her shoulders stiffened that she wasn't thrilled about it, either. Her reaction pulled him in two different directions.

Part of him wanted to hurry and reassure her and let her know she had nothing to fear from him. He wasn't there to shout from Main Street that they'd slept together.

The other part of him wanted to march up those steps and demand to know why she'd not only run out on him in San Antonio, but earlier today, as well. Well, she hadn't literally run away because she couldn't with a wrecked car and a bum knee, but she hadn't been happy to see him then, either, and she'd refused his help until he'd practically had to beg her to let him.

He wouldn't lie. Her reaction hurt. Because he'd treated

her with respect. Hell, he'd worshiped her. There'd been no coercion. In fact, he'd asked her multiple times between them leaving the bar together and their getting naked if she was sure. She'd said yes. And when she'd screamed his name later, it sure as hell hadn't been in anger or fear.

He could understand regret, as he carried some, as well. He'd been extra careful in high school to treat her special.

So when he'd first woken up in that hotel room and remembered what had happened, he'd initially felt a little panicked.

Everyone in Last Stand knew about her mother's wild ways. He'd always suspected that was part of the reason she'd been so reserved.

Because of that, he'd been careful not to flirt with her at first. He hadn't wanted her to think he was befriending her to get laid. He hadn't known, at the time, the relationship she had with her grandmother, but he had known she wasn't happy. And he'd wanted her to be.

Once she'd shared her life with him, and he realized he'd been right, he'd tried to show her she was pretty and smart and fun to be around. That it wasn't a hardship to spend time with her.

He'd never gotten completely through to her. When they spent time together, whether it was after he drove her home from one of the times he'd snuck her out of the house or when he'd walked her to her locker, she'd thanked him like he'd done some chore for her. And if he happened to stop and talk or ask to sit beside her outside or in the cafeteria, she'd always look around first. As though the only reason he could possibly want to was if nobody was watching.

Nobody was watching now.

Pushing away from the Jeep, he reached in the back and pulled out the crutches he'd stopped to get at the pharmacy. Carrying them in one hand, he skirted the front of his vehicle and stepped onto the sidewalk.

The Stone house wasn't anything fancy. An older, rectangular shaped two-story with a porch off to the right. But one thing about it remained the same as it had been in high school. It was well maintained. The lack of peeling paint on the wood siding told him the pale cream color had been recently applied. The front door that had once been plain white was now the color of the Caribbean ocean.

Faith's grandma had pots of pink flowers lining the deck and flanking the door while bright, multicolored blooms flourished in the flowerbeds tucked up against the house. The sweet smell of them blended with that of a neighbor grilling meat. Both scents followed him up the stairs.

"I thought you could use these," he said as he stepped onto the porch.

Her lips tipped upward. "Thanks. It *was* a bit tricky getting out here."

"Didn't have help I take it?"

"Yeah, right," Faith scoffed.

He set the crutches at her feet.

"You didn't have to do that, Gage," she said, keeping her eyes lowered.

He took the chair next to hers, careful not to bump her elevated leg. "It wasn't about *have to*, Faith. I wanted to."

She nodded.

He leaned forward, braced his elbows on his knees. "I

don't mind helping out my friends. And once upon a time, Faith, we *were* friends."

She raised her head. Her hazel eyes met his. "That was a long time ago."

He cocked his head. "What happened in San Antonio wasn't that long ago."

Color poured into her cheeks. He sat back, satisfied. After her walking out on him at the hotel and then her reserve at the accident site earlier, he'd feared that night hadn't affected her.

Because it sure as hell had had some effect on him.

Normally, when he looked back on a night with a woman, he relived the moments. What she'd done, what he'd done. How it had felt. How he'd want to see her again. Do it all over again. While he'd thought all those things with Faith, he'd actually spent more time thinking of other things than he had of the actual sex.

What was she doing? *How* was she doing? Was she regretting what they'd done? Why didn't she call?

Okay, they hadn't exchanged numbers that night, but the Diamond G still had a landline. It would have been easy enough for her to find the number if she'd wanted to. Since he'd never received a message, despite having asked Ryker every day for the first two weeks after that weekend in San Antonio if anyone had called for him, it was clear she hadn't wanted to.

Because she'd cut the ties after high school, he didn't know much about her anymore. Other than the fact she lived and worked in San Antonio. But he didn't know where exactly. Had no idea if she had a roommate. She could have

MICHELLE BEATTIE

twenty cats for all he knew.

The point was, he knew nothing about her, and she knew as little about him now, other than he lived and worked in Last Stand.

So really, had this been any other woman, there was no reason she would have consumed as much of his thoughts as Faith had. Their hookup would have been easy to move past.

But it wasn't just any woman. It was Faith and, three months later, he still couldn't let it go.

What had started out as friendship in high school had changed into more for Gage. But he'd always known his life was in Last Stand, and Faith had made it clear hers wasn't. Instead of starting something that would break his heart, he'd never pursued his feelings. But that hadn't stopped him from missing her over the years. From wishing things had been different.

The moment he'd kissed her in that bar, he'd known. This time, he wasn't going to let her go without a fight. He didn't care if she lived in San Antonio. They were adults now. They could find a way to make it work. He could convince her life in Last Stand would be good. With him.

But she'd taken away that possibility when she'd disappeared in the night. Now he'd found her again, and he was going to make sure she didn't disappear on him again.

"Faith, about that night…"

"Shh!" Her head swiveled toward the screen door.

Despite hearing muffled voices coming from the television inside, she was clearly worried Alice would hear. He sighed. Dammit, he really wanted to talk. But he had to agree. With Alice within earshot, it still wasn't the time or

36

place.

"Fine. But you're not getting away—"

He was interrupted by his phone ringing. He pulled it from his pocket, saw it was Ryker.

"Sorry. I should grab this." Likely, his brother was just looking for his supper, but in case he needed something else from town, better Gage find out now rather than after he was home.

"Yeah, Ryker, what's up?"

"I'm freaking starving. You bringing supper, or do I have to throw a pizza in the oven?"

"I've got it. Just had to make a quick stop."

"Well, finish it already. Cam and I've already chewed through a bag of chips."

Gage scowled. "The smoky bacon ones were mine."

"*Were* being the operative word. And unless you want us to dig into the stash of bagels you hide at the back of the freezer, you'd better get here with supper."

Gage heaved a breath. "I'm on my way. Don't touch the bagels."

"Someone holding bagels for ransom?"

Gage slid his phone back in his pocket. "Ryker and Cam are starving and looking for their supper." He shrugged. "My night to cook, so I got takeout from The Hut."

"Can't go wrong with barbecue."

"Yeah. Anyway, it's in the Jeep, so I better get going. I just wanted to make sure you had crutches for tonight."

"And now I do. Thanks to you."

He stood up but he didn't walk away. Instead, he looked down at her. "I'm off for the next two days. Since you can't go anywhere until your car is fixed, how about I pick you up tomorrow? We can go somewhere and talk."

He'd expected her to come up with excuses, list a dozen reasons why they shouldn't. So it surprised him when she nodded instead.

"How about I swing by after lunch? I have some chores to do in the morning." He gestured to her propped leg. "Since a walk is out of the question, we could go for a drive. Or we could go back to the ranch. Up to you."

"Not the ranch. Maybe just a drive."

He wasn't sure why the ranch was out, but location didn't matter. He just wanted to talk.

"Works for me. I'll see you around one thirty."

Though he didn't look back, he swore her gaze followed him to his Jeep and down the residential street until he turned the corner.

He took a deep breath, filling his senses with the aroma of barbecue. All in all, it hadn't been a bad day. No major emergencies. He had a delicious meal waiting for him, and he'd finally found the woman that had haunted his thoughts for the past three months—six plus years, if he were honest.

He wasn't sure if it was normal to hang on to feelings for a woman that long. But then, when had his life ever been normal?

His dad had emotionally shut down when his mom had gotten sick with cancer. His oldest brother, Dallas, had taken over as head of the family and tried to be both mother and father. What he'd ended up being was closer to a general.

By the time their dad had emerged from his depression—or whatever had kept him closed off and living as a stranger for years—every relationship in their household had been damaged.

They'd lived more as acquaintances than family for almost a decade now. And likely would have continued on that way indefinitely if, nearly two weeks ago now, his dad hadn't had a heart attack and been brought in by a mysterious woman nobody knew. She'd slipped out, and since vanished, before anyone could find out who she was.

They suspected she was the reason Joe'd had the attack, but until he regained consciousness, the woman came forward, or they found their dad's car—which could give them some insight as to where he'd been and what he could have possibly been doing—they had no way of knowing.

Gage rubbed his temples.

And he'd thought his relationship with Faith was complicated.

Chapter Three

BEYOND CATTLE, THE Diamond G had about a dozen horses and also farmed several hundred acres of hay fields. It had always been Joe Granger's dream that his sons take over the ranch. And maybe that dream would have come to fruition if their mom hadn't gotten sick.

But once she had, it had been the start of the end. Not only for their mom, but for the family. Her terminal diagnosis had changed Joe. Not that he'd ever been particularly touchy-feely, but until the cancer had been confirmed, he'd at least been active in their lives.

He'd gone to their football games, taken them on trail rides and overnight camping trips. He'd taught them to fish and hunt, how to dress the meat after, and how to fillet a bass with the least amount of bones left in the meat. And he'd always been close to their mother. They'd loved sitting on the front porch after supper, and it hadn't been uncommon to see them walk down the lane hand in hand.

At first, it hadn't been so bad. As long as his mom hadn't shown signs of the disease, Joe seemed fine. Almost as though he was living in denial. If she didn't look sick, she couldn't be sick. But when the ravages of chemo started to affect her and she'd decided not to pursue further treatment, his dad had become a different man.

He'd buried himself in ranch work. He'd left the house before dawn and stayed out long after sunset. He never went into the sickroom for longer than a minute or two, and it had been left to Dallas, as the oldest, to ensure meals were on the table, homework was done, and that someone was always with their mother, as she'd decided to die at home.

The fishing had stopped. There'd been no more camping trips. It hadn't been fun for anyone and it had caused rifts between not only them and their dad, but also between each other. Because everyone was hurting and instead of leaning on each other, they'd fought.

It was always someone else's turn to do the dishes or the laundry. And who the hell had left the gate open this time and why were the whites now pink? The smallest thing had led to doors slamming and later, fists flying.

By the time Dallas had left, their mom had been dead for a year, and their dad was starting to come around. But the damage had been done. Hudson had gone off to serve their country by then, and though Dallas visited on occasion, their dad saw Dallas's decision to leave and pursue his own dreams as the reason the rest of them had.

While Cam came by and helped between rodeos and Gage pitched in on his days off, Ryker was the only one who'd truly stayed. The only one fully committed to the ranch. And like their father, Gage suspected Ryker felt some sense of resentment.

He wasn't alone.

Although Gage's feelings didn't center around the ranch—but rather those of a ten-year-old boy who'd lost his mom and had his dad essentially abandon them, he'd needed someone to stand in. Not just an adult to see to his basic needs the way Dallas had, but someone who would have seen that he'd been a boy drowning in grief with nobody to help him through it. Nobody who'd take the time to ask if he was okay. Nobody to set a reassuring hand on his shoulder and tell him things were going to get better.

He figured that was what drove him to be an EMT. He could be that person at an accident scene who held the patient's hand, who ensured that no matter how scary the situation, they weren't alone. Who checked up on the hospitalized patients so they knew they mattered, that they hadn't been forgotten and weren't just another body.

Gage put the Jeep in park and rolled his shoulders. Apparently, seeing Faith again had brought back more than just his past with her.

He shook it off as he got out and grabbed the bags of takeout from the passenger side.

"Need help with that?"

Gage looked over his shoulder. Roy was coming from the bunkhouse.

"I've got the bags," Gage said as their new ranch hand sauntered over in his jeans and ratty sneakers, "but you can grab the door."

"Sure," Roy answered as he loped up the porch steps.

The man was easily old enough to be Gage's father, heck all their father, but in the week or so he'd been there he'd had no problem taking orders from any of them. Not that Gage made a habit of ordering people around, but Ryker had been known to. And Dallas had been all about orders until he'd moved out.

"Ah, there it is." Cam half-rose from his seat at the kitchen table to grab the bags from Gage's hand. "I thought I was going to have to go for a second bagel there for a minute."

Gage caught Cam's smirk before he took the bait.

"For you," Gage said as he slid the white box containing the pie in front of Ryker. "For taking care of Faith and her car."

Ryker's brows arched. "She already paid me for the tow bill. And I won't know how much the car is until I have a chance to look at it."

Gage kept pulling containers from one bag while Cam continued to fish them out of another. Roy, having been told to make himself at home when he'd been hired on, went to the cupboard to pull out plates.

"The pie is thanks for heading straight over. I couldn't stay and didn't like the idea of her sitting there alone for too long."

Cam paused. "You going to rekindle that high school romance?"

Despite the tug in his chest, Gage shook his head. "It was never more than friendship."

Faith had made it clear, not only in high school when she counted down the days until she could leave Last Stand, but the day she'd driven away as well. And if that hadn't been clear enough, when he'd missed her so much that he'd tried calling her a few weeks later, the automated message in his ear saying the number was no longer in service brought her point home.

On the off chance he'd forgotten any of that, she'd mentioned it again before he'd laid her on his hotel bed in San

Antonio. She wasn't interested in a relationship. Least of all with someone who was tied to Last Stand.

And he was. He might have gone on to be an EMT, but he was still a rancher, too. While he enjoyed the semiannual weekends in San Antonio with the buddies he'd met in EMT school, he was happiest to stay out of the city. Maybe it was because his job could be hectic and traumatic. All Gage knew was he loved the wide-open spaces, the sight of cattle dotting the rolling hills, and the peace of hearing nothing but nature through his open window at night. Not to mention the memories of his mom that were everywhere on the ranch.

The memories that were the only part of her he had left.

"I was just looking out for a friend, Cam."

And since when did they discuss each other's love lives? Hell, usually if it didn't have to do with the ranch, and lately their father, they hardly talked at all.

Ryker opened his box. "Let's hope your friends need a tow more often." Then he glared over the top of the open box to Cam. "Keep your paws off my pie."

Cam was too busy scooping out forkfuls of barbecue to even glance up at Ryker. "Then I suggest you eat it quick."

It was common knowledge that when Cam came home, he helped himself to whatever was in the house. Sure, he was just as well known to leave some bills on the table when he left again, but that was cold comfort when he'd been craving something all day and got home only to find Cam had filched it.

Gage ignored them both as he waited for Roy to fill his plate. He had no idea how long the man had been homeless before Dallas offered him a job at the ranch but judging by the way his jeans hung loose around his narrow waist, it had been long enough to lose a substantial amount of weight.

"There's lots, Roy. Don't be shy," he said when the man only took one scoop of mashed potatoes.

The man's cheeks went a little pink, but Gage was happy to see him take another heaping spoonful. Roy took a can of soda from the fridge to go along with his meal, thanked them all, then took his supper back to the bunkhouse.

No matter how many times they told him he was welcome at their table, he never ate at it, instead choosing to go back to the bunkhouse.

Gage filled his own plate then took his seat at the table.

The food wasn't steaming hot anymore, but the tangy barbecue aroma still filled the country kitchen. Gage slathered some butter onto his corn biscuit.

"You need me around here tomorrow?" Cam asked Ryker as he gnawed the meat off a beef rib.

"Why? Where you heading?"

Cam set the bone he'd picked clean onto his plate and licked the sauce of his fingers. "I figured if Gage and Roy can finish the last bit of haying, I'd head up to Vernon for the Santa Rosa Roundup. It's too late to enter, but it would give me chance to keep an eye on my competition, get a sense of who'll be coming to Last Stand for the rodeo next month."

Ryker looked to Gage. "You're off tomorrow, right?"

Gage finished swallowing his bite of corn muffin. "I am. And I can give you the morning, late afternoon, and evening. But I've got something planned after lunch. Not sure how long it'll take."

If Faith had her way, they'd be done in thirty seconds.

Gage had other ideas.

"That should be fine. I think he only has a few acres left, and other than Faith's car and checking in on Dad, I can help, too."

"I looked in on Dad this afternoon when we were picking up our patient to transfer. No change. I can sit with him a bit tomorrow when I'm in town."

Ryker used his biscuit to wipe up the bead of gravy that threatened to drip off the edge of his plate. "Sounds good. Let's plan on picking up the last of the bales after supper. We'll let Roy drive the tractor. Gage, you and I can stack them on the wagon."

"That works," he answered.

"Dallas coming this weekend?" Cam asked.

"Sunday. While Ashley's up in Dad's office working on getting the books caught up, he'll be helping Roy in the bunkhouse," Ryker said.

"What's wrong with the bunkhouse?" Cam asked.

"It needs a bunch of work. I hadn't realized how run-down it had gotten in there until Roy asked if he could do some fixing up."

Ryker scowled. "It not only needs a good cleaning, but it needs some general upkeep. Paint's peeling. There's some water stains on the roof from a leak somewhere. That kind of thing." He gulped some water. "Roy's handy with tools, so he'll give Dallas a hand."

With business taken care of, they fell into their usual silence. A silence Gage had come to loathe.

He might've been young when his mom had gotten sick, but he still remembered how it had been before then. How the house had been noisy with them chasing each other playing cops and robbers, or how they'd all tried to talk at the same time over supper until their mother, laughing, would remind them to speak one at a time.

And outside. Man…outside had been the best. Tree houses, playing hide and seek, going fishing, going riding. Now the only thing they did together outside was work. He'd noticed all this, of course, before their dad had the heart attack. It was hard not to when Dallas hardly ever came home, and when he did, the tension was thick enough to choke on. But Joe ending up in the hospital in a coma had snapped Gage out of the complacency he'd come to accept.

He'd been the one to call Dallas, the one who'd told him to get his ass home. Then Ryker had forced a schedule on Dallas to get him to keep coming back. Ryker had done it only to get some help around the ranch, not to rebuild the fractures within them, but as far as Gage could see, the reason didn't matter. He was more concerned about the end result.

Because seeing his dad in the hospital had been a wake-up call. It proved none of them were invincible. They could have easily lost Joe. And though he was stable, and his vitals were good, he remained in a coma. Heck, he might never come out for all they knew.

It gutted Gage to think he might never speak to his dad again. Not that he and Joe were any closer than he was to his brothers, but the man was still his dad. And Gage was too young to have both his parents buried in the Last Stand cemetery.

Ryker wiped his mouth with a napkin, balled it up, and

set it on his empty plate. He pushed away from the table.

"I'm going to go look at Faith's car."

Cam was on his feet before Ryker had left the kitchen. "I'm going to go pack my stuff."

"Hey! I brought supper. It's your turn to clean up."

"I'll do it before I leave. Besides," Cam added with a nod at the food left on Gage's plate. "You're not done yet."

With both his brothers gone, Gage finished the last of his meal. He left the cleanup to Cam, knowing his brother would get to it before he left. The clock on the microwave said seven. He could do the chores early and head into town. Friday nights were usually hopping at the Last Stand Saloon.

But he didn't feel like the noise tonight. After seeing Faith again, on top of the emotions he was feeling regarding his family, he just wanted to be alone with his thoughts. There were a lot of things he wasn't happy with, and maybe some time on his horse would give him some inspiration as to how to change them.

But since he was still in uniform, he'd need to change first.

He passed the fridge, stopped, and backtracked. Opening the freezer door, he pulled out a couple frozen pizzas and bags of frozen veggies. Tucked at the back was his bag of bagels.

"Goddammit, Cam," he swore when he saw there was indeed one missing.

FAITH HADN'T SLEPT much, and her eyes were gritty when

she hobbled into the bathroom the next morning. Placing her hands on the counter, she looked into the mirror.

She'd done okay with what she'd been given. Her poker-straight hair was cut in a fashionable bob that grazed her collarbone. She splurged on copper highlights every eight weeks to give her dark brown hair some pizzazz, and thanks to good genetics, she didn't need much in the way of makeup as her skin was naturally clear and even-toned.

And none of that was going to help her talk to Gage this afternoon. She'd had a couple weeks to come to terms with the pregnancy and what she planned to do. While she was ready to explain, she didn't expect Gage to go along easily. Not knowing the kind of man he was. Which, though she wasn't sure it was possible, made her feel worse about herself.

Sighing, Faith looked into her tired hazel eyes. She wished she could blame coming back to Last Stand for her insecurities, but the truth was they were a burr she'd never been able to pluck free.

She turned from the mirror and stripped. She'd called the doctor yesterday while she'd waited in the ditch for Ryker, and she needed to get ready so she'd make the eleven forty-five appointment they'd squeezed her in for.

Once she'd showered, she blow-dried her hair, added waterproof mascara to her lashes, and brushed her teeth. Figuring it would be easier for the doctor to examine her knee if she wore shorts, she pulled on her favorite denim pair along with a V-neck, lavender T-shirt. Then, with the crutches in one hand and the handrail gripped firmly in the other, Faith hopped down the stairs.

Her grandmother was working at the small island, an

apron once again tied around her waist. She never did anything in the kitchen without one. Not a gray hair was out of place. Flour dusted her cheekbone. It could have been a cozy scene. But there was nothing warm about the look Alice gave her.

Well, it wasn't going to get any warmer.

"Morning, Grandma."

"Faith," she answered as she continued to stir the batter.

"I was hoping I could take your car to the doctor?"

The rubber spatula stopped mid-stir. "Why are you going to the doctor?"

"I thought the crutches gave that away."

Her grandmother shook her head, continued stirring. "It's just a bruise. Likely the doctor will tell you the same. Don't know why you'd want to waste their time, not to mention the money and the gas."

Well, they were all hers to waste, but that didn't seem to occur to her grandmother. "I work on my feet all day. I want to make sure it's nothing more serious before I go back to work on Monday.

"I'll put gas in it," Faith added when her grandma's stern mouth didn't say anything more—even though it wasn't more than a five-minute drive to the clinic.

"The keys are on the rack," Alice finally relented as she poured the batter into a glass cake pan.

Though it hurt to bend it and put weight on it, her knee wasn't serious. Yes, she wanted to make sure she could work without further injuring it in case it was more than a bruise, but it would have been nice to have her grandmother show some concern.

"I won't be long."

"I should hope not. And don't take it out to the Granger Ranch. I heard Gage on the porch yesterday."

For a moment, Faith went completely still. But then she remembered she'd shushed Gage before he could say anything incriminating. A good thing since she had no intention of letting Alice know about the pregnancy. The only person in Last Stand she planned on telling was Gage.

She took her purse from the back of the chair, slung it crosswise across her body, then snagged the keys from the rack by the door.

"Did you need me to pick anything up at the store?"

"I've been doing my own shopping since you left. Anything I've needed, I've gotten myself."

Okay then. No guilt there.

Last Stand was a one-stop shop for all things medical with the dental and medical offices located across the street from the hospital. Parking the car in a stall that faced the hospital, Faith couldn't help but think of Gage. Her hands tightened on the wheel. If only that stupid dog—or whatever it was—hadn't raced out and caused her to lose control...she could've maybe bought more time before facing him.

But then, she'd already taken as much time as she could spare. So there was no hiding. No delaying.

Besides, all of this had very little to do with Gage. Well, other than the obvious part. The truth was Gage had always been nice to her. It had been her own insecurities that had driven her to gather her clothes in the dark and slip out the door.

It had bothered her since, no matter how much she'd

tried to pretend differently. So, she'd just have to suck it up and deal with it. Besides, she was already getting anxiety from worrying about telling him. She needed to get it done. Then maybe she'd be able to sleep again.

She rested her forehead onto her hands. "Let's hope."

Screaming sirens yanked her attention to the hospital across the road and the ambulance that drove into the emergency bay. The bad part about small towns was that everyone knew almost everyone. Although she'd been gone over six years and that wasn't the case for her anymore, she nonetheless sent up a quick prayer that whoever was in there would be okay.

Faith watched a moment as the EMT and paramedic efficiently removed the stretcher from the back of the ambulance and quickly wheeled it inside. Gage did that. He was responsible for saving lives and helping the sick while she served food and drinks and wiped tables.

"And there's nothing wrong with that," she stated firmly.

Yanking the keys from the ignition, Faith pushed open the door. Maybe she didn't have a career, but she had a good, honest job, and while her grandmother had never encouraged her to reach for more—the opposite, in fact—one thing she'd instilled in Faith was that there was no such thing as a menial job. Making her own way in the world, supporting herself no matter the path, was still an accomplishment.

But it hadn't taken away her desire to do more. So, despite her grandmother's cutting remark of "Do you think you're smart enough?" when Faith had mentioned college back in high school, Faith had taken some general education classes online through community college and would have enough money saved by next fall to pursue her dream of being an X-Ray technician.

The excitement she used to feel at the thought of college was no longer as vibrant and shiny as it had once been because to pursue her dream, she had to cut out a piece of her heart. But there was no way around it. If she didn't go to school, she'd always regret it. More, she'd resent not having taken the opportunity. And there was no way she'd put that on a child. Not when she knew all too well what would happen if she did. To both her and her baby.

Sighing, Faith hobbled into the reception area of the medical offices. The clerk behind the counter was wearing cute pink scrubs with white llamas on them. Faith's heart squeezed because not only did she want to wear cute scrubs to work, but the pattern would also make a cute receiving blanket.

Don't think about it. It's not possible.

Her smile was brittle when she approached the counter. "Hi. I'm Faith Stone. I have an appointment for eleven forty-five."

The clerk looked at her screen. "If you just want to have a seat, it shouldn't be too long."

The waiting room only had two other people waiting, so Faith had her choice of chairs to sit in. She opted for one that let her see the TV mounted in the corner. She was engrossed in a rerun of *Friends* when her name was called.

Faith followed the nurse to the examining room. She sat on the paper sheet covering the bed and leaned her crutches against it. The nurse did a preliminary exam, jotted down notes, then stepped out of the room. A few moments later, there was a light tap on the door, and the nurse came back, followed by the doctor. Dressed in a white lab coat over a blouse and pair of slacks, the doctor peered at Faith over the frame of her hot pink glasses.

"Good morning. I'm Dr. Schmidt. I understand you have a sore knee?"

Faith ran through what had happened and how the EMT had suggested she come. She specifically didn't mention Gage by name, not wanting the conversation to veer into personal territory.

"Let's have a look."

Dr. Schmidt checked her head first, but even Faith had noticed the bump had gone down since yesterday. Still, she checked her eyes and asked her about headaches. Then she moved down to her knee. With gentle fingers, she pressed, probed, and checked her range of motion.

"The EMT was right. It's just a bad bruise. I don't think an X-ray is necessary." She sat in her chair as the nurse stood by, writing in a file. "Ice it. Take some anti-inflammatories. You can use the crutches for another day, but no more. The longer you stay off of it, the more it'll stiffen. Best to keep it limber, even if it hurts."

"Okay."

"Anything else? Any bruising from the seat belt?"

"A little." She tugged aside her shirt to show her the purple and blue bruise on her shoulder.

"No other pain?"

"No, but I'm about eleven weeks pregnant. Can we make sure the baby is okay?"

Worrying about Gage last night had only been half the

reason sleep had eluded her. She'd been afraid the baby might have been hurt when she'd been jostled about in the car.

Dr. Schmidt set her glasses on the desk. Without the bright pink distracting her, Faith saw the woman's eyes were the color of the sky right before a rain.

"Any pain or cramping? Any spotting?"

Faith shook her head. "No."

"Well, those are good signs." She removed a paper gown from the cabinet on the bed. "Put that on. I'll do an internal just to be sure."

Faith changed into the gown, assumed the position. After a quick internal exam and a confirmation the baby's heartbeat was still strong, the doctor and nurse left her to change into her clothes.

"So, no ibuprofen or anti-inflammatories for you. Stick to ice packs and acetaminophen if you need something for the pain."

"That's what I've been doing. My doctor in San Antonio had told me to stay clear of ibuprofen, and I haven't taken any anti-inflammatories."

"Good girl." The doctor slid the glasses to the end of her nose. "Anything else?"

"I don't think so."

"Then you have a good day."

Good day. Yeah, right. It had already started out crappy with her grandmother. Next, she had a meeting with Gage at one-thirty, which was sure to be anything but enjoyable.

Faith blew out a long breath.

Apart from the fact she hadn't hurt the baby, she couldn't think of a single good thing about the day.

Chapter Four

FAITH SHUFFLED UP the porch steps. Opening the door, the smell of warm, fresh-baked chocolate cake assaulted her. Faith grimaced at the thought of eating it—of eating anything. Her nerves were strung so tightly from knowing what she was about to tell Gage that the smell of food turned her stomach.

She hung the keys on the rack and stepped into the kitchen.

Her grandmother hurried in from the living room, dust cloth in one hand and lemon spray cleaner in the other.

"Did you hang the keys up?"

"I did."

"Good." Then she turned and went back to presumably finish her dusting.

Hurt, Faith turned and hobbled back outside. Sitting heavily on the lawn chair, she closed her eyes. Her grandma hadn't cared enough to ask how the appointment had gone.

Would it have killed her to ask? To show a little worry, a little concern? To act like she cared more about her granddaughter than she did about the damn dusting or where the frigging keys were?

Faith pressed the heels of her hands against her eyes. It was like high school all over again when she'd often sat on the porch feeling alone and miserable.

Her grandma had her own life and seemed to think as long as Faith had food and shelter, she was fine. Alice had never, not that Faith could recall, asked her how her day had gone. Or how she was doing in general. Or why Faith spent so much time alone in her room.

Likely because that was how Alice preferred it.

From the day her mom had dropped her off in Last Stand, her grandmother had never altered her routine for Faith, or made a point of spending quality time with her. It was a bit like a car merging into traffic. Her grandma might have let her in, but she'd made sure it hadn't affected the flow of her life.

Sighing, Faith lowered her hands and opened her eyes.

And startled when she saw Gage standing there.

He offered a sheepish grin. "Sorry. I didn't know if you were meditating or had found a way to sleep with your arms up like that, but either way, I didn't want to interrupt."

"You're early," she stated.

"I know. I can come back later, but I thought if you were free now..."

He leaned against the support post and crossed his arms over his chest. He'd looked sexy in his dark blue uniform, because—uniform—but in jeans, a black T-shirt, and a matching Stetson, he took sexy to a whole other level. Just as he had that night in San Antonio. Coupled with the fantasy she'd harbored about him since high school, was it any wonder she'd accepted his hand and his offer to go back to his room?

Before that, though, he'd asked her to go out with him

for some fresh air. Once outside, he'd backed her against the building, pressed the length of his hard body against hers, and slid his tongue intimately along hers in a soul-searing kiss. Despite the fact she'd been more than sober enough to know what she'd been doing, she'd wondered since if *he'd* have done what he had if he hadn't been drinking.

Faith sighed. Probably not.

"No, it's fine," she said, referring to his comment about being early. "We can go now."

It wasn't as though she planned on eating lunch anyway.

"Did you get to the doctor? What did he say?"

For a moment, Faith panicked. Her heart lurched and she forgot to breathe. Why would he care what the doctor had said? Had he realized the condom had failed and was waiting for her to say something? Could he somehow read on her face or see some sign she was pregnant? But then she realized he was referring to her knee, and her breath whooshed from her chest.

"She said it was bruised. That it was okay to use the crutches for a day to help get around, but that I should still walk on it, too, even if it hurts. If I keep it immobile too long, it'll just tighten up more."

"Ice and anti-inflammatories?"

"Yeah." She didn't bother correcting him on the medicine. He'd learn soon enough. And this wasn't the place.

He nodded. "So, all in all, it could've been worse."

Knowing she could have lost the baby, she nodded.

He pushed off the post and picked her crutches from the porch. "You ready?"

Sure. If he meant about ready to throw up.

He followed her down the steps but cut across the grass to get ahead of her. He opened the passenger door on the Jeep.

He drove out of town, taking the gravel road that followed Hickory Creek Spur until he reached the first turnoff where a sign advertised a day-use area. Slowing, he turned down the narrow road toward the sparkling water.

The small clearing was empty, and they had the picnic table to themselves. Combined with the thick bushes of willows on either side, it was as private as one could find without staying home or riding out in the middle of a field.

"No, it's okay. Just leave them," Faith said when Gage reached into the back for her crutches. "It's not that far to the picnic table."

He reached into the back anyway and pulled out a small, insulated cooler bag.

"In case we get thirsty," he said as he slung the bag over his shoulder.

It was just like him to think of that. Using the door as support, Faith hopped a few steps. By the time she swung it shut, Gage was beside her, offering his arm. She looked at his muscled forearm and her insides clutched. Golden skin, blond hair, and the same substantial watch he'd had on the other day. The one containing a bunch of small dials within the face.

Faith was a sucker for hands and the black watch perfectly accented the strength of his—and reminded her just what his hand was capable of.

Her breath jammed in her lungs. Everything about this would be so much easier if he were an ass. Or a troll. Or if she didn't know him well enough to know nothing about his behavior was fake or contrived. He didn't do anything with an ulterior motive in mind. If he was offering his help, it was because he genuinely wanted to give it.

And she'd be the ass for refusing to take it.

It's just an arm, for Pete's sake. Stop being ridiculous.

Stretching her lips into a smile, Faith reached for him.

But it wasn't only an arm, and she'd been a fool to tell herself otherwise. The moment she touched his skin, a blast of heat shot up her arm, through her chest, and sizzled down her legs. It also electrified all the womanly parts in between. A soft mew escaped her lips.

"Knee still hurts pretty bad, huh?"

"Yeah," Faith managed. "Pretty bad."

It wasn't a lie. Every time she put weight on her left leg, even with his support, needle-like stabs of pain jabbed her knee. Of course, she'd made that mewling sound before taking an actual step. But he didn't mention it, so neither did she. She just kept her gaze on the glittering water and her legs moving forward. The gravel area was flat, without roots or rocks to trip over, and it wasn't long before they reached the table and she was able to let go of him.

"Thanks."

He set the cooler bag onto the faded, scarred table. "No problem."

They settled side-by-side on the bench with their backs to the tabletop so they could watch the water slip by. Usually, nothing relaxed Faith like campfire or water, but there wasn't anything relaxing about sitting next to Gage, knowing they had to talk about their night in San Antonio. Knowing what had resulted from that night had tension settling like a rock in the pit of her stomach.

The heat added another layer of discomfort. With the sun high in the sky, the trees provided no relief from the blazing rays. Even in shorts, sweat trickled down her spine and at the back of her neck. She didn't know how Gage tolerated it in jeans and boots. But then it was better he had on more clothes than less. Not that he didn't look spectacular in jeans, because he did. The way they hugged his thighs and...

"You wouldn't happen to have water in there, would you?"

The skin at the corners of his eyes crinkled as he smiled. "I do. Ice cold, too."

Grabbing the bag by the strap, he dragged it across the surface of the table. Faith bit her lip as he pulled on the zipper. She remembered not so long ago, when the only sounds between them had been their ragged breathing and the sound of her inching his zipper down.

"For you," he said as he handed her a clear bottle.

"Thanks." Faith yanked it from his hand.

She pressed the chilled plastic to her heated cheek, closed her eyes, and sighed.

"Sorry, I guess I wasn't thinking about the sun." He looked around. "Stand up."

"What?"

"Stand up. I'll move the table over there."

He pointed to the copse of willows on their left and the thin band of shade they provided. Since she felt as though she were burning up, Faith stood. She shifted her weight to her good leg while Gage scraped the table across the gravel to the edge of the silvery-leafed bushes. She managed to limp her way over before he turned for her. If the point was to cool her off, then the less she touched him, the better.

They were able to settle into much the same position, facing the creek with no noise but that created by nature. The soft whisper of the water trickling past. The skittering of birds rustling the leaves.

"Did I hurt you?"

Of course he'd lead with that. And it only made her feel worse. He was more worried about her feelings than whatever she had done to his. Feeling her throat tightening, Faith uncapped her water and took a long sip.

"No," she answered.

She kept her gaze firmly on a gray rock that stuck out of the creek, watching as the flowing water swirled little whirlpools around it. She heard his relieved exhale loud and clear.

"That's good. I'd wondered—"

"I'm sorry."

The bottle in his hands crinkled as he flexed his fingers around it. "You're sorry you slept with me, or you're sorry you left without a word?"

As far as shots went, that one hit the bull's-eye. But it wasn't anything she didn't deserve.

"I thought leaving the way I did was best."

"For you, you mean."

She dared look at him. Beneath the brim of his Stetson, his gaze pierced hers.

"And for you. I didn't want you to feel uncomfortable or obligated to say something you didn't mean." She shifted her gaze when his narrowed.

"What made you think I'd feel uncomfortable?"

She scoffed. "Oh, I don't know. The fact we hadn't seen or talked to each other since high school and the first time we did, we ended up sleeping together."

"That was your decision."

Her head came up so fast she made herself dizzy.

He held up his palms. "I wasn't talking about sleeping together. I think it was pretty clear we both wanted that. I meant the not keeping in touch after high school. When you had your number changed without telling me and never bothered to inform me when you came to town, I took that as a pretty clear sign you wanted nothing to do with me."

She sipped some more water. Too bad her regret didn't go down as easily.

"It wasn't you, specifically. It was everything." She tucked her hair behind her ear. "I wanted a clean break—or as much of one as I could with my grandma still living here."

He leaned back, hooked his elbows onto the tabletop behind him, and stretched his legs out in front, crossing his ankles. Faith's gaze shifted to his brown boots. Gage might spend most of his time as an EMT, but the scratches, scuffs, and dirt marring the well-worn leather on his feet proved he also spent a lot of time working the ranch.

"Did you get it?"

Faith thought to what she'd envisioned when she'd packed her bags and moved and where she'd ended up. She'd hoped to have made more of a change than she had. It was depressing to realize the biggest difference she'd made was her address. These many years later, she was still insecure about who she was. Still had a crush on the same guy. Still had no future with said guy.

"Well, I have a job and a nice little apartment, a newer car, a few good friends. I can go wherever I want and don't have to worry about everyone knowing my history. Feeling sorry for me."

Which had been a big reason for the move. Everyone in Last Stand knew she'd been abandoned by her mother. That Linda hadn't cared enough about her only child to keep her. But even worse than that was the fact that Linda was a slut, and everyone knew it. Everyone knew the real reason she'd abandoned Faith. Because the men in Linda's life had started to look at Faith.

Linda hadn't left Faith to protect her from those kinds of men. She'd done it to keep the attention on herself. And Faith had felt eyes watching her ever since, starting with her grandma's, just waiting for her to turn out the same. Waiting for her to end up unwed and pregnant.

Well she'd proved them right, hadn't she?

Like mother like daughter.

Only she wasn't going to risk making the same mistakes her mother had. The similarities ended at the unplanned pregnancy. Faith was forging a different path. One where her baby wouldn't suffer the same fate she had.

She'd spent most of her life feeling as though she didn't matter. As though she was a burden. She was going to ensure that never happened to her child. No matter if it broke her heart in the process.

First, though, she had to tell Gage.

Feeling green, Faith leaned forward.

Gage shifted down the bench. His strong, warm hand settled between her shoulder blades.

"You okay?"

She pinched her eyes closed. Nope, she wasn't. But stalling wasn't going to change that.

She forced herself to look up, look at him. "I'm okay."

His green eyes searched hers. "You always were a terrible liar."

She looked back at the water. Though she'd never told him how she really felt about him, she'd always been able to tell him everything else.

"I just thought I'd have more to show for my life at this point, you know?"

"It's not like we're old, Faith. There's lots of time. And you don't have to prove anything to anyone." He leaned forward until she looked at him. "You never did."

She fiddled with the cap on her bottle. "I just wanted to show everyone that I was better than my mom. I tried my whole life to prove I was."

"You are better than her. You always have been. You just never believed it."

It was an old argument and one, clearly, she wasn't ever going to win. She'd never been able to convince him she had something to prove, and he'd never succeeded in convincing her she didn't.

So, instead of beating a dead horse, she changed the subject.

"You were right. It was clear we both wanted sex that night. You didn't force or coerce me. And I'm sorry if my sneaking out made you feel like you had done something wrong. I'm not mad at you. Wasn't then, nor am I now. I just thought it best to leave it as a one-night stand."

Gage rubbed his thumb over her knuckles. "Well, that's just it. What if that's not what I want?"

SHE GAPED. "DON'T be ridiculous."

Her words would have made him angrier if it weren't for the deer-in-the-headlights look that glazed her hazel eyes.

"I'm not. In fact, I'm quite serious."

She zipped the cooler closed, shoved it toward him. "Let's go."

Instead of grabbing the cooler, Gage grasped her arms. Though he was careful not to hurt her, he increased his grip when she tried to wriggle free.

"Faith, this isn't high school. You're not running away this time."

Her mouth pinched. "I'd always told you I was leaving right after school. And you came by the day I left. You helped me pack my car, so don't tell me I ran away."

"You'd never said you were leaving the very next day after graduation. By the time I'd heard through the rumor mill, you'd already had half your car loaded. You were so excited to be leaving, I doubt it would've mattered what I said."

When she didn't so much as blink, he knew he'd been right. And it made him feel as shitty now as it had then.

"That didn't stop me from trying to call you two days later." His gaze drilled into hers. "Which was when I discovered you'd changed your number."

"I didn't see the point in keeping in touch. I knew we'd hardly see each other."

"And that night in San Antonio?"

"It just made sense. We live in different cities and have different lives. And we'd already had sex so…"

"So, what? You think that's all I was after?"

She shrugged.

"I'll have you know I've driven past your grandma's place so many times since that night in San Antonio, hoping you'd be home, that I'm surprised nobody on that street has called the cops on me."

He finally got a reaction he was happy with when she jerked.

"Yeah, it's true. And maybe I could've asked Alice for your number, but I didn't think you'd want her wondering why I wanted it. Which was why I've been to that bar on the River Walk three times since then. I was trying to find you. But all I accomplished was spinning my wheels."

He expected that would get her back up. That she'd fall back on her usual defensiveness to say something along the lines of, *"Then why are you here if everything about me is so difficult?"*

Instead, she looked stricken. The color drained from her cheeks.

Shit. He'd just wanted to show her how much he'd tried to find her. To prove to her she clearly meant something to him for him to go to those lengths. Instead, he'd made it sound like it had been a pain in his ass.

Smooth, Gage. Real smooth.

"I didn't mean it like that." He hurried to explain.

She shook her head. "No, you're right. From the beginning, I've inconvenienced you."

Needing to make light of things, he nudged her good knee with his. "I wouldn't call what happened in San Antonio an inconvenience."

Instead of lightening the somberness that filled the small picnic area, his joke had the opposite effect. Like an incoming storm, he watched as shadows filled her eyes. Despite the heat that had his T-shirt sticking to his back, she held herself close, shoulders curved, like she was bracing for disaster.

He didn't know how else to reassure her. As his mind scrambled to think of something, she angled herself toward him. He wouldn't say her eyes were swimming with tears, but they shone with them. Despite the fact her jaw was clenched tight, her chin wobbled with suppressed emotion.

He'd only ever seen her looking that distressed once before—when he'd caught up with her in the middle of the football field with her locker contents overflowing her arms. She'd looked at him then as she did now.

Like her world was over.

Then, he'd known how to help her. Now, he hadn't the slightest—

"I'm pregnant."

Chapter Five

"You're…" He blinked. Shook his head. "But—"

"Yeah," she agreed. "Those were my first reactions, too. Apparently, the only way to ensure an unwanted pregnancy is to not have sex in the first place."

He was glad he was sitting because his head was suddenly spinning. She was pregnant? That meant they were going to be parents. That meant there weren't going to be any more disappearing acts. That meant… And then…

He fought to rein in his scattered thoughts. God, he had to take this one step at a time.

"The condom. It must have broken. Well, obviously it did. I just"—he held out his hands—"never noticed." How could he not have noticed?

She looked at him, her eyes wide.

"What?" he asked. Did she blame him?

"You're not even questioning that the baby is yours." Her lips trembled.

Even with his thoughts going a mile a minute, that one was a no-brainer.

"First of all, unless you've changed a lot in the past six years, you were never one to sleep around." In fact, talk in the locker room had run more toward she was frigid that anything else.

"Second, I don't imagine you'd be telling me if it wasn't mine. Especially since we haven't talked since that night." And not six years before that night.

She stared at her hands. "I figured with my mom being who she is—"

He placed his hand over hers. "Stop. It never entered my mind. I know you're not like her."

Her choppy breaths told him she was struggling not to cry. He remained as he was until it evened out. It gave him some time to settle his thoughts, to focus on what came next.

Number one, he wanted her near. He wanted to be there for her, to be part of the process. As for a relationship with her, that was another no-brainer. He just had to convince her to move back.

"So what do we now?" he asked.

She moved her hands, forcing him to do the same. She rubbed her palms over her hips. If he didn't know better, he'd say she was nervous, but he didn't know what she'd have to be nervous about. Surely telling him had been the worst—

A ball of dread landed in the pit of his stomach. Looking into her eyes didn't alleviate it any. A tornado of emotions swirled within them. There was more she wasn't telling him.

He forced himself to ask what he feared most. "Were you thinking of having an abortion?"

Immediately, she shook her head. "No. That never entered my mind."

He heaved a sigh of relief. Thank God. Then they still had a chance at—

"But I have decided to give it up for adoption."

His jaw literally fell open.

"I know, for you, this all seems very sudden, but I've thought about this, Gage. I've had weeks to weigh the options and this is the best one."

Best? For who?

"But you haven't even talked to me about it yet. Faith, I'd never leave you to do this alone." He reached for her again. "We can do this. You can move back and—"

Faith gaped, like the idea he'd want their child had never occurred to her. For a split second, the clouds in her eyes cleared. For a moment, his heart raced with possibilities. But then her face set and she leaned away from his touch.

"It's not in my genetics to be a good parent, Gage. And I won't do to my baby what was done to me." Her gaze hardened. "I won't."

"But your mom was alone. And your grandma, too. You have me, Faith. I'll be with you every step of the way."

She flinched as though he'd told her he could care less rather than the fact he'd just promised his support.

"I'm going to college next year. Finally. I've waited a long time to do that, Gage, and if I don't go, I know it's just a matter of time until I resent the baby for missing my chance, for not chasing what I wanted."

Past hurt darkened her eyes. "I know what it's like to feel resented. Nobody deserves that." She took a deep, shuddering breath. "I'm sorry, Gage. My mind is made up. I just came to Last Stand because you had a right to know."

It scared him. It scared the shit out of him. Because he knew Faith Stone, and when she decided on something, there was no changing her mind. Which meant she was serious about adoption.

He dragged his hand over his mouth. He really only had one option. And while it scared him just as shitless, maybe more, he already knew he'd do it.

Because the alternative was unthinkable.

"Fine," he said through lips that suddenly felt numb. "If you're serious about giving up our child, then I want it."

GAGE DROPPED FAITH off at home and headed to the hospital. He was vaguely aware of parking between a red minivan and a dusty SUV. He was pretty sure he waved a greeting and nodded at some of the staff he encountered, though he couldn't have said who.

The whole thing was like some sort of out-of-body experience.

He hadn't felt like himself since he'd been told about the baby.

But, hell, it wasn't as though he'd been expecting Faith to lay that kind of news on him. He'd replayed that night in his head and how he distinctly—despite the lust that had wiped his brain of everything but Faith and getting her naked—remembered protecting them both before he slid into her.

And then to add the bit about adoption…

Though his mind had still been reeling, he'd known instantly he wanted the baby. He hadn't needed to think about it. He rubbed a shaking hand through his hair. He wasn't going to lie. Being a dad freaked him out a little bit. Not because he didn't want kids, but he hadn't wanted them now. And, if he couldn't convince her otherwise, he'd sure as hell never planned on raising one by himself.

Not that he'd told her he was going to try to change her mind. No, that wouldn't work. The fastest way to get her running was to tell her his intentions. And he didn't want her to run. Because, God forbid, if he wasn't able to get her to change her mind, he didn't want her disappearing again until the baby was born.

Because he already wanted to do more than just pick up the baby when it was born. He wanted to go to doctor's appointments, wanted to be a support for her through the remaining months. He wanted her in Last Stand, dammit. But not just in town, at the ranch. Because living with Alice was toxic for Faith.

There were too many bad memories there for her. Too many ghosts telling her she couldn't be the kind of mother he knew she could be. So, no, staying with Alice wasn't happening.

He needed to get Faith and the baby to the ranch, where, despite the fact he and his brothers still weren't the tight-knit group they'd once been, they at least loved each other. Gage didn't doubt that. And they stood together, even if it was awkward at times. He wanted to show Faith the kind of home their child could grow in. Grow and thrive in.

But what she'd laid out was enough for one afternoon. Besides, she'd suddenly looked wiped out, and between her sore knee and head, not to mention the pregnancy, he'd taken her back to her grandmother's to rest.

And now, there he was, walking through a fog on his way

to his dad's room.

Joe was as Gage had last seen him when he'd checked on him after his shift yesterday. Cords still ran from the heart monitor, up the right sleeve of his gown, to the pads taped to his chest. An IV line still dripped clear fluids into his left hand. Country-western music still played from the small radio Gage had brought him a few days ago.

He'd talked to enough patients who'd woken from comas to believe them when they said they'd sensed what was going on around them while they'd been unconscious. Maybe his dad wouldn't remember the station or the exact type of music, but Gage believed he'd remember there was music. And that it had made him feel less alone.

Assuming, of course, Joe ever woke up.

Gage rubbed the back of his neck as he took the lone chair in the room and stared at the man who'd sired him. His feelings toward his dad were complicated, to say the least.

He missed the dad who'd taken them fishing and riding. Who'd put the first Stetson on his head. Who'd nodded with pride when Gage had ridden his bike for the first time without training wheels.

He was angry at the man who'd pulled away from his family when they'd needed him most. When Gage had needed a hug and some reassurance that life was going to be okay, even without his mom in it.

Though Joe had come around some by the time Dallas had left, it had never been the same since. He'd seemed to think that just showing up again, being present again, was enough. Without a word of apology. Without any consequences for his actions.

He'd just stepped in where he'd left off. The fact he'd assumed they'd just be so grateful he was once again willing to be part of their lives hurt Gage as much as Joe's absence had. His brothers felt the same. Even without discussing it, it was obvious in the stilted relationship they had with their dad to this day.

So when Gage had gotten older and needed an opinion on the Jeep before he'd bought it, it was Ryker he'd asked. It was Ryker who'd gone with him and looked over the engine, who'd told him the secondhand Jeep was worth the money. And it had been Cam who'd told him about women when Ryker had stumbled over the words.

As much as Gage appreciated what his brothers had done, it had never made up for the resentment he'd felt toward his dad. If he'd manned up, been accountable for what he'd done instead of just trying to pretend it had never happened, or worse, hadn't affected them, then maybe they'd have a relationship now. As it was, his dad was more a boss than anything else.

Gage might still be reeling from Faith's news, but one thing he already knew was that he couldn't imagine any circumstance where he wouldn't be there for his kid.

His kid.

"Oh, God."

Spreading his knees, Gage braced his forearms on his thighs and hung his head.

"I don't know what you're looking at, but I'm pretty sure God isn't there."

Gage scoffed as he lifted his head. Like Ryker and Hudson, Dallas was pretty serious. Of all of them, it was more himself and Cam that were the jokesters. But there'd been a change in Dallas the past two weeks. His girlfriend Ashley was likely responsible for some of it, but Gage suspected the change had a lot to do with their dad's heart attack as well.

Which stood to reason. Gage couldn't be the only one affected by the possibility of losing Joe.

"Don't say that to Cam," Gage said as his brother strode further into the room, his work boots clomping on the shiny linoleum. "I'm sure he'd argue differently."

Dallas snorted. "That's because Cam thinks his dick *is* a God."

It felt good to laugh after the afternoon he'd had. But it didn't last long. Dallas stopped at the side of the bed, looking down.

"No change?"

"I haven't been here long, but doesn't seem like it."

Dallas's deep sigh reflected Gage's thoughts exactly. Though their dad had suffered a heart attack, all the tests had shown he only suffered mild damage. Medically, there was no reason for Joe to still be unconscious. It didn't make sense.

But then, not much about his dad's circumstances made sense. He'd been brought in by a young woman that had slipped out of the hospital while the staff was busy. By the time Gage had been notified that his dad was in emergency and he'd contacted the others, she was nowhere to be found. Joe's car was nowhere to be found, either. So the woman, whoever she was, had cared enough to bring Joe in, but clearly didn't want anyone to know who she was.

Why? What did she have to hide? Had she upset their father so much he'd had a heart attack? If so, what could she have possibly said to him to have that kind of effect? And where the hell was the car? At her house? It sure as heck wasn't at the Diamond G or anywhere in town. Gage, Ryker, and Cam had all driven around looking for it.

And frankly, the fact he'd taken the car and not the ranch truck he usually drove added to the mystery. As a rule, they only used the car if they were short wheels or one of the trucks broke down. Since that hadn't been the case the day Joe was hospitalized, then the reason for the car was even more suspect. As though he'd deliberately driven it to keep from being recognized.

At first, they'd all suspected perhaps his dad had a girlfriend. But then Dallas had pointed out that if she was as young as the nurses thought, it was possible she could be his daughter.

Which meant his dad would have cheated on his mom.

The thought ripped Gage in half. So he tried not to come to conclusions until they got some more facts.

"Where's Ashley?" Gage asked, referring to Dallas's girlfriend.

"At home. There's some concert tonight at the AT & T Centre in San Antonio. Brittany and her friends are going to see it. One of the other moms is going to drive them to it, but Ashley volunteered to pick them up."

It was strange to think of his brother dating a woman with a sixteen-year-old daughter. That meant if they got married, and Gage would bet it was heading that way, he'd be an instant uncle. But then, he'd just become an instant dad, so go figure.

"They're both coming tomorrow. Ashley's going to work some more on organizing dad's office, and if Ryker doesn't have every hour I'm there already booked, I was hoping to take the girls for a trail ride."

"Ryker mentioned the bunkhouse needing work. About you and Roy working on that."

"Yeah. It's probably years overdue."

Dallas scraped his hand over his stubbled jaw. It was always like that. Gage didn't know how he stood it. The itch would drive him crazy. Gage ran his fingers along his own jawline. Still smooth, thanks to his shave before going to see Faith.

The nurse came in then, on silent rubber soles. She smiled at them as she checked Joe's vitals and made notes in his file before tucking the chart back into the slot at the foot of the bed.

"How long are you planning on staying?" Dallas asked Gage once the nurse had left.

Gage shrugged. "I'm in no hurry."

"Do you mind if I head out? The sooner I can get to Ryker's to-do list, the more time I'll have for that trail ride tomorrow."

Gage gave him a knowing look. "You'll go on that ride no matter what Ryker says."

Dallas's lips curved. "Well, yeah, but I'll have to hear less bitching if I get more done first."

"Sure, go ahead."

"I'll see you there." Dallas took three steps then turned around. "Whose turn is it to make supper?"

"Cam's."

"Thank God. I wasn't in the mood for frozen pizza."

Without another word, Dallas left. Gage slumped in his chair. Dallas could've stayed. It wouldn't have killed him to pass an hour with his brother. They could've talked. Dallas had had an issue with one of his employees not too long ago that had resulted, due to a bad judgment call by Dallas, in his brother serving some community service.

The community service was lending his expertise as a builder to help erect a House of Hope. The recipient happened to be his new girlfriend and her daughter.

Gage would've liked to know the progress, look at the pictures he was sure Dallas had on his phone. Dallas could've asked what else had been going on that week, both at the ranch and at work. Though Gage doubted he'd have told him about Faith and her news, it would have been nice to share the rest. To know his brother cared about the rest.

Dallas talked about wanting to take Ashley and her daughter for a trail ride, but had he asked Gage? Or Cam or Ryker?

But then, had Gage asked him?

His loud sigh filled the room. No. No, he hadn't.

He rubbed his palm across his tight chest as he came to his feet. His thoughts were too big for the small confines of the sterile hospital room. He couldn't take a full breath without the antiseptic smell clogging his senses. Not to mention looking at his motionless father lying there, the jagged line of the heart rate monitor and the slow rise and fall of his chest the only indication his dad was alive.

Gage's gaze shifted to the window ledge where three vases of mixed flower arrangements perched. They'd been there a few days now, given by the local businesses in town the Diamond G patronized. Business was where Joe Granger excelled. It was the personal aspect he needed to work on.

What they all needed to work on.

"I'm not sure where to start mending fences, but I'm going to try, Dad. Because I miss the way things used to be before Mom got sick."

And because he wanted his family back together, emotionally, before his son or daughter came into the world.

Gage pressed hard against his chest where his breath suddenly caught. Geez, he was going to have to get used the idea of being a dad before he gave himself a heart attack when the reminder snuck up on him.

"Hopefully, that gives you something to fight for, Dad."

A new grandchild might, too, but Gage wasn't ready to say those words out loud yet. Not when just the thought of it felt as though he was being pressed in a cattle squeeze.

"Anyway, one of us will be by tomorrow." Gage set his hand on his dad's arm. His throat tightened, but this time for a whole other reason. "We need you, Dad. To be part of this family. To be part of our lives."

There was a knock at the door. "Is this a bad time?" a deep, masculine voice asked.

Gage turned. Some of the heaviness of the room lifted as he recognized Doc McBride.

A retired general practitioner, Doc McBride had delivered Gage and the rest of his brothers, and was—besides a good friend of Joe's—inarguably, one of the nicest people Gage had ever met.

"No, not at all." Gage met the man halfway and shook his strong, calloused hand. "In fact, your timing is perfect. I was just leaving. I have a patient I want to check on before I head out to the ranch." He smiled. "I'm sure Dad will enjoy your company."

The man walked past Gage to the bedside. "No change yet?"

"No."

Doc took off his tan Stetson. "That's a shame." He turned to Gage. "You ever find that woman that brought him in?"

"Not yet."

"Well, for your sake, son, I hope they do. If nothing else, to get some answers."

Gage nodded. "Yeah, that would be nice. In the meantime, though, I should be on my way. Nice to see you again, Doc."

They shook hands and Gage left him to his visit. He checked his watch and winced. He really should get back to the ranch. He'd promised Ryker he wouldn't be gone all day. But he could spare a little time to check in on one of his patients.

In the hallway, instead of turning right toward the front door, Gage veered left. He zigged and zagged down a few corridors, past stretchers lining the wall and two nurses' stations until he arrived at the room he was after.

The door was open, and the elderly woman was sitting in bed, glasses hanging off the edge of her nose as she did a crossword puzzle. She had more than three vases filling her windowsill, and it made Gage smile. Though she was alone at the moment, it was clear the woman was well loved and hadn't been without visitors.

He knocked softly before walking in.

"How's my favorite patient today?"

THANK GOD HER grandma was in the backyard fussing with her small garden when Gage dropped Faith off.

It gave her time to hobble up to her room and, with the window closed and the drapes drawn, take some time to contemplate her life. Why was this even happening? They'd used protection. It was why she'd never thought about her period being late.

Until she'd gone in the bathroom and seen a tampon wrapper in the garbage. Her and her roommate, Soraya, tended to have similar cycles, so it wasn't until she'd seen the wrapper that she'd realized she, too, should've been having her period.

When it hadn't come a week later, she'd finally bought a test. And cried at the results.

Thinking of Soraya, and needing a friend, she shot off a quick text.

Because it was Saturday and her roommate was a school-teacher, hopefully, she wouldn't be too busy for a call.

Got time for a chat?

The answer was almost immediate.

Yes! I've been dying to know how it went.

Faith peered around the edge of her curtain. Her grand-ma was at the back of the yard, weeding her small raspberry patch. Without fear of being overheard, Faith dialed her friend.

"Oh, my God. I'm so glad you called," Soraya said by way of hello. "Tell me everything!"

Settling in on the bed, Faith did indeed tell her everything. From hitting the ditch and having Gage happen by, to Gage bringing her crutches, and to finally telling him everything that afternoon.

"Wow. He wants to raise the baby. Did you see that coming?"

Faith pressed her fingers to her eye. "No, but once he said it, I can't say it came as a total surprise, either."

In fact, it was more surprising she hadn't thought of the possibility herself. He'd been raised by two parents until his mom died. And while his dad might have withdrawn, he'd never physically left. He had relationships with his brothers, and she knew by how he'd spoken of his mom back in high school that he loved his family. Gage had always been kind and open to strangers. He had a generous heart. Of course he'd want his own child.

But she hadn't been thinking about Gage or his family. She'd been thinking about her own life, her own past. How she'd grown without a father and how the parade of men that had walked through her mother's life had never looked at Faith as anything but a nuisance, a cramp in their style. And those were only the men who stayed longer than a week. Most had left after one night.

"So now what?" Soraya asked.

"I don't know. There's more to think about now, and it was a lot for both of us to take in, so he took me home.

We'll get together again tomorrow to discuss things some more. But, Soraya, this changes things for me."

"I know, hon," she agreed, her voice soft with compassion.

"The point is to give my baby the best life possible. How is that going to happen when it's being raised in Last Stand? Where most everyone knows its mother? Where it will grow being reminded almost daily, like I was, that its mom had chosen to give it up?"

Her heart ached just thinking of it. She wanted better for her baby. So much more than she'd had. And while Gage would be a great dad and give it unconditional love, it wouldn't change the fact it would be raised in a town where everyone knew its mother and her history.

"It's not the same. Your mom couldn't be bothered. She was too interested in partying. You're doing it for the right reasons."

Maybe. But she wondered if her child would see it that way. And the thought of it growing up hating her as much as she hated Linda…

"It would be so much easier if it went to strangers."

Which was an absolute lie, because nothing about this was easy. The thought of the baby with Gage was actually a reassuring one, because there would never be any doubt it was loved. She'd never have to wonder if her child was in a safe home, if it had everything it needed.

But picturing Gage holding it? Walking to calm the baby if it had colic or was fussy? Laying it down in a crib? It ripped her heart out. Because she wanted to do all those things, too. But she couldn't. She wouldn't risk being the kind of mother Linda was. The kind of cold, heartless woman her grandmother was. She wouldn't subject her child to that.

After a long pause, Soraya asked, "Is there anything I can do?"

"I wish. We're just going to have to figure this out, I guess."

"It'll mean spending more time with him."

"I know." Faith blew out a breath. That was going to be difficult. Because when she was with him, looking into his green eyes, all the feelings she'd had in high school came back.

Combined with the ones she'd experienced that night in San Antonio, it was a deadly combination. Because all it was going to do was hurt her even more. There was no future for them. She'd worked hard to save for college, and she wasn't giving up on that when it was finally within reach.

And with him wanting to keep their baby, a future was even more impossible. There was no playing "happy family" when she didn't have the right genetics to be a good mother.

With her heart hurting worse than her knee and head, Faith ended the call after promising to keep her friend in the loop. Then, with the weight of the world pressing in on her, she limped across the hall and into the bathroom. She splashed cold water on her face before hobbling back to her bedroom and lying down.

Rolling onto her side, she pulled the light throw blanket from the foot of her bed. Tucking it in close, Faith closed her eyes, wishing for sleep. Anything that would give her a reprieve from the mess her life had become.

Chapter Six

"THANK YOU FOR supper."

Alice dabbed at her mouth with her cloth napkin. "You know I like to eat at five."

"I know. I'm sorry. I was tired. I didn't expect to sleep so long."

As she'd already explained three times since limping down the stairs thirty minutes ago.

"When I was your age, I didn't have time to nap. I had a daughter to raise and a household to run. On my own."

"I know, Grandma. It's not like I don't have a job. I just happen to have the weekend off and thought I'd take advantage of it and come visit."

"Day off," she scoffed. "As if I ever had such a thing."

Faith rolled her eyes as she helped clear the table, ensuring her back was to Alice when she did. She didn't need a lecture about her attitude on top of her laziness.

They finished the dishes without talking. The kitchen clock ticking away was the only sound besides that of dishes and silverware clanging.

When her grandmother was done, she wrung out the dishcloth and set it over the divider between the sinks to dry. Then she wiped her hands on the decorative tea towel hanging from the stove's handle.

She looked over at Faith. Her face was as cool as the air conditioning blowing through the house. "I'm going over to the library. They're having a speaker in tonight."

Her grandma didn't bother asking if Faith wanted to go or how her granddaughter was going to spend the evening. It didn't matter that Faith might want company, that she might also want to get out.

It had been the same growing up. Faith hadn't minded at first. The nights she had the house to herself were, if not fun, at least stress free. She'd watched the TV shows she wasn't allowed to watch normally. Had long baths where she wasn't nagged about the amount of water she used or the length of time she spent in the bathroom.

She'd played her music loud and talked on the phone with Gage, which she never did when her grandmother was home. But after a while those nights just got lonely and boring. She hadn't wanted to be alone. She'd wanted company. Someone to talk to in person, do things with.

She'd tried telling her grandmother. It had fallen on deaf ears. Why was she complaining when she had everything she could possibly want? And after all Alice had done for her, Faith shouldn't begrudge her some semblance of a social life.

She hadn't cared that the thing Faith wanted most was the thing she was most denied.

Her grandma strolled back in, purse over her shoulder and a light sweater draped over her arm.

"I won't be long," her grandmother said. It was the same thing she'd always said when leaving Faith alone. No doubt to ensure her granddaughter toed the line, as she'd have no idea when her grandma would return.

In this case, a quick search of the library's event section on their website would tell Faith what she needed to know. Because, despite not being invited along, she had no intention of staying home. Provided, of course, her grandmother didn't take her car.

"Have fun."

With a disgruntled harrumph, Alice marched out of the kitchen. Faith held her breath as the woman neared the key rack. Then let it out in a long whoosh when her grandma walked past it.

Faith grinned. Thank God for her grandma's frugalness.

She watched through the living room window until her grandma turned the corner onto Main Street. Then, as fast as she could manage on her crutches, grabbed her purse and her grandma's keys.

It wasn't until she was on her way out of Last Stand with George Strait crooning through the speakers that she realized she really only had one place to go. The Diamond G.

Well, crap. She didn't have anything else to say to Gage at the moment. She chewed her lip as she slowed. But where else could she go?

To heck with it, she decided. She'd go check on her car. Nothing else. With any luck, she wouldn't run into Gage at all.

WHILE GAGE REAPED a lot of satisfaction from his day job, he much preferred the smells of the ranch. He'd take the stench of cow and horse manure over that of blood, fear, and death any day. Which was good considering what he smelled like after cleaning the corrals.

He parked the skid steer in the long machine shed where the tractors and other equipment were stored and followed the well-worn path that led first to Ryker's garage, then on to the main yard. Long shadows from the house and surrounding trees spread across the ground.

He hadn't asked about Faith's car when he'd first returned from town. He'd been anxious to get to work and have something else to focus on besides the news she'd dropped on him and just how he felt about it. He could've asked at supper, but he'd decided to finish the job rather than fill the house with his stink.

Now he was ready for both a meal and a hot shower.

Hearing the clang of tools coming from the open door of the garage, Gage decided to stop in and ask about the progress on Faith's car. Like hospitals, garages carried with them their own distinct smell and it was that of grease and oil that welcomed Gage when he stepped inside.

Ryker was just locking up his tall red toolbox. Though crime wasn't a prevalent issue in Last Stand, Ryker's tool chest was worth thousands of dollars and it was his habit to keep it locked unless he was working in the garage.

His brother swung around the moment Gage stepped inside. "Geez, don't bring that smell in here," Ryker said, his mouth twisted in a grimace. "Get out before you stink up my garage."

Gage backed out as Ryker started pulling off his greasy coveralls.

"You all done with her car?" he asked.

"Not quite. The exhaust got bent when she hit the ditch. The muffler shop in Luckenbach didn't have one in stock that would fit, but it'll be in Monday afternoon."

"Not till Monday? What if she has to work Monday?"

"Out of my hands. It was the best I could do."

Gage nodded. Ryker would have done his best. "But everything else is done?"

"Yeah. A buddy of mine owns an auto wrecker near Fredericksburg. I was able to get a new rim for her tire and an oil pan, since she'd ruptured hers."

"That's good. Save her some money."

Ryker scowled as he hung up his coveralls next to the overhead door. "I don't believe in people paying more than they need to."

They started walking. It didn't go unnoticed that Ryker kept a fair distance between them. Not that Gage blamed him. He could barely tolerate his own stench.

"I didn't realize you guys were still friends," Ryker said.

"We aren't, necessarily. But we have a history together." And a future, whatever that was going to be, but Gage kept that to himself. There were things he and Faith needed to figure out and sort through before he told his brothers they were going to be uncles.

He'd had a lot of time to think while he was cleaning out the corrals, and while his thoughts included Faith, they'd included his brothers, as well. And what he'd told his dad—that their family was broken and he wanted to fix it.

He'd broken out in a sweat more than once while he'd been scraping out shit, and it had nothing to do with the heat of the afternoon or the odor he'd stirred up. It had everything to do with the only way he'd come up with to start to mend things with brothers. By talking. *Really* talking.

Though the idea made his throat clamp shut, Gage pushed the words out. "Do you ever miss it?" he asked.

"Miss what?"

"The way things used to be before Mom got sick. The way *we* used to be."

Because Gage was looking at Ryker, he saw his brother frown. "That was a long time ago."

"Too long, don't you think? Or are you okay with the distance between us?"

Ryker looked annoyed. "You're close enough you're making my eyes water."

"I'm not talking about literally. And you're the one who asked me to clean the corrals."

"Yeah, well, I wasn't planning on having to be this close to you before you'd had a shower."

Gage stopped. His gaze searched Ryker's. "Don't you think we've avoided this long enough?"

The panic in Ryker's green eyes told Gage his brother was as uncomfortable with the idea of talking as he was. Too bad. They weren't going to get anywhere otherwise.

His brother shifted his feet. His gaze darted around the yard, bouncing from one thing to another. Like Dallas, Ryker preferred a thin layer of stubble on his cheeks and he raked both his hands over it, leaving a streak of grease smeared from his cheekbone to his jaw. He cleared his throat once. Then again.

"It's not that—"

His words were cut off by a car coming down the driveway.

"I'll see who it is," he said eagerly before turning to Gage. "You really need to shower."

Usually, when company showed up, Ryker scowled down the laneway, mostly because he preferred to be left alone. But this time his gaze latched onto the approaching plume of dust as though it were a lifeline. He made a beeline toward it.

"I'm not giving up on this," Gage called.

Though the yard was quiet and there was no way Ryker hadn't heard him, his brother gave no indication he'd received the message. Gage ambled toward the house and the shower he was craving. Ryker might have bought himself a bit of time with the unexpected visitor, but Gage wasn't done with him.

Chapter Seven

FAITH BLEW OUT a deep breath when Gage angled toward the house. Like a moth to a light, her gaze had zeroed in on him the moment the yard came into focus. And like a moth, her stomach had fluttered wildly. It shouldn't, damn it. Nothing about him should make her flutter. Not when they had no future.

She parked next to barn, in front of the corrals. It was far enough from the house that even with the screen door open, Gage shouldn't hear her. So as long as he didn't look out the window...

By the time she got out of the car, Ryker was there. Three of the horses had ambled over and were stretching their necks toward him, seeking his attention. Since the parking area practically butted up to the fence, he was able to greet her and rub their chins at the same time.

"I was going to call you once I'd showered. I actually just finished with your car," he said.

Her spirits lifted. Finally, some good news.

"So it's done?"

He gnawed on his lip. She wondered if he knew he had a smear of grease running down his face. Coupled with the fading yellow bruising beneath his eyes, he looked a little foreboding. If she hadn't known him from before or been on the receiving end of his gentleness and helpfulness yesterday—she'd have taken a step back.

"Not quite. I'm waiting for some parts, and they won't be in until Monday afternoon."

Her stomach sank. "But I have work on Monday."

"I'm sorry. You bent the exhaust system. I was able to get some of the other parts from an auto wrecker, but the muffler is something best gotten new. And unfortunately, the parts store didn't have the right one for your car."

Faith's shoulders drooped. "I guess I can borrow grandma's car." And wouldn't that be fun?

He shrugged. "Sorry. The good news is with getting the other parts from the auto wrecker, I saved you some money."

She forced her lips into a smile. She'd pay double, triple even, if it meant she could head home tomorrow and not have to come back. Of course, that was impossible; she and Gage still had loads to sort out.

"Why don't you come to the house for a sec? Normally, all my paperwork is kept in the garage, but I was working on your estimate over supper and I left it on the table. I've ballparked the amount it'll take me to install the new exhaust, but it should be close to what I've figured. I've done them before, so I know about how long they take."

Faith balked. Gage was in the house. And she really wasn't ready for another face-to-face with him yet.

"I—"

He shook his head. "Sorry, I wasn't thinking. I can get your crutches if you need them."

He opened the back door, pulled them out, and handed them to her.

"I'm sure whatever you've come up with is fair."

"It won't take long. Besides, I'm thirsty and could use a cold drink."

Without looking like an idiot for refusing, Faith tucked the crutches under her arms and started moving. He altered his pace to her slower one. At the bottom of the steps, Faith stopped. Eyeing the door, she sighed deeply.

"Are you sure you can manage?"

"Yes." After all, it wasn't the idea of climbing three little steps that presented the problem. She managed a flight at her grandma's to get up to her room. No, the problem was seeing Gage. Her emotions were still all over the map and, with her grandma's comments earlier, she didn't feel as strong as she needed to see him again.

Should have thought of that before coming over.

No kidding. Despite the fact she and her grandmother had never been close, Faith always held the hope that the next visit would be the one where they connected. Where they finally started to build the relationship Faith had always wanted to have with her.

And though the main reason for her coming to town was Gage, Faith had still held that hope. Her grandmother's words and actions tonight had once again ground that dream to dust, and she'd just needed to get away before the walls closed in and suffocated her.

But she should have gone somewhere else. If wishes were horses...

Using the railing, Faith climbed onto the porch and through the door Ryker held open. She hadn't been inside the house in over six years and was surprised to see it hadn't changed a bit.

The front door still opened into a long mudroom where coat hooks and boot racks dominated one wall. On the other were a chest-style freezer and a white front-load washer and dryer with heaping piles of laundry stacked on top of both machines. A bathroom was tucked at the back. The mudroom led to the kitchen with its dark oak cupboards and matching kitchen table and chairs.

"Have a seat." Ryker moved past her to the fridge. "Can I get you anything? There's soda, water. I'm having a beer, but you shouldn't as you're driving."

"I'm fine, thanks. I really can't stay."

She heard water running upstairs. She imagined Gage was in the shower. Well, she tried not to imagine it, but her mind kept conjuring the image of soapy suds dripping over his muscles.

"Actually," she said as her mouth went dry, "I could use a glass of water."

"Sure." He poured her one before twisting off the cap of his beer and taking a long drink. He let out a loud sigh. "Better."

"You said the estimate was here?"

"Right." Ryker took another sip, set the bottle down. He looked from the table to the counter, frowned. "I could've sworn—"

He shook his head. "Shit. I *had* taken it back with me to the garage." He shot Faith an apologetic glance. "Sorry. I'll go get it."

She scraped her chair back, but Ryker was already across the room. "No, don't move. I'll be right back."

He was gone before she could argue, but worse—so much worse—was the moment the door slammed behind him, Gage shouted from upstairs. She hadn't noticed until then that the water had stopped running.

"Hey, Ryker, didn't you do the laundry?"

Faith froze. She eyed the stairwell warily.

"I know you're down there. I heard your voice. I need a pair of jeans. Can you bring me a pair from the dryer?"

She had to assume because he wasn't asking her to fetch them that he hadn't heard her voice. Which meant maybe she could—

"Goddammit, Ryker! It was your turn to do the damn laundry."

His heavy steps came barreling down the stairs, and within seconds, Gage stepped into the kitchen wearing nothing but a towel and a scowl.

GAGE COULDN'T HAVE said who was more surprised, him or Faith. After the tension between them after he'd dropped her off earlier, he sure hadn't expected her to be in his kitchen a few hours later. But then, judging by the size of her eyes and the flush riding her cheeks, she hadn't expected to find him nearly naked, either.

As a gentleman, he should have excused himself to get dressed. Though he recognized he was making Faith uncomfortable, and even *he* felt a little exposed given the circumstances, he didn't want to chance leaving the room to put some clothes on. Not when her gaze kept shifting from his chest to the mudroom as though she were looking for the first opportunity to bolt.

"I'm sorry. I didn't know you were here. Not that I'm not glad you are," he hurried to add, "but I would have ensured I was decent before coming down."

Although, how he'd have done that, he couldn't have said, given that Ryker hadn't brought up any of the laundry he was supposed to have washed. Still, while he imagined Cam would enjoy parading around nearly naked in front of a woman, it wasn't Gage's style. At least, not when he wasn't dating said woman.

But she was having his baby, so it wasn't as though Faith hadn't already seen and touched all there was to him. Gage dropped his attention to her hands. They might have been wringing each other at the moment, but he distinctly remembered how they'd felt raking through his hair, trailing down his back. Latching on to his ass.

A flush of his own rose from waist to neck. His breath chugged heavily through his lungs.

He shouldn't be thinking about that night, given the fact his draping towel wasn't doing much in the way of masking any...reactions.

Faith jerked her gaze from his abdomen. She stared at him with an intensity that carried all the way down to her tight jaw, leading Gage to believe her thoughts had been running along the same track as his.

When his body responded naturally to those thoughts, he anchored his hand on the knot at his waist. *Shut it down, Gage. Now.*

"It's fine. I don't..." She shook her head, then started

again. "I came to check on my car. Ryker thought the estimate was here but then he remembered it was in the garage after all." Clearing her throat, she straightened her shoulders. "It's probably best if I just meet him outside."

Gage was right on her heels. A task made easier by her crutches.

Reaching toward her, he gently took her arm, turned her toward him. "Can you stay a little? Let me get dressed. Then we can talk."

She stood hipshot, favoring her sore knee. "I know we have things to say, but I think it best we wait until we've both had time to get used to things. I have a lot to sort out. I'm sure you do, as well."

"I do. But don't you think it's better if we sort them out together?"

Her eyes filled with doubt. He hated that her first instinct was to pull back. It didn't surprise him, given what he remembered about her, but it still hurt. Maybe he hadn't pictured every detail in his head, but he'd assumed the day he learned he was going to be a dad would be a happy one. It gutted him that instead of being a joyful time, it was one of uncertainty and trepidation.

Movement behind her caught his eye. Over her shoulder, he saw Ryker standing on the other side of the screen door. With brows arched high over his green eyes, his brother looked pointedly at Gage's towel and then toward Faith.

With a sigh, Gage lowered both his hands and took a step back.

Faith must have sensed they were no longer alone. She angled away from Gage as she looked toward the door.

"You found it," she said, gesturing to the white sheet of paper in Ryker's hand.

The screen door squeaked open as Ryker walked in, handing the estimate to Faith. "It's pretty self-explanatory, but I can go through it if you want."

She was already shaking her head. "No, I'm sure it's fine. Thank you. If you can text me when it's done Monday?"

He nodded. "No problem. Should be shortly after lunch."

"Thank you." She smiled at Ryker. It faltered when she turned toward Gage. "I guess I'll see you tomorrow?"

She hobbled outside and down the steps before he could think of a reason to keep her there—other than he wanted her to stay. Wanted to talk and hold her and figure out their future. The more time she had to herself, the more she'd convince herself giving him the baby was the only way.

Keeping his voice low, Ryker asked, "Is there a reason you're standing here practically naked?"

Gage's gaze snapped to Ryker's. "I won't be much longer, and unless you want an eyeful, I suggest you leave."

He aimed for the dryer, growled at the pile of clothes stacked on top of the machines and in the basket.

"You know," he called to his brother's back as Ryker disappeared into the kitchen, "your turn to do laundry includes folding and putting it away. If you'd done that," he said as he pulled out the first clean pair he found out of the pile, "I wouldn't have had to come downstairs mostly naked."

Thank God it had been Faith waiting in the kitchen and not some other customer of Ryker's.

"I was busy," Ryker called from the kitchen.

"We're all busy," Gage grumbled as he dropped the towel. Forgoing underwear in his need to hurry, he yanked on the jeans and jammed his feet into his boots. Ignoring his brother's next excuse, Gage slapped open the screen door and hurried to catch up with Faith.

How the hell had she reached the car already?

"Faith! Wait up."

Though he ran, she was already in the car with the door shut when he reached the passenger side. He tapped on the window.

He wasn't sure at first if she'd lower it, but after a few long moments, she did. Then she turned her pained expression his way.

"Please don't look at me like that, it's killing me," he said gently. "I'm not trying to make this more difficult."

"I know you're not. But I don't have anything else to say tonight. We agreed we'd meet tomorrow for breakfast. That's the best I can do right now, Gage."

"Okay," he agreed, though nothing about the whole situation was okay. He backed away, feeling as helpless as he'd ever felt in his life.

Chapter Eight

G AGE WAS STILL standing in the middle of the yard when Dallas's voice came from beyond the barn. He'd forgotten all about his older brother and Roy working in the bunkhouse. But judging by the words that carried on the light breeze, they were done working for the night and heading to the house for a beer.

Not wanting to have to explain why he was half-dressed in the driveway, Gage trudged back to the house. She'd said they'd talk more tomorrow. But, dammit, he wanted to talk tonight. Talk about the most important decision she'd already made. The one she'd made without him.

To give up their child.

It gutted him to think of that. To imagine his baby without a mom. To know Faith truly believed the kid would be better off without her in its life.

The hell kind of thinking was that?

The screen door slammed behind him as he entered the mudroom. He narrowed his gaze at the pile of clothes his brother had yet to deal with. How the bloody hell was he supposed to find anything in that mess? Kicking off his boots, his marched into the kitchen.

Ryker turned from the open fridge, beer in hand. His brows knit together.

"Aren't those my jeans?" he asked.

Gage stopped and glared. "Don't even. If you'd finished the damn laundry, I wouldn't have had to come down here half naked and rifle through that mess you've left. These were the first I found."

Ryker closed the fridge. "You could've looked a little harder."

It took a lot for Gage to lose his temper. Growing up, he'd witnessed enough brawls and shouting matches between his brothers that, somewhere along the way, he'd decided someone had to keep a level head. Not that he wasn't capable of holding his own if pushed, but as a rule, he opted to be the voice of reason. Such as last week when he'd come into the kitchen to find Ryker and Dallas throwing punches at each other. He'd managed, with Cam's help, to break them up, but not before Dallas had broken Ryker's nose.

Gage eyed the fading bruises under his brother's eyes and struggled not to add to them. "And you could've done your job. You're always riding our ass to help around here…Well that goes for you, too."

"I said I've been busy."

"We're all busy. Next time you want me to clean the corrals, I'll leave the pile of shit in front of your garage instead of on the manure pile. See how happy you are when I only do half my damn job."

Knowing if his brother came up with another excuse, Gage would indeed deck him, he spun on his bare foot and went up to his room, taking the stairs two at a time. Luckily, he at least still had clean underwear and socks in his drawer. And a few T-shirts. He pulled off Ryker's jeans and got dressed properly. It gave him great pleasure to put his brother's jeans back on.

The TV was on when Gage got back downstairs. Even knowing he wouldn't be happy about what he'd see, Gage poked his head into the living room. Sure enough, there was Ryker, sprawled on the couch, beer in hand as he watched a baseball game. Gage's hands fisted at his sides. He had to remind himself he was in the profession of treating injuries, not inflicting them.

That didn't make his blood boil any less. Frustrated and pissed off, Gage marched across the kitchen. Hearing Dallas and Roy coming in the back door, laughing and talking, further aggravated him. Maybe because, at the moment, he didn't have anything to laugh about. And too much on his mind to sit down, have a beer, and enjoy a ball game.

He stalked into the mudroom.

Dallas, with his usual ball cap facing backward, nodded to Gage. "Where are you off to?" he asked.

"Out," Gage answered in a much harder tone than the congenial one Dallas had used.

He jammed on first one boot, then the other. When he stood Dallas was there, concern filling his blue eyes.

"Everything okay?" he asked.

"Fine," Gage all but snarled. "Be better if Ryker finished the damn laundry."

Gage gestured to the teetering pile of clothes as he moved around Dallas and came face-to-face with their ranch hand. Gage reined in his temper a notch. The man had only been at the Diamond G a week, and they needed his help. While a little anger wasn't likely to send the man running, Gage wasn't going to take out his frustration on him. His brothers, on the other hand, were fair game.

"Roy," he acknowledged.

Roy tipped his head as he stepped aside. "Gage."

Gage felt a little less snarly once he was outside. He took a deep breath, pushed it out of his lungs. The sun was low in the sky, but he had a good hour before it set and about another hour of daylight after that. More than enough time. He saddled his horse.

There were a handful of trails on the Diamond G and, knowing what he was after, Gage took the one that started behind the house. It was a narrower trail with more trees and hills than if he were to go out toward the pastures, and it wasn't conducive to having a riding companion, but since he was alone, it suited him just fine.

He could've done without the mosquitoes that converged on him when he was in the shade, but when he finally broke from the trees and crested the hill he'd been climbing since shortly after leaving the yard, it was all worth it.

From there, he could see the pastures and fields that made up the ranch as well as several of the surrounding spreads. The houses, outbuildings, and animals were small enough from where he stood that they reminded him of an old farm set he used to play with as a young boy. The one with the white plastic sheep, eraser-pink pigs, and the red barn door that mooed like a cow when he opened it.

He couldn't make out Last Stand, but he looked in that direction anyway.

Faith would be back at her grandmother's now. Likely alone in her room. It twisted him up that she was determined to go through this alone. That she wouldn't lean on him. Wouldn't trust him to look after her. After them.

His sigh drifted over the hilltop as he secured his horse then settled against the trunk of a towering live oak. His stomach growled, reminding him he'd left before taking his supper. But more than the food, he wished he'd have taken the time to pack a couple beers. If he were going to brood, he'd just as soon do it over a cold beer.

Although it soon became clear he wasn't going to be brooding alone. His horse nickered a greeting just as Gage heard the steady clomp of another rider coming up the trail. Bending his knee, he set his forearm on it as he waited for Roy to clear the trees.

It wasn't going to be one of his brothers, 'cause they weren't the sort to follow. Especially if they knew he was in a bad mood. That was when they tended to give each other the most space. Because the alternative was to actually communicate.

The idea of Roy following him was strange, though. They'd only known each other a week and, while the man was pleasant enough, it wasn't as though they'd developed the kind of fast friendship that would have Roy coming to check on him. And besides, he was a grown man. He didn't need to be checked on.

Though a part of him wished his brothers cared enough to do it.

But it wasn't Roy who rode out of the trees. It was Dallas. And Gage couldn't have been more surprised if the clear evening sky above had suddenly gone gray and started dumping snow on his head.

"You lost?" Gage asked.

Dallas only ever wore a cowboy hat when he was riding, and he tipped up the brim as his horse meandered forward.

"Nope," he answered.

Dallas dismounted, loosely tied his gelding's reins around a branch then pulled out two cans of beer from the saddle-bags he'd brought along. His brother strode forward, folded himself next to Gage on the grass and passed him a cold can.

"Thanks," Gage said.

"You looked as though you could use one."

Gage cracked the can open, took a refreshing gulp. "Wouldn't have been so bad if Ryker had done the damn laundry like he was supposed to."

"Well, he'll be doing it now," Dallas answered.

Gage studied his brother. "You didn't break his nose again, did you?"

"No," Dallas chuckled, as he pulled the tab on his can. "I set the basket and the piles on the couch next to him. Figured he'd get the point."

"I'm not sure he will," Gage grumbled, not yet ready to let his anger go.

"You're not one to lose your shit over laundry." Dallas tipped his head. "Does this have to do with the woman in the yard earlier? The one you were talking to half naked?"

While Dallas had come back home a few times during the years, once he'd moved to San Antonio it had only been on holidays and those Faith had spent with her grandmother.

"Her name is Faith."

"She your girlfriend?"

Gage took a long drink. "No."

"Your tone suggests you wish she was."

Gage flicked the tab on his can. "Are you just making conversation, or do you really want the answer?"

Funny how he'd just wished his brothers cared enough to come after him, and now that one had, Gage was hesitant to trust what it meant.

Dallas's gaze dropped to his beer. "I deserve that. I know I wasn't around much."

"No, you weren't."

His brother nodded, took a drink. He picked at the grass. A few times, he opened his mouth then shut it again.

Finally, he seemed to find the words. "I can't change the past, not sure I would even if I could. That doesn't mean I'm happy with the way things are." He took another drink. "You know. Between us."

The fact that Dallas struggled with the words and couldn't quite look at Gage as he spoke went further toward convincing Gage that he meant them than the words themselves. But as much as they were what Gage wanted to hear, it didn't make answering his brother any easier. Past hurts and years of treating each other more like strangers than brothers wasn't going to change overnight.

But they'd get there if they kept taking steps toward that goal.

Swallowing his own discomfort over the idea of opening up, Gage forced himself to say, "I told Dad the same thing last time I was at the hospital. That I wasn't happy with how things are in our family."

Dallas raised his head, looked at Gage. "How bad do you want to fix it?"

Gage's mouth twisted to match his guts, which felt as though a Boy Scout was practicing tying knots with them. "Bad enough to be having this conversation."

Dallas snorted, ran a hand across the back of his neck. "Amen to that."

Knowing Dallas was as uncomfortable as he was eased the tension in Gage's stomach. Maybe they *could* do this.

However, fifteen minutes later, they were still sitting in silence. The sun was melting into the horizon. They needed to start heading back while it was still light enough to see where they were going. But Gage wasn't ready to go yet. He'd been working on how to phrase something, and if he had another few minutes, he just might get it past the hard lump in his throat.

Dallas pulled the empty, dented can from Gage's tight fingers.

"I can hear the gears grinding. Just spit it out, Gage. If you need to yell at me for leaving when you were so young, go ahead. I know it wasn't fair to you—you more than anyone."

Emotion rose in a swell up Gage's chest. He'd always wondered if his oldest brother had ever realized the hole he'd left in Gage's life when he'd left.

"Thanks." He cleared his throat. "But that's not what's on my mind."

Gage wished he still had something to fiddle with. He didn't know what to do with his hands now. He clasped them together as he looked down the valley. Cows that looked no bigger than the die-cast cars they'd once played with dotted the green pastures.

"Faith and I were friends in high school. Not at first. At first, I approached her because she looked so sad. And one day I caught her emptying her locker. Figured she was going to quit school. I was right."

"You stop her?"

"Yeah. Anyway, from then on, we slowly built a friendship. And once we had that going, I started to wish for more."

"Did you ever tell her?"

"No. She made it clear she wanted out of Last Stand as soon as high school was done, and I knew I wasn't leaving. Figured it would hurt less when she left if I just loved her from afar."

"How'd that work out for you?"

"Not worth a shit," Gage scoffed.

"But you never got over her?"

Gage shrugged. "It wasn't like I pined after her and was unable to move on, but I never forgot her. I'd hear something that would remind me of high school and think of her, or see someone that had the same hair color or smile, and wonder where she was and if she was happy."

"And now she's back?"

"Only until Ryker gets her car running again."

"So that's the vehicle he's working on?"

"Yeah."

"And this is the first time you've seen her since high school?"

Gage cleared his throat. "Actually we just, uh, reconnected by fluke in San Antonio a few months ago."

Dallas's lips twitched. The gleam in his blue eyes told

Gage he knew just what "reconnected" entailed.

"Anyway…" Gage sighed. "Now, more than ever, I'd like to have a real relationship with her, but I'm pretty sure that's impossible."

He knew her past. Knew she'd always felt like a burden to her grandmother. Of course, the old biddy had made a point of telling her, but still. Faith believed it. It was why she'd fled Last Stand. She didn't want to be anyone's obligation anymore.

If she'd have stuck around in San Antonio, he could have told her he had feelings for her. That he'd like a shot at dating her. She might have believed him then.

There was no way she would now. She'd take it that he was only saying that because of the baby. And, sure, to an extent, the baby played a factor. How could it not? It was his, after all. But he'd had feelings for her for years that had nothing to do with the baby.

"I had a hard time convincing Ashley my feelings for her were real, too."

"Yeah?"

"She figured because she was a single mom working hard to make ends meet that I couldn't possibly be interested in her. She even tried convincing me what my type should be."

"How'd you change her mind?"

"I didn't give up. I kept showing her she was the only woman I wanted, and when I screwed up royally, I swallowed my pride and begged."

"You? Beg?" Gage gawked.

Dallas grinned. "It wasn't pretty."

Gage blew out a breath and rolled to his feet. He gathered the empty beer cans. "I have a feeling, no matter what I do, Faith will find an excuse to discount it. She's damn stubborn."

Dallas stood. Walking over, he took the cans from Gage's hands.

"So what are you going to do about it?"

Gage thought of Faith and the baby they were going to have. One way or another, he'd be part of the baby's life moving forward, but he didn't want only that.

He wanted to be part of hers, too. He wanted her to be part of theirs. The thought of never seeing her again, never kissing her again, never holding her in his arms, never being the reason she smiled… Yeah, that wasn't going to happen.

Straightening his shoulders, he said, "I'm going to do whatever it takes to prove to her my feelings are real."

And if that didn't work, he wasn't above begging, either.

GAGE KNOCKED ON the Stones' front door at ten the next morning. He'd hurried through the morning chores and, feeling charitable after finding his clean clothes folded neatly on his bed after returning from his ride with Dallas the night before, left his brothers and Roy two heaping piles of pancakes. He'd also left them with the dirty dishes, but that was the unwritten rule in their household. Whoever cooked didn't do dishes.

Which was always a little satisfying since Ryker's idea of cooking was slapping together whatever frozen foods were in the freezer, usually pizza, which didn't leave much in the way of dishes for the rest of them. Gage, however, liked to cook and, having to take his turn regularly at the fire hall, had gotten used to making more complex meals. Which also meant more dishes.

But since Ryker made them eat tasteless food, Gage figured leaving his brother with more dishes when it was his turn to cook was only fair. Especially on the nights Dallas was in San Antonio and Cam was on the circuit.

He was chuckling about the last time he'd cooked chicken cacciatore and the stack of dirty dishes he'd left Ryker when Faith's grandmother answered the door.

God, she should have been a school marm in the eighteen hundreds with that stern expression.

"Good morning, Mrs. Stone. I'm here for Faith."

"Again? Weren't you just with her yesterday?"

"Yes, ma'am. I was."

He didn't explain further. Faith was an adult, and her grandma didn't need to know her every move.

"I suppose you're the reason she wouldn't eat the breakfast I cooked for her this morning."

"Can you tell her I'm here? Please."

"No need," Faith said as she limped up to her grandmother's side, crutches free.

"When will you be back?" Alice asked. "I thought you were coming to church."

"Unfortunately, not this time. Gage asked me out for breakfast."

Her grandmother's disdain raked over him. "You're not going to church, either?"

"Not today, ma'am. But I hope you enjoy the service."

With a look that said he has going to hell, she elbowed past him. "Lock the door on your way out," she said by way of goodbye to Faith.

Once she was out of earshot, Gage couldn't help saying, "I don't know why she bothers with an air conditioner. Surely, it's cold enough in her house without one."

As he'd hoped, Faith's mouth curved. "It is, trust me."

He leaned against the doorjamb. "So? Are you ready to go?"

She eyed him carefully. "You know us going out for breakfast together will stir up the gossip mill."

He lifted a shoulder. "Let them talk. I just want to eat and spend time with a friend I've missed." He gave her his most charming grin. "Even in your grandma's eyes, that isn't a sin."

She shook her head as she stepped onto the porch. "I swear you can get anything you want with that smile."

"Not everything," he mumbled as he waited for her to lock the door.

It had never gotten him her.

Not that he'd ever told her that. He'd remained silent instead and let her slip through his fingers. Not a mistake he planned on repeating.

He was glad to see she hardly favored her knee as they walked to his Jeep and the, ten minutes later, into Hilde's Haus, the local diner. They settled at a table next to the window overlooking Main Street. Being a Sunday, and with church service starting soon, the street was quiet.

Gage ordered a rancher's breakfast consisting of three eggs, bacon, grits, toast, a side of pancakes, and coffee. Faith chose coffee and a cinnamon bun.

"It's the same as I remember it," Faith said as the waitress took their menus and headed to the kitchen with their order.

"Yeah." Gage settled into the booth. "That's what I like about it. Brings back memories."

She looked around, and he knew by the slight downward turn of her mouth that Last Stand didn't hold many good memories for her. But there were some good ones, and he intended to remind her of those.

"I took you here on our first date," he said.

She slanted her gaze his way. "That wasn't a date. Grandma had gone visiting a friend in Fredericksburg that afternoon, and we took advantage of her absence."

"It was fun, though, wasn't it?" He didn't mean breakfast so much as the afternoon they'd spent at the ranch afterward. An afternoon he hoped to recreate. "I was hoping, after breakfast, you'd come back to the ranch with me. Spend the day there."

Faith didn't answer until the waitress, who had been on her way over, had delivered their drinks and left again.

"I thought we'd just go somewhere by the river again," she said as she stirred sugar into her coffee.

"It'll be better at the ranch," he said. "We can talk, maybe go for a ride if your knee is up for it, and you can stay for the cookout."

"Cookout?"

"Since I have the day off and lots of time to prep, I was planning on grilling steaks. Dallas and his girlfriend will be there, so you'll finally get to meet him. And with Ashley and her daughter there, you won't be the only female."

And, since Ashley was a mother, too, maybe it would bring the two women together. Give them something to bond over.

"I don't know," she hedged. "You didn't cook worth a damn in high school."

He waited until the waitress set their food down before answering. "I've gotten better at a lot of things since high school."

She rolled her eyes as she smiled. "Your double entendres sure haven't."

He grinned. It was the first real smile he'd gotten out of her since that night in San Antonio.

He'd been sitting with his buddies when he'd caught a glimpse of her out on the dance floor. At first, he hadn't believed it possible. What were the chances after years of thinking about her that she'd suddenly just be there? Like fate had handed him this perfect gift?

But despite the low lighting and packed dance floor, he'd recognized her easily when she'd spun in his direction. The dark brown hair she'd worn to her mid-back had been shortened to her collarbone and highlighted with copper. It framed her face beautifully. That night, she'd added some soft curls to it. Today, it was straight and glossy. It was pretty either way.

That night, like today and most times in school, he hadn't been able to take his eyes off her. Leaving his friends to their drinking and laughing about their last four-wheeling trip and the mudhole they'd had to tow three of their side by sides out of, Gage had woven through the country-western bar. His attention was on the brunette with the tight-fitting denim shorts, long tanned legs, white button-down blouse tied at the waist, and dark red cowboy boots.

He'd caught her elbow just as the line dance ended. Flushed and bright-eyed, she'd spun toward him. Whether it was the alcohol or the momentum, either way, she'd lost her balance and he'd had to hold her to keep her from tripping.

He'd looked into her startled eyes. "Hi, Faith."

"Gage!"

She'd hugged him, pressing her warm body and all her curves flush against him. He hadn't let her go the rest of the night. They'd line-danced, two-stepped, and slow-danced. Though she'd also come with a few friends, they were both content to stay together. They hadn't done much talking. The fast songs weren't conducive to conversation, and the slow ones, he'd been satisfied to simply hold her. Finally hold her.

But when her fingers had crept into his hair, when he'd felt her warm breath on his neck, it hadn't taken long to want more. He'd buried his face in her neck, inhaled her like a drug.

She'd responded instantly, dragging him even closer. His blood had shot south of his belt, and though Lonestar's hit ballad was still drifting through the speakers, he'd pulled back.

The other couples had continued to sway around them despite the fact he and Faith had come to a halt.

It had taken a long time for Gage to find his tongue. Mostly because it wasn't talking he'd wanted to do with it.

"How about we take a break? Maybe get some air?"

Faith's hand had slid from the back of his neck, crept

down his spine, and curled around his ass. While his heart had tripped over itself, her lips had curled enticingly.

"How about we go back to your place?"

Had it been up to his body, he'd have been out the door with her before she'd finished speaking. Luckily, his mind had still been mostly working.

"I'm not so sure that's a good idea." Which was a blatant lie. It was the damn finest idea she'd ever had. Just not the right timing. "We haven't seen each other in years, Faith."

Her hand, which had still been firmly gripping his ass, squeezed. "Then we have lots of time to make up for."

A mountain climber at the top of Everest couldn't have had a lighter head than he'd had at that moment. Oxygen had definitely been hard to come by.

"I've thought about you, you know," she said. She sidled closer, brushed her breasts against his chest. "I've thought about you *a lot.*"

Brain cells fried like flies in a zapper. The hard nubs of her nipples pressing against his chest, the grip of her hand on him that had him wondering what else she'd grip like that, and the scent of her hot, heated skin worked together to rob him of sense. And yet, he'd tried one more time.

"I don't want you regretting this." Because he already knew it was going to be a highlight of his life.

She'd pushed onto her toes. With one hand still on his ass, the other had wrapped around the back of his neck. Her hazel eyes had gone dark with desire. Her mouth had inched toward his.

Her voice had been like cool silk rubbing against his skin. "My only regret is that you never let me do this in high school."

Then she'd had her mouth on his, her tongue slow danc-ing with his. His body had caught fire. He'd had to fight the urge to walk her against one of the square wooden pillars and ravish her right then and there.

It was exactly why he hadn't kissed her in high school. Because there would've been no turning back. Just like there hadn't been that night.

He'd kept his head while she grabbed her purse and told her friends she was leaving and he told his he was heading back to his hotel early. Other than a sizzling kiss on the side of the bar, he'd managed to mostly keep his hands off her while they made the short trek to his hotel. But the moment the door closed behind them, it had been a whole other story.

Funny, he didn't remember anyone knocking that night.

He blinked, surprised when the darkened hotel room gave way to the bright restaurant. Surprised when instead of a lust-filled gaze, Faith stared him with a quizzical look on her face. She rapped the table again.

"You still with me?"

"Yeah." He shook his head to clear away the last of the memory. Which was a damn shame given how perfect it was. "Sorry."

"Everything okay?"

"Yeah." He reached for the small packet of jam, stalling as he tried to remember what they'd been talking about before his mind had veered so far off course. Oh, right, the cookout.

"So how about it, Faith? What do you say to coming

back to the ranch for the day?"

Faith picked off a piece of her shrinking cinnamon roll with her fingers. While his mind had trekked back three months, she'd eaten half her pastry. Though, by the solemn look on her face, she wasn't necessarily enjoying it.

"I guess we do have lots to sort out." She lifted the dough to her mouth.

He paused as she licked the cinnamon sugar off her lip. Oh, the things she'd done with her tongue. Raising his cup, he gulped some coffee. He winced as the hot liquid scalded the roof of his mouth. But at least it shifted his thoughts from the gutter.

Putting down his cup, he said, "We do. But we don't have to do it all today. I want us to have some fun, too."

She snorted. "I'm not sure we can afford to have any more fun. Look what happened last time."

It certainly hadn't been planned and, no, it wasn't the ideal circumstances to bring a child into the world, but he couldn't say he was sorry, either. The more he thought about the baby, the more the idea grew on him.

He could teach him or her to ride a horse, to drive a tractor. They could join Little League or dance. Whatever their interest was, he would be there, cheering them on. As for providing for it, he had a good, secure job. Financially, he could afford it. The mother was someone he respected and liked—and found sexy as hell. They had chemistry and several things in common. They'd always enjoyed each other's company.

He took a slower sip of his coffee, studied Faith over the rim of his cup. As much as the idea of being a father was growing on him, the best thing, to Gage's mind, was having Faith back in his life. He lowered his cup.

"I certainly didn't plan things to turn out as they did, but I'm not sorry, Faith."

She shook her head. "How can you not be?"

He reached across the table, took the fork she'd been toying with from her fingers, and covered her hand with his. He looked into her troubled eyes. "Because it's with you."

Chapter Nine

G AGE STROLLED THROUGH the supermarket as though they'd done it a hundred times. As though they were a couple. As though they had a future.

"Because it's with you," he'd said.

Her heart had stumbled and, for a bright, shining moment, she'd envisioned a whole other reality. One where he put his hand over her swollen belly and went all soft when the baby kicked. One where they smiled at each other as they looked at the sonogram pictures.

She'd had to thrust those images aside before they tempted her believe such a future was possible when it wasn't. Not only did she have a job and a life in San Antonio, she wasn't mother material. And she was going to college.

Oblivious to her churning thoughts, he ambled around the produce section and up the aisles, mindful of her slightly slower pace. He asked her preferences when it came to veggies, salad dressings, and side dishes.

"Just get what you guys normally eat," she said. "You don't need to make exceptions for me."

"I know I don't. But I want to." He tossed in more food.

"Gage, that's too much," she protested.

The cart was already loaded with corn on the cob, a large head of romaine with the assorted vegetables to make a garden salad, four cans of baked beans, and two plastic containers, one full of potato salad the other coleslaw. Not to mention the steaks he said were marinating back at the ranch.

"You haven't seen how much Ryker and Dallas can eat," he answered before backtracking and adding another tub of potato salad to the cart before wheeling it toward the checkout. There, he tossed in three packages of orange Tic Tacs.

Faith scowled at his back. She knew exactly what he was doing. Using his brothers as an excuse so she wouldn't feel bad, wouldn't think he was doing her any special favors. Except she knew him. And she knew he was. Even if his words were kind and came from the heart, she couldn't help hearing her grandmother's voice screeching in her head about how much it cost to feed her.

"You're quiet," Gage commented.

They'd left Last Stand fifteen minutes ago, and she'd been staring at the rolling countryside ever since, wondering how she'd let him talk her into going back for a cookout. With most of his family present.

"Have you told your brothers about the baby?" she asked.

The question had been weighing heavily on her mind since she'd been there yesterday. Ryker hadn't let on that he knew anything, but...

"Not yet." Gage reached out and took her hand. "But when I do, it'll be okay. You don't need to worry about that."

Her hand tingled where it touched his. She focused on the passing pastures instead of how much she wanted to grasp his hand and hold on.

"I don't need to worry about them judging me?"

He shot her a quick glance before returning his gaze to the road. "First of all, I don't think people have ever judged you as much as you think they have."

"You didn't see the looks I got at church and at the grocery store. And at work."

This time when he looked at her, his gaze lingered longer than she felt comfortable with. Both because he was still driving and because he was about to argue with her.

"I don't think they ever judged you the way you always thought. You believed they were looking at you and seeing your mother, expecting you to be like her. Or Alice. I happen to think they were looking at you in awe."

Faith nearly choked. "In awe?"

"That's right. In awe that you turned out so well despite your mother and grandmother."

"I don't—"

"I know you don't," he agreed. "But I'm telling you, as someone who's spent his life here, the people in Last Stand don't judge anyone based on who their family is. They base their opinions on who a person is, and I can tell you I've never, from the time you arrived in Last Stand until now, ever heard anything negative about you."

Faith's thoughts reeled. God, was it possible she'd let her mother's heartlessness and her grandmother's disdain toward her cloud her judgment so badly that she'd misread a whole town?

Granted, she'd always been reserved and quiet, so she hadn't exactly invited conversation, but she'd been sure—so sure—they'd looked at her with the same low expectations her grandma did. Could she really have been so wrong? Her stomach jittered at the thought.

"Secondly," Gage continued as though he hadn't just knocked her world off its axis, "Ashley's a single mother. She has a sixteen-year-old daughter she's raised on her own and Dallas is head over heels for her. I'm pretty sure neither one is going to ostracize you when they find out."

"That's because they don't know I plan on giving it to you to raise alone."

"About that," he said. "I had a thought last night. How about we don't tell them that part yet? Why don't, when we do decide to tell them, we leave it as we're having a baby and we're working out the details. They don't need to know, *nobody* else needs to know, until it's time."

"And you don't think they're going to wonder why I'm in San Antonio instead of here?"

"Of course they will," he agreed. "We just tell them we're taking it day by day. That this wasn't planned and we're figuring it out as we go."

She fisted her hands on her lap. "There's no figuring, Gage. My decision has been made, and I'm assuming yours has as well."

And being around Ashley, who'd managed to raise a daughter on her own for sixteen years when Faith wasn't prepared to even handle a day, wasn't the way to make her feel any less shitty about herself.

Faith pressed her temple to the sun-heated window and closed her eyes. The green fields and tidy farms were too pretty for the ugliness she felt inside.

"You're not a bad person, Faith."

She squeezed her eyes tight as a tear slipped down her cheek. "I feel like one."

"The fact you're tore up about this proves you aren't. You're doing what you believe is best for the baby and that's all anyone can ask of you."

Wiping her cheek, she turned and faced him. "Even you?" she asked.

"Even me," he answered.

Faith had no doubt he wanted to believe that, but the tightness around his mouth told her what she already suspected to be the truth.

He wasn't buying his own lies.

IT WASN'T SO bad at first. Ryker and Dallas were outside somewhere, and it was only her and Gage in the kitchen. Sunshine streamed into the room casting a thick yellow wedge on the hardwood floor.

Gage's home life hadn't been perfect, but she'd still envied him. He'd had wide-open spaces to lose himself in. He'd had other siblings to do things with, and anytime he wanted, he could go out and be with the horses.

Faith had been stuck in the same small house in town. Other than school, church, her part-time job, and the occasional trip to the Diamond G when Gage managed to sneak her out, she'd had little options. Her grandma wouldn't drive her anywhere or, when she was older, let her borrow the car. Not even if Faith offered to pay the gas.

Luckily, she'd been able to buy herself a cheap cell phone with the money she'd earned at her job. Texting Gage meant she hadn't felt quite so alone or as confined.

Gage came up behind her, placed his hands on her shoulders. "You're thinking again."

"I can't seem to turn my brain off."

"I have an idea that might."

Instead of saying something flirty, though, he removed his hands and walked out the room. He was back within moments, an oblong, black, wireless speaker in his hand. He set it on the counter next to a package of store-bought muffins then pulled his phone out of his pocket. A few taps later, Florida Georgia Line's newest single filled the kitchen.

"What are you doing?" she asked as he strolled toward her, his hand outstretched.

"I was hoping you'd dance with me."

"Here?" she asked.

He tipped his shoulder. "Why not?" He stopped, waited. "Come on, Faith. It's just a dance."

Then why was her heart beating faster than the music? Still, she had no excuse that wouldn't make her look like more of a coward. Besides, it would hardly be the first time they danced together.

Just the only time since they'd slept together and she'd learned she was carrying his child.

"Stop thinking," he said and took the decision from her. Wrapping an arm around her waist, he took her hand and pulled her close.

Oh, God. She'd thought he'd smelled good that night in San Antonio when his skin had smelled of soap and tangy cologne. Though she still smelled his soap, and the hint of his laundry soap, she also smelled sunshine, wind, and the natural salt of his skin.

Never mind the food that remained in bags on the table and the steaks marinating in the fridge. Right then, the only thing she was hungry for was him.

And he wasn't hers to have.

Faith stepped out of his embrace. Luckily the sound of a car's tires crunching on gravel filtered through the closed window. Hopefully, he'd think that was why she pulled away.

"We should deal with the food," she said.

She took the bag with the produce to the sink, pulled out lettuce, radishes, peppers, and mushrooms. She started washing the romaine.

A slamming car door drew her attention outside. A petite blonde with a long, wavy ponytail stepped out. Almost immediately, a man strode out of the bunkhouse. Tool belt slung low on his hips, tan work boots, and ball cap pointed backward. It had to be Dallas. Just as the young girl running toward the corrals had to be Brittany.

But Faith's attention was on Dallas and his smile as he met Ashley halfway across the yard. It wasn't until they reached each other that Faith noticed the height difference between them. Ashley barely came to Dallas's shoulders. Not that it seemed to be a problem. The woman clutched Dallas around the neck as he lifted her off the ground.

Even from a distance, Faith saw the passion in the kiss, the way they melted into each other. She was sure if the horses that had come to the fence suddenly jumped it and ran free, neither Dallas nor Ashley would notice.

What would it be like to have that kind of love? To know, unequivocally, that when she reached for someone, they'd be there for her? Not out of obligation or resentment, but because they wanted to be. Because they wanted to show her in every way that their life was better with her in it.

She'd always wanted that kind of love. Used to dream of the day her mom would realize what she'd given up and come back for her. Or that her dad would come find her, tell her he was sorry he'd never stuck around.

She'd even fantasized about Gage walking into her restaurant, his gaze fixed only on her, despite the fact the place was bustling with people. But he'd ignore everyone else and, without breaking stride like Dallas had just done, walk straight up to her, lift her off the ground, and kiss her breathless.

Jealousy wasn't a foreign emotion to Faith, but right then, it sank its green teeth into her heart and bit down hard. She wanted that. God, did she want that.

Yanking her gaze from the yard, Faith grabbed a bunch of radishes and started ripping the leaves off. By the time she'd decapitated them and scrubbed them clean, Dallas and Ashley were walking into the kitchen.

Faith's stomach clenched. She had no idea how Gage was going to introduce her or how she should act. When she'd been there as a teenager, it had been easy. She was just Gage's friend. Now she wasn't sure what she was. But she tried not to show how anxious she felt when she turned around.

It helped that she was greeted by two welcoming smiles.

"Dallas, Ashley, I'd like you to meet a special friend of

mine. This is Faith Stone. We went to high school together. Faith, my brother Dallas and his girlfriend, Ashley. Once Brittany has her fix with the horses, you'll meet her, as well."

Faith wiped her hand on her hip. "Nice to meet you," she said as she shook both their hands.

Dallas looked to the vegetables piled on the counter. "What are you building?"

"Garden salad," Faith answered. "For supper."

"We bought all the fixings for a cookout," Gage said. "We thought if we prepped everything now, Faith and I could go for a ride this afternoon as there won't be much left to do at supper other than toss the steak and potatoes on the barbeque and boil the corn."

"You mean we're having a real meal that isn't takeout or out of the freezer?" His blue eyes sparkled at the prospect.

Ashley, on the other hand, didn't seem the least bit impressed by the food. Faith wondered if maybe the woman was a vegan or on some sort of a strict diet, not that her petite figure indicated she needed one.

"You're going on a ride?" the woman asked longingly.

Faith liked her immediately. Between Ashley's unreserved reaction to seeing Dallas, the lack of judgment on her face when Gage had introduced her—what did "special friend" mean, anyway?—and the slight pout at the idea of missing a horseback ride, it was clear Ashley was an open and real person.

Faith's favorite kind.

"You're welcome to join us," Faith suggested.

She didn't miss the slight frown that creased Gage's forehead.

"No, I can't. I'm working on the ranch books while Joe is in the hospital, and I've barely started making a dent in the piles he'd accumulated before he was hospitalized." She smiled. "But maybe another time."

Maybe. But Faith wasn't sure when that would be. She'd asked for another day off since her car wouldn't be ready until tomorrow afternoon, but she needed to get back. She couldn't afford to get fired. Not now.

Once her car was done, she needed to head back to San Antonio. Not only to keep her job, but to find another place to live.

The night she'd bumped into Gage at the bar, she'd been there with Soraya and a group of friends celebrating Soraya's engagement to her boyfriend, Darius. Which was only part of the reason Faith had drunk more than usual that night. She'd also known what that would mean for her. No newly-wed couple wanted a roommate. Besides, their little apartment wasn't big enough for three even if they wanted to.

It was just before Faith had found out she was pregnant that Soraya had sat her down and gently told her she wanted Darius to move in. The sooner the better, but she'd given Faith three months.

"What time do you plan on supper?" Dallas asked Gage.

He looked to Faith. "Seven?"

That left a whole lot of time between now and then. Time she'd spend listening to the rumble of his voice, smelling the tang of his skin. Looking at his gorgeous body that turned her on even when he wasn't around, let alone when he was right beside her. Her attraction to him seemed exponentially stronger since seeing him again on Friday.

"Seven is fine," she answered tightly.

"Okay. I'll let Roy know." Dallas pulled three water bottles out of the fridge. He handed one to Ashley, kissed her. "Nice meeting you, Faith," he said before striding out the room.

"I guess that's my cue," Ashley said. "I'll see you two later." She disappeared down the hall.

Gage turned to her. "That wasn't so bad."

"No. They both seem very nice."

He tipped his head. "I am, too."

"Yeah, I know."

He raised a brow. "Then why were you trying to get out of riding alone with me?"

"I wasn't trying to get out of it. I just thought it would be fun with more people."

"Or maybe you're afraid of what'll happen if we're alone together."

She rolled her eyes. "We've been alone, Gage. We were alone yesterday when I told you about…" Her eyes darted to the hallway and she lowered her voice. "About *things*," she said. "And we were alone this morning at breakfast."

He walked closer. The gleam in his eyes had her retreating until her hips pressed into the hard counter. He bracketed his hands on either side of her, closing her in. The hunger in his green eyes ignited her blood and sent it pulsing to all her erogenous zones.

"First of all," he drawled, "yesterday our minds were both rightly on something else." He tucked a strand of hair behind her ear.

She shivered as his fingers trailed the sensitive area behind her ear.

"As for this morning, a restaurant is hardly the place for anything...intimate."

His gaze lowered to her mouth. His lips parted as though he was going to kiss her. Lust clenched her belly. Her hands gripped the edge of the counter to keep from reaching for him.

"I think dancing with me stirred you up. And that scared you."

It did more than scare her. It terrified her.

"And I think you're afraid of what you can feel for me if you allow yourself."

He stared into her eyes, challenging her to deny it.

But the lie wouldn't come.

FAITH HADN'T RIDDEN in over six years, but it didn't take her long to get her rhythm back, to move with the horse instead of against it. But though she was settled in the saddle with the reins loose in her hand, there was no relaxing.

Not with Gage riding beside her, looking all kinds of sexy.

It was hardly the first time she'd seen Gage ride a horse, but he'd filled out substantially since high school. Now his shoulders stretched the dark blue cotton of his T-shirt, and his biceps tested the cuffs with each subtle movement of his arms. Somehow, his jean-clad legs looked longer, and the way he sat the horse, hips tilting with each stride, reminded her how he'd ridden her with the same easy skill.

Not something she should be thinking about when her own movement kept rubbing her pelvis up against the saddle horn. She'd much rather rub herself against Gage.

Stop it! Ever since learning she was pregnant, she'd felt like a horny teenager. Worse, actually. In high school, while she'd wanted hugs and kisses and maybe a little petting, she hadn't been ready for more. She hadn't known what she was missing. Now she did and it was a constant craving. But not a random one. There was only one man who could satisfy her.

And what was wrong with her that she still felt such desires? Pregnancy brought on hormones, but she'd assumed it would be more related to mood swings and food cravings. But her cravings had nothing to do with food.

"We can stop, if you need," Gage said.

She turned to look at him. Green eyes. Black Stetson. Sitting a horse like he was born on one. All he needed was to be holding a bottle of cologne and his picture could sell millions.

God knew she was tempted by him, and he wasn't even selling anything.

"No, I'm good, thanks."

"Are you sure? 'Cause it looks like you're having a hard time getting comfortable."

Her cheeks burned, but she chose not to address his comment. Instead, she asked, "Where are we headed?"

"I thought we'd ride over to the creek like we used to. Is that okay?"

She'd loved going there. A few times, Gage had snuck

some beers. Sometimes, they'd dropped in a line. But mostly, they'd sat and watched the water float by, talking when they felt like it and sitting comfortably in silence when they didn't.

For Faith, the peacefulness had been a balm and a welcome reprieve from her grandmother's criticism and complaints. There, the silence didn't mean anyone was mad at her or was staring at her as though they wished she didn't exist. There, she'd had someone who listened to her and, when she was too far in her head, told stupid jokes to bring her out of it.

"That sounds good." And leave it to Gage to pick a spot that had always brought her comfort in the past.

It was a nice day for a ride. The sun was high in the sky, but there was a nice breeze and enough fluffy clouds to keep the temperature from crawling into the scorching zone. As long as she didn't look toward Gage.

So she didn't. She focused on the pale red Longhorns they passed. The calves frolicked while their mamas sprawled on the ground chewing their cud. A hawk soared overhead, moving in large circles without so much as a flap of its wings.

It didn't lessen the awareness she had that he rode right beside her, but at least it helped distract her somewhat. As did her having to concentrate as they navigated though some rocky terrain before reaching the flat, grassy area by the creek.

Dismounting, they let their animals have a drink before ground-tying them in the shade of some live oaks. Luckily, the trees were tall and full enough to provide respite for both the animals and themselves.

Digging in his saddlebags, Gage passed her a blanket then dug out two bottles of water and a baggie of chocolate chip cookies.

Faith eyed the bag. "You told me those were for dessert after supper."

He grinned, humor dancing in his green eyes. "I lied." He nodded toward the blanket. "Want to spread that out?"

They settled across from each other onto it. He offered her a water bottle and three of the six cookies he'd brought. Though they were store-bought, he'd picked them up in the bakery section, so they weren't hard and tasteless. They were chewy and fudgy and just plain delicious. Faith didn't hesitate to devour her share.

He was looking at her, an intense look in his eyes when she finished.

"What?" she asked as she whisked her fingers over her lips and chin. "Do I have crumbs on my face?"

Planting a hand at her hip, he leaned forward. He brushed the corner of her mouth with his thumb. "Chocolate," he said before licking the smudge off his thumb.

Her insides clamped hard at the sight of his tongue.

Faith ran the back of her hand over her mouth. In case there was more, she wanted to get it before Gage got any more ideas.

"Party pooper," he said with a wink.

She turned her attention back to the water. It wasn't much of a defense against his charm and the pull she felt toward him, but it was all she had at the moment.

Accommodating as always, Gage said nothing more. He seemed quite content to just sit and stare out at his family's land.

Eventually, he broke the silence. "Can you walk me through the thought process that led to your decision about adoption?"

Faith bowed her head. She'd known he'd want deeper answers than she'd given him so far. And though they didn't make her feel great, he deserved to hear them.

"You know I don't have a history of loving women in my family," she began. "My mom got rid of me when she started seeing me as competition for her boyfriends. My grandma might have kept me, but she made it clear every day of my life she resented the obligation. I can't do that to a child, Gage."

"What makes you think you would?"

"Do you know what my first thought was when I found out I was pregnant? *There goes college.*" Faith shook her head. It sounded even more awful said out loud than it had in her head.

"That was just shock at hearing the news. You know what one of my first thoughts was yesterday when you told me? That I'm going to need a new car. My two-door Jeep isn't going to work with a baby." He tipped his lips. "I love that Jeep, Faith. I don't want to give it up. That doesn't mean I won't be a good parent."

"But you come from better people," she argued. "Your dad was there for you before your mom got sick, and you could always count on your mom. You never had to live knowing you were resented, knowing you were never really wanted."

"Maybe my mom didn't choose to leave me like yours,

137

but my dad did."

"It's not the same."

He cocked a brow. "How's that?"

"He withdrew and stepped away, but did he ever say a bad word to you? Did he ever make you feel as though you never should have been born?"

He stared at her for a moment. Then he sighed as his shoulders fell. "No, he didn't," he admitted.

"Exactly. You have family. You've always had it, even when it wasn't ideal. You knew where you belonged. You have your brothers, and when your dad comes out of this, you'll have him, too. I've got nobody, Gage."

His gaze softened. He scooted forward, his eyes never moving from hers, until he was right before her. He settled his hand on her bare knee.

"I'm right here. I'm not going anywhere."

No, of course he wasn't. His ranch, family, and job were in Last Stand.

"I know," she said.

He shook his head, something shifting in his eyes. "I don't think you do."

Like he had moments ago, Gage planted a hand at her hip and leaned toward her. At first, she thought maybe she'd missed another smudge of chocolate, but his hand didn't reach for her mouth. It curved around her neck, brought her closer as he leaned in that last little bit and brushed his lips over hers.

It was unlike any kiss they'd shared before. In San Antonio, fueled by alcohol and a crush she'd never gotten over, their kisses had been deep, hot, and hungry. Even slightly tipsy, she'd known she hadn't wanted him to change his mind. So she hadn't given him the chance.

But this was tender and sweet. There was more here than lust and the anticipation of sex. There was no hurrying, no ripping off clothes as they raced to the bed. Though her belly clutched at the memory, this softness had her trembling almost as much as she'd been that night.

He seduced her mouth with soft kisses that stole her breath. He scraped his teeth against her lip, igniting a fire in her blood. By the time he finally curved his tongue against hers, she was reaching for him. The brim of his Stetson bumped her forehead, but it didn't slow her down.

Locking her wrists behind his neck, Faith surrendered to his kiss. He was sweeter than chocolate and even more addicting. Maybe it made her weak, but when he held her, when his mouth made love to hers as though she was the most important thing in the world, she held him tighter. Anything to keep wrapped in those feelings.

His hands splayed across her back and pulled her closer. Faith flicked her tongue against the tip of his. Though his hands flexed, and he moaned low in his throat, he ended the kiss and leaned back.

She wanted to reach for him and push him onto the blanket. She didn't want to go back to reality. Everything felt simpler in his arms.

Which was why she didn't do any of those things. Because there was nothing simple about them, and some kissing, no matter how hot and arousing, wasn't going to change that.

Between the passion and the bright sunshine, it took her

eyes a moment to clear. If he'd had the same issue, it didn't show. His gaze was firmly fixed on hers with an intensity her fuzzy brain couldn't have managed in that moment.

"When's your next doctor's appointment?"

She blinked. "In two weeks. Why?"

"I want to go."

"You want to go?" Apparently, her brain was slow to clear because what he was saying didn't make sense.

"I do."

"Why?"

For a split second, no longer than a few beats of a hummingbird's wings, a shadow darkened his green eyes. It was over so fast Faith questioned whether it had been real or a trick of light as the sun disappeared behind a cloud.

"I don't just want to pick up this child when it's born, Faith. I intend to be part of the pregnancy. I'm not going to let you go through this alone. This isn't only your responsibility."

The last lingering effects of his kiss fizzled with his words. Setting her jaw, Faith grabbed her half-full water bottle and scrambled to her feet.

He was right behind her, grabbing her arm.

"Faith, that's—"

She whirled on him. "I will take myself to my own appointments. I told you from the beginning I wasn't asking for anything from you, and I sure as hell don't want to be your *responsibility*."

"You might not want to be, and I know you well enough to understand why, but the truth is until *our* baby is born, you are. You both are." He leaned down, kissed her softly.

"It's not a hardship, Faith."

Something in his tone caught her attention, and she looked at him a little closer. He was too calm about this. Too accepting of her...

Her jaw dropped. "Oh, my God," she said. "You're hoping to change my mind, aren't you? That's why you haven't tried to talk me out of it, why you're offering to go with me to my appointment."

He shook his head. "I'm just trying to be supportive. The decision is yours."

She yanked her arm free. "You're full of shit. You forget that *I* know you, too. This is exactly something you'd try to do. And I won't fall for it."

Unconcerned, he tipped his shoulder. "Then you have nothing to lose by letting me go with you."

"Damn right I don't," she agreed as she headed toward her horse.

"Where are you going? We just got here."

"I'm hungry," she answered. Which wasn't a lie. The cinnamon bun was long gone, and the three cookies hadn't made a dent in her appetite. She was starving. No, that wasn't the lie. The lie was telling him she had nothing to lose by him coming to the appointment.

It wasn't that she was afraid he'd succeed. She was set on doing what was best for the baby, even if the thought of it kept her up at night. But she feared the more time they spent together, the better the chance she'd fall in love with him.

And there was no way she'd survive giving up both Gage and their baby.

Chapter Ten

"IT WASN'T SO bad, was it? Spending the day with me?" Gage asked.

He shot her a glance across the cab of his Jeep. It was dark, and the bluish glow of his dash controls wasn't quite enough to see her clearly. Not that he needed to. Because, despite how her pause told him she was trying to play it cool, she'd had a good day.

He'd worked damn hard to ensure it.

After their ride, he'd asked Faith to help take care of the horses, a task she enjoyed and one that didn't tax her sore knee too much. Then, knowing what was hiding in the "feed" room, he'd sent her to get some treats for the horses.

When she'd squealed in delight, he'd chuckled as he'd eased the bridle off his horse. "Kittens. Works every time."

Not that he'd used that ploy much, just enough to know women couldn't resist them. By the time she'd come back with a tiny ball of grey fluff cradled against her breasts, both horses had been seen to. Locking the stall behind him, he'd been content to watch her fuss and coo over the six-week-old kitten.

He'd made her fresh-squeezed lemonade like he used to in high school, and they'd sat on the shady side of the wraparound porch until she'd fallen asleep, her head on his shoulder. That, he hadn't planned. But he hadn't minded one bit. He'd bought the padded swing a few years ago when Ryker had had him stop in at the chain home improvement store in San Antonio when he'd gone to the city to spend the afternoon of his day off with Josh, his little brother. He'd spotted the swing on his way in and had immediately pictured himself sitting on it with a beer at the end of the day. It helped that, of the two on sale, the one he'd chosen had navy-and-white striped cushions. If a man had to buy a swing with a frilly canopy, at least it wasn't going to be a pink floral one.

He'd sat contentedly while she napped, her head an enjoyable weight against his shoulder. He'd breathed in the scent of her shampoo and the sunscreen he'd lent her before their ride and thought this wouldn't take much getting used to. Especially when she'd woken up looking soft and disoriented.

There were only two things he regretted from their night in San Antonio. One, that she'd left without a goodbye, and two, that he'd been robbed of waking next to her. It hadn't been the same having her wake on a swing wearing shorts and a tank top rather than in a bed wearing nothing, but he'd enjoyed it nearly as much.

By then it had been time to get the rest of supper ready and she'd finished putting the last touches on the salad while he'd tossed the steaks on the grill. The seven of them—he and Faith, Dallas, Ashley, and Brittany, Ryker and Roy— had had a nice meal outside at the picnic table. He hadn't been surprised when Ryker and Roy had disappeared shortly after they'd had ice cream. He had, however, when Dallas and Ashley had stuck around to visit.

While it could have been a desire to humor Brittany, who'd gone off to play with the kittens, Gage had nonetheless enjoyed the fact his older brother had stuck around for a bit.

"You and Ashley seemed to hit it off," he said as he turned out of the driveway onto the gravel road.

"She's easy to get along with. So is Dallas."

"He's getting better," Gage admitted.

Who'd have thought a few weeks ago he and his oldest brother would not only go riding together but would spend an evening sitting outside together with their women.

Gage smiled as he thought of Faith as his woman.

He wisely kept his mouth shut about that as he slowed for the next turn.

"Roy seems nice, too." She turned in her seat. "What's his story?"

"I don't know much. He was homeless when Dallas found him trying to help around Ashley's house."

"I still can't get over how they met. That is a great story."

"It really is," Gage agreed.

Even though, at the time, it wouldn't have been for either Dallas or Ashley. When Dallas had been trying to return a stolen tool one of his employees had taken, the police officer who'd identified the company truck based on an eye witness and had pulled Dallas over had had to charge him with possession of stolen property, despite Dallas's claim he was en route to return it.

The judge had issued him a fine and community service, and the probation officer, learning Dallas was a carpenter, had ordered the service be completed on a Houses of Hope project. And the recipient of that house, who was also obligated to put in many hours on the project, had been none other than Ashley.

"Roy has mentioned a family to Dallas, though we don't know where they are."

"He seems so nice. I can't imagine the circumstances that left him homeless." Faith sighed. "I'm glad you guys gave him a job and a home."

"Well, to be honest, he's done us the favor. He used to farm, so he's familiar with all the machinery, and he's just one of those jack-of-all-trades kind of guys. He's helping Dallas spruce up the bunkhouse. He fixed the bailer when it broke, and I know he's helped Ryker in his garage a time or two. Not to mention, with him around to help with chores, it gives the rest of us more time."

"But aren't you curious?" she asked as he turned into Last Stand.

"I guess so. But I figure when he wants us to know, he'll tell us."

He pulled up in front of her grandma's house, put the Jeep in park. Hoping for a goodnight kiss and wanting to walk her to her door, Gage got out of the vehicle. He rounded the hood, but she'd stepped out before he could open her door.

"Well, um, thanks for everything. I really did have a nice time."

"Me, too," he said. He leaned in. Cupping her cheek, he opened his mouth over hers. Her response was a bit hesitant at first, but it didn't take her long to melt into it. Soon, her hand was on his chest and his was splayed in the middle of her back, drawing her closer. A hard thunking noise on the porch interrupted them.

Faith sprang out of his arms.

Together, they looked toward the house. What the hell?

Her grandma, dressed in pleated slacks and a stiff blouse that was buttoned right up to the neck, stood there watching. She had a small carry-on style suitcase at her feet. It didn't take a rocket scientist to figure out whose suitcase that was or who was the target of her furious scowl. But what he couldn't understand was why.

First of all, they'd only been kissing, and Faith was twenty-four—it was hardly scandalous. Second, they hadn't been at it long enough for her grandma to see it from the window and get Faith's belongings together. Which meant she'd had the bag packed before they'd gotten home, and she'd been lying in wait. Why the hell would she do that?

Faith walked toward the porch. "Grandma, what are you doing?"

"I knew it," the older woman raged. Her eyes were narrowed like two lasers. "I knew you weren't just here for a visit like you claimed. Especially not when you've been spending most of your time with *him*," she said scathingly.

Winding up like a pro ball player, she tossed something at Faith. Gage couldn't see what it was until Faith held up the bottle of pills.

His stomach lurched. Surely, she wouldn't...

"Did you really think I wouldn't find out?"

"You went through my things?" Faith asked incredulously.

Gage stepped closer, peered at the bottle Faith held in her hands. His breath rushed from his lungs. It was nothing but prenatal vitamins.

"Of course I did! I knew you were lying from the moment you arrived on Friday. Knew you had to want something. Did you even damage your car or was that just the excuse you gave me for having a man carry you home in the middle of the day?"

Her flinty gaze raked over Gage. "Which one of you Granger boys is responsible? Or was it someone else altogether? Wouldn't surprise me if you didn't even know." She harrumphed.

Gage was stunned speechless. There was no love lost between Faith and her grandmother, but for the woman to imply Faith was a slut... That she didn't even know who the father of her baby was...

"Oh, I know," Faith answered. She marched up the porch steps and looked her grandma in the eye. "It could be any of the three men I had an orgy with that night." Ignoring her grandmother's shocked sputter, Faith continued on. "As for Ryker and Gage, well, I was already pregnant by the time I took those two to my bed."

She yanked her suitcase off the porch and, with no sign of a sore knee, stomped back down the stairs. Head held high, she didn't even look at him as she passed him. He was still standing there, gaping, when he heard her get back into his Jeep.

FAITH HAD NEVER been so furious in her life. She and her grandma had never been close, so it wasn't the fact she was mean to Faith that hurt. It was the words she'd chosen to use. Normally, her go-to digs were how much she'd cost Alice over the years. How her grandma had had to sacrifice so much to put a roof over her head and feed her all those years.

But to have her assume she was anything like Linda when she'd gone above and beyond her whole life to prove she wasn't cut deep. Faith had been a model student in school. She hadn't gone to parties, hadn't tried drugs, and only ever drank those few times Gage had snuck her out to the ranch. She'd gone to church every Sunday with her grandma. She'd helped with housework, and despite her grandma's constant bitching, had never fought back.

Oh, she'd wanted to. More times than she could count. But she hadn't. Until tonight. When something inside of her had snapped. After years of respecting her grandmother and following her rules, of doing everything to be a model child, to be what her mother hadn't been, only to have none of it matter? To have the one mistake she made be thrown at her in such a hurtful way had been the last straw.

Her grandmother knew nothing about her because she hadn't cared enough to try. Okay, Faith was pregnant. But Gage was only the second man she'd slept with, so she was hardly a tramp. And the first one had been when she'd been twenty-one. And unlike her mother, who'd just dumped her without a thought, Faith wasn't going to do that.

Maybe she wasn't going to go with the private adoption she'd originally started looking into, but her child was still going to be raised by someone who wanted it and would love it. Unconditionally. Who would never spew hatred and disgust from the top of the porch steps.

It had been petty to lash out, but damn if she regretted it. She'd followed the rules, done everything right, and it had gotten her nothing. Nothing! And since there was no point defending herself, Faith had used her grandmother's words and made them even uglier. The sad part was Alice was likely to believe them.

Why was it easier to believe the worst in her than the best?

Faith clenched her hands into fists. Her heart pounded in her ears and against her ribs. Who does that? Who treats family like that?

Shaking, she tried to calm down, but the words and images just kept replaying in her mind, and the more they did, the more the fury inside raged. The more tears stung the back of her eyes.

Gage got into the vehicle and, God bless him, didn't say a word. He pulled out onto the darkened, quiet street, drove them through the sleepy neighborhood and back toward the ranch.

The miles he put between her and her grandma helped a little. But then, she'd always felt better the further she was from Alice Stone. The obligatory times she came back always eroded the progress she'd made since the last time she'd left. She'd worked hard, with no help whatsoever, to support herself.

She'd found a roommate to share expenses and a job close to her apartment so she could walk to work and save money. She'd done it with a purpose in mind. Not for a trip, or a bauble, or a fancier car. For Faith, it was always just about having a reserve. Having a cushion so she wouldn't ever have to go back and have Alice tell her she'd failed. Tell her how much trouble she was.

Fighting the tears that tickled her nose and pushed against her chest, Faith leaned her head back against the headrest and closed her eyes. Even with her impromptu nap earlier, she was exhausted.

"I know we're supposed to respect our elders," Gage said after another few miles had passed, "but that woman has a stick so far up her ass, she must choke on the splinters."

Faith sputtered, a mixture of laughter and tears. It was a gift he had to somehow know the best thing to say at the right time. Had he offered sympathy, she'd just have felt worse. And too much silence would accomplish nothing but more stewing and silent raging.

So he'd opted for crass humor.

It was the exact perfect thing to get her out of her head.

"I've tried to give her the benefit of the doubt over the years. I've tried to put myself in her shoes and imagine what it must have been like to raise a child as a young widow and then have that child turn out like Linda. And then to be stuck raising her granddaughter." She rolled her head to the side so she could see him. "It had to have been difficult."

"Of course it was," he agreed. "But a lot of people have difficult lives. It doesn't give them permission to treat everyone around them like shit."

Though the gravel road was empty save the two white beams of his lights cutting through the night, he nonetheless signaled as he turned onto the ranch's driveway. He parked in front of the house, cut the lights, then the engine. Unfortunately, they hadn't been gone long, and the glow in the windows indicated Ryker was still awake.

At least they wouldn't have to explain her presence to Dallas and Ashley as they'd headed back to the city shortly after supper. But she didn't know how Ryker would feel having an overnight guest, especially an unplanned one.

"Will Ryker mind?"

"He shouldn't. And besides, it's not just his house."

"I know but—"

"It'll be fine. Come on. I'll get your bag."

He hauled out her suitcase and met her on the brick sidewalk. Though the houses weren't alike at all—her grandmother's a tidy, little two-story while this one a sprawling ranch house—it nevertheless felt a little déja vu as they walked toward the porch steps.

"I'm really sorry about this, Gage. I'll explain to Ryker it's just for tonight."

"Don't worry about it, Faith. It's not an imposition."

Maybe not to him, but she felt uncomfortable walking in knowing she was staying the night. She stopped dead.

"What's the matter?"

She turned. Between the yard and porch lights, and the fact he was within two feet of her, she was able to see him clearly. He appeared his usual calm self. At least one of them was. She was suddenly a ball of nerves.

"I hadn't given a thought to sleeping arrangements."

His expression gave away nothing. "Okay."

"I'm not... I don't think it would be..."

He reached out squeezed her shoulder. "Faith, relax. You can have my bed. I'll bunk in Dallas's room for the night."

The combination of his touch and tone reassured her, and her muscles relaxed. But she had difficulty looking him in the eye.

"I just didn't want you to assume...anything."

He moved his hand to her chin and gently raised her head until she was looking at him. "There's nothing to assume. You need a place to stay tonight and I'm offering you one. No strings, Faith. Okay?"

"Okay."

His expression suddenly shifted, and she watched as mischief danced in his eyes. "I do have a few requests, though."

She knew by his expression she had nothing serious to worry about. Nevertheless, she crossed her arms. "Okay. What are they?"

"One. You don't sleep with Ryker. Ever. Two. If you're ever going to have an orgy, I want to be invited."

Laughing, she slapped his hand away.

It wasn't until she was settled in his bed, smelling him on the blankets and yearning for what couldn't be, that she realized he'd done it again. He'd taken an uncomfortable moment, added humor, and eased her mind.

She felt a tug on her heart and pinched her eyes closed as she realized what it meant. She was starting to really fall for him. Which meant she needed to get back to her life in San Antonio before she did the unthinkable—fell in love.

Good thing her car would be ready tomorrow. No telling what would happen if she had to stay longer.

NOBODY WAS AROUND when she woke up. It felt weird walking around the house without anyone there. Almost as though she was trespassing.

At supper the night before, it had been mentioned Cam wouldn't be back from his rodeo in Vernon until today, and she suspected, as it was eight thirty, Gage and Ryker were outside working. And since Ryker had told her the parts wouldn't be in until that afternoon, she had nowhere to go.

"So, I'm stuck for now."

Almost as bad was the fact she was starving. Hands on her jean-clad hips, she looked over the counter. The only food she saw were the crumbs dusting the area in front of the toaster. She didn't feel comfortable riffling through their cupboards or fridge. Which meant, despite the enticing smell of coffee coming from the half-pot in the corner, she'd have to go without that, too.

No food or coffee to start her day. She frowned. This had better not be a sign of how the rest of her day was going to go. With her stomach giving a loud growl, Faith turned to go outside. She'd find a way to make herself useful.

That was when she noticed the kitchen table and what was on it.

"He didn't."

But as she walked toward it, she realized he had. Sitting on a placemat was a cereal bowl stacked over a small plate, cutlery, a coffee mug, and a tall glass. Next to it a box of granola cereal, a banana, and an orange. Faith picked up the note he'd left sitting in the bowl.

Good morning! The milk and juice are in the fridge. You'll find bagels tucked at the back of the freezer. There should be coffee in the pot unless Roy drank it all. Ryker and I are moving cattle to the east pasture. Should be back by lunch. Please make yourself at home. Gage

Faith wasn't sure how it was possible, but her heart both swelled and broke at the same time. It was so sweet. *He* was so sweet. And for the briefest moment, she imagined this was their home and that it would be common occurrence to wake and find he'd left her something thoughtful like this. Because it was Gage, and he would.

But because it was Gage, she also knew he'd have done the same for any other guest in his home. Suddenly, she wasn't so hungry. But until she delivered the baby, she needed to take care of it, so she ate, had the one cup of coffee a day she allowed herself, cleaned up, then went outside.

The roll-up door on Ryker's garage was open, and her car was up on the lift. Curious, she headed that way. The smell of oil and grease wasn't unpleasant as she strolled in and looked around. Situated on a ranch, one might think it wouldn't have all the amenities of a big city garage, but from what Faith saw, it wasn't any different.

Shelves stocked with boxes of parts, containers of oil, and other necessary fluids. Serpentine belts and various windshield washer blade packages hung off two rows of hooks. And in the middle of it all was a hydraulic lift that currently held her car.

She walked closer, saw all the grass and dirt Gage had said was stuck under there was gone. Other than that, Faith really didn't know what she was looking at. She walked out of the shop. When she heard whistling coming from the barn, she aimed in that direction. In the corrals next to the barn, several horses lifted their heads to watch her progress. Like the note Gage had left her, Faith could get used to seeing them every day. Though it was silly, she waved to them before stepping into the dimness of the barn.

"Good morning."

Though she recognized Roy's voice from last night, it took her eyes a moment before she could actually see him. He was standing in the aisle, pitchfork in hand and a wheelbarrow of soiled straw beside him. With both end doors of the barn open, a draft blew through. She smelled horseflesh and hay as much as the manure he was mucking.

She gestured to the wheelbarrow. "Need help?"

His bristly brows arched. "You want to muck stalls?"

"No." She laughed. "I want to keep busy. The Grangers were nice enough to let me stay over last night after an, um, incident with my grandmother. And since I also ate their food for breakfast, seems only fair I do a little something in return."

His brows drew together. "I don't think they expect that of you. They've been nothing but generous toward me."

"Oh, I know they don't expect it. It's just something I want to do."

His blue eyes crinkled at the sides when he smiled. "Well, then, I'd love some company."

After he finished the stall he was on, he showed her where the fresh straw was kept. Ripping off two flakes from the bale, he set one down. Taking the other, he demonstrated how to shake it out to make it nice and fluffy for the animals.

He picked up the other flake. "Your turn."

When she grabbed it, a sharp piece of straw jabbed into her palm. She yanked her hands back.

"Ouch!" she said as it fell to the floor.

"Sorry," Roy apologized. "I should have offered you a pair of gloves."

"No, that's okay." Faith sucked on the sore spot a moment then bent to retrieve what she'd dropped. She must have come up a bit too fast because suddenly the barn swirled around her. Instinctively, she reached out for something to steady her. Her fingers closed around Roy's arm.

"Easy, there," he crooned. His free hand grabbed her other arm. "You all right?"

"I think I need to sit."

She lowered herself to the stall floor. She hadn't asked Gage how old Roy was, but given the lines around his mouth and eyes and the grey peppering his hair, she pegged him for somewhere in his early sixties. It didn't stop him from folding himself right down beside her.

"Do you need me to get you some water?" he asked.

She took a breath, sagged against the rough wood sides of the stall. "No, thanks. I'm starting to feel better."

He pulled off his gloves. "Does this kind of thing happen to you often?"

"It didn't used to," she answered. "But it's happened a few times lately."

"Maybe you ought to get it checked out. In case it's something serious."

Faith scoffed. Oh, it was serious all right. Just not life-threatening the way Roy was thinking. But she didn't know how to answer him. She didn't think Gage had told anyone about the baby, and it wasn't her place to do it. On the other hand, she was the one carrying it. And, dammit, she was really curious about Roy's life. Maybe if she said a little something about hers, he'd do the same.

She looked at Roy. He had kind eyes. A relaxed, easy-going demeanor. His jeans and T-shirt were old and fraying, his dirty sneakers were bursting at the seams, and his greying hair was in desperate need of a trim. In contrast, his cheeks were clean-shaven, and he smelled of Irish Spring. She couldn't help liking the man. She'd never met her grandfather, and though Roy didn't resemble the man she'd seen only in photographs—although he was decades older than her grandfather had been when he'd died—he was everything she'd imagined a grandpa should be.

"I'm not sick, Roy," she said. "I'm pregnant. And in case you're wondering, yes, Gage knows. It's his."

Delight spread across his face until he noticed she wasn't smiling. "You're not happy about it?" he asked.

"Actually, my gut reaction was delight," she admitted to him, even though she'd told Gage her first thought had been about college.

"But then reality set in. I've been saving up for college and finally have enough to go. I've worked too hard to give that up."

She grabbed a piece of straw, twisted it within her thumb and forefinger. "I was looking into private adoption, but Gage wants it, so I'll sign whatever I need to give the baby over to him."

Roy goggled. "I know it's none of my business, but why won't you do this together? You seem to like each other."

"We do."

"Then I don't understand. He can help with the baby and you can still do college."

She shut down his words before they had a chance to root and give her false hope. "I come from an abusive background. Not physically, but mentally. My mother chose cheap flings with men over me. When I was in eighth grade, she left me with my grandma who made sure, every single day, I knew just how much she didn't want me. I'm not passing that on to any child of mine."

He frowned. "But you said, initially, you were happy. That doesn't sound like someone who'd make their baby feel unwanted."

"It wasn't planned. And it's not like Gage and I are even dating. Sure, my gut reaction was excitement, but it was closely followed by the fact I wanted college. What happens when, a year or two down the road, I can't go anywhere or do anything without worrying about getting a sitter? When I'm stuck in the same dead-end job instead of having gone to college like I'd always wanted? Then what?"

"You're forgetting Gage. If he's willing to raise it on his own, then you have to figure he'd help you if you decided to keep it, too."

She shook her head. "I can't chance that I'll eventually treat it like my mother and grandmother treated me."

Sadness softened his eyes. "I'm sorry you went through that, Faith. But more than that, I'm just as sorry for your mother and grandmother because having children is the best part of life, and they both wasted the gift."

Gladly putting aside her own worries, she focused on Roy. "Did you have kids?"

His lips curved. "I did. Two daughters. They were my pride and joy."

"Were?" Oh, God, had something happened to them?

He held up his broad hands. "They're still alive. At least, I assume so." He lowered his gaze to the straw. "I haven't seen them in almost ten years."

"I know it's none of my business, but can I ask why?"

"I always liked to have a drink or two. But over time, it got to be three, then four a day. Gradually, even more than that. My wife tried everything. She'd pour it down the sink, refuse to have any alcohol in the house. Even declined to go out with friends or have them over because, inevitably, someone brought booze."

He clasped his hands in his lap. "I just learned to be sneaky. I'd keep a bottle hidden in the garage somewhere. I even had one under the seat of my car. And I kept telling myself I wasn't an alcoholic, because I could stop anytime. It wasn't until I'd lost everything that I realized it was the very fact I *hadn't* stopped that made me one."

Hearing the hurt and shame in his voice, Faith regretted having asked. Her curiosity wasn't worth his pain.

She put her hand on his shoulder. "I'm sorry, Roy. I had no business prying."

She moved to stand, but he put his weathered hand over hers.

"Actually, it's nice to have someone care enough to ask."

He shook his head. "Living on the streets, you get used to people either going out of their way not to look at you or looking through you as though you're not even there. As though you don't matter."

Knowing she'd done exactly that, more than once, Faith settled back in to listen.

"You matter, Roy," she said, her voice choking up.

He squeezed her hand. "The more I drank, the less I felt as though I did. I lost my job by coming in drunk. I saw the disappointment in my girls' eyes, heard the anger and bitterness in my wife's voice. But instead of that driving me to be better, it drove me further into the bottle. I felt useless. I knew I was a burden. But it wasn't until I overheard my oldest telling her mother she didn't want me to come to her high school graduation because she was embarrassed that I truly realized they were better off without me."

"I'm sorry."

"So was I. Sorry enough to leave. I grabbed what I could fit in a backpack. I left a note apologizing for the hurt I'd caused, and I haven't seen them since."

His sigh sounded as though it came from the depths of his soul. "Even after that, it took me over five years of living on the streets, years of being miserable and alone, before I admitted I needed help. Before I was ready to do something about the addiction.

"Luckily, one of the people at the homeless shelter helped connect me with an organization that would help me with my recovery." His tired eyes met hers. "I failed twice but, luckily, neither they nor I gave up."

"And now?"

His lips slowly curled into a smile. Faith was relieved to see the shadows clear from his blue eyes. He even sat a little straighter. "I've been sober for almost two years."

"That's fantastic! Good for you."

He looked up toward the dusty window. Following his gaze, Faith watched the dust motes trickle through the veiled sunlight like tiny snowflakes.

"Unfortunately, getting back on one's feet isn't easy. Nobody wants to hire you when it's clear you haven't washed and shaved in days, and your clothes have gone even longer than that without being cleaned. When you don't have an address, a car, or even respectable clothes to wear."

"But you're here."

Again his smile spread. "Because of Ashley and Dallas. Ashley worked it so I could volunteer on her house, and once Dallas got to know me better and learned I'd once had a farm, he hired me on here."

Gage had already told her how Dallas had met Roy, but enjoying the conversation and not ready for it to end, Faith pretended she didn't know.

"You volunteered on Ashley's house?" she asked.

"I know." He chuckled. "Probably doesn't make sense, but it made me feel useful. Like I was still good for something." He patted her hand and winked. "And now I'm getting paid to work, so I better get back to it."

He rose, held out a hand to her. Studying her closely, he said, "Maybe you should go inside? Take it easy."

She wiped the straw off her butt. "I'm fine. Really."

He didn't look convinced, but he didn't stop her from grabbing the flake of straw. Then he watched her shake it out over the floor. When she was done, he nodded his approval.

"Okay. I have those three already cleaned." He gestured to three stalls across the aisle. "Have a look once you're done, but five or six flakes per stall should be enough. You might need more. Use your judgment."

He walked out first, sliding his hands back into his gloves. He gripped the wheelbarrow, but he'd no more than lifted the back end off the floor when he set it back down again. The somber expression on his face made her pause.

"Faith, my biggest regret is leaving my family behind and knowing I chose the bottle over them. Now, I know it's an addiction and not nearly that black and white, but I also know that's what my wife and daughters believed."

He pierced her with his gaze. "There is nothing better, nothing more humbling and beautiful, than holding your child in your arms. Than having them look at you with absolute love and trust." His eyes shone with tears, and it took a moment before he could continue.

"You have a chance, Faith, a chance at something wonderful. At the most beautiful thing life has to give us. I'd hate to see you lose out on that because you're scared. We're all scared. Nothing about life is easy or guaranteed."

"I know that, but—"

He shook his head adamantly. "I have to make a choice every single day not to drink. And lots of times, I have to make that choice more than once a day. But you know what? My sobriety is worth it. My life is worth it. Maybe you'll falter. Maybe one day, when you're frustrated and at your wit's end, you'll say something you'll regret. It's called being human. But if every day, you make the choice not to be your mother or grandmother, if every day, you give your heart and soul and your tears into fighting it, into being a better person, then guess what—you will be."

Faith stared at him. She wanted to believe him, but if it was that simple, than why did cycles of abuse continue from generation to generation?

Roy cleared his throat, ran the back of his glove over first his right eye, then the left. "Just think about it."

Think about it was all she did as she finished the stalls and the other few light chores Roy gave her. Then, realizing lunch was approaching and the guys would be hungry, not to mention she was starving, Faith headed back to the house.

She would set aside her discomfort at going through their fridge and cupboards so they'd all have a good meal. Then, Gage would go off to work, Ryker would pick up her parts to finish her car, and she'd be free to get back to San Antonio.

Chapter Eleven

"WHY WOULD I do that?" Ryker asked.

The last of the herd had just passed through the gate. Ryker was on the ground, dragging the section of fence they'd set down to let the cattle in back toward the post on the other side of the opening.

Then, putting his shoulder into the post, he drew it tight to the other one so he could secure the small loop of barbed wire over the stationary post, effectively locking the Longhorns in.

"Because I need her to come back and she won't if she doesn't have a reason."

Giving the wire a tug and deeming the fence sturdy, Ryker took off his gloves, tucked them into the back pocket on his jeans. He eyed Gage from under the brim of his Stetson.

"And how do you think she'd feel if she knew you were lying to her?"

Gage grinned. "I'm not. You are."

Ryker shook his head. "I never said I would."

His brother grabbed the reins he'd left draped over his horse's neck before gripping the pommel and lifting himself into the saddle. He tapped his heels against the mare's flank to get her moving. Gage fell into step beside him.

"Come on, Ryker. It's not a big deal. Tell her the parts were delayed a day. That they missed getting on the truck or something." He sighed. "I'll get you another peach pie."

Ryker quirked a brow. "Two peach pies for the same woman. Keep this up, I'll get fat."

Gage snorted. Good genes and hard work ensured none of the Granger men had an ounce of fat on them.

"Will you do it?"

"I don't want to get involved in your drama, Gage."

My drama or my life? But since he needed the favor, he kept his caustic comment to himself.

"Fine," Ryker finally relented. "But I won't make a habit of lying for you."

"You won't have to," Gage promised.

But Gage might. Because Ryker's lie would only ensure Faith came back one more time. Gage had no idea how to ensure she'd back after that.

A GOOD THING Faith was standing at the kitchen sink. The receptacle would catch the drool forming in her mouth at the sight of the two cowboys striding from the barn.

Oh. My. Goodness.

Long legs. Stetsons shadowing their faces. Tight T-shirts showcasing their taught abdomens and muscular shoulders. Belt buckles that showcased their...

Faith might have been too young for a hot flash, but surely, this must be what one felt like. A fever that started in the belly and spread like hot lava, burning everything in its path.

Her eyes drawn to one particular cowboy, Faith drank in all his deliciousness. If he were hers, she'd do exactly what Ashley had done with Dallas last night. She'd run toward him, launch herself into his arms, and kiss him with all the heat sizzling inside her.

Until he'd do as he had in San Antonio, where he'd stroked her, hands, tongue, and sex, until she'd broken into a million pieces in his arms.

"Oh, God."

Mortified to feel her cheeks burning, not to mention the throbbing between her legs, Faith turned on the tap. Cupping cold water in her hands, she splashed the chilled liquid over her face until the worst of the fire had been subdued.

She doubted, when it came to Gage, it would ever die completely.

While he and Ryker washed in the mudroom, she finished setting the table and brought out the shepherd's pie she'd put together for lunch.

With Roy taking his back to the bunkhouse, it was just Faith, Gage, and Ryker. They didn't talk much over the meal. Faith asked about their morning and then Gage asked about hers. There was a lot of awkward silence in between.

She was all too happy when it was over. She turned her attention to Ryker.

"So you'll go get the parts this afternoon?" she asked.

"Actually," he said. "I got a call on my cell while we were out moving cattle. The supply store in San Antonio forgot to send it on the truck. So it won't be here now until tomorrow."

Faith sucked in a breath. "But I work tomorrow. I need to be back in San Antonio tonight."

How was she going to get there? There wasn't a taxi service in Last Stand, and she couldn't ask her grandmother. Not now. That bridge had not just been burned, it had exploded.

"Take my Jeep," Gage said.

"But how will you get to work?"

"You can drop me off on your way to the city. I just have to shower quick and change into my uniform and I'll be ready to go. Ryker can pick me up after my shift tomorrow."

Ryker scowled. "I can?"

Gage rolled his eyes. "Or you can send Roy." He faced Faith. "What time do you work tomorrow?"

"Seven in the morning to one in the afternoon."

"Okay, that works. Ryker should have your car done by the time you get back here, right?" he asked, looking at his brother.

Ryker's scowl remained fierce as he looked at Gage. But it morphed into a smile when he looked at Faith.

"I'm sure your car will be ready by then," Ryker agreed.

"Great," Gage said. "Then it's settled."

Yeah, settled. Except for the fact she once again had to come back to Last Stand.

NORMALLY, A DAY at work without a call was a good thing. It meant nobody was hurt. Or worse. But there was only so much TV a guy could watch, so many games of cards or basketball a man could play in a shift. Even cooking for the crew and volunteering to clean up after hadn't been enough to keep Gage's mind off the one thing it was fiercely determined to remain fixed on—Faith.

He'd hated the idea of Faith and his baby in another city last night. And that was only one night! Now what was he going to do? She was bringing his Jeep back later that afternoon, and she'd want to head back. Dammit, he didn't want her to go.

He wanted her and the baby close. Wanted to be able to take care of them, and he couldn't do that effectively when she lived over an hour away. How would he know if she needed anything? He knew Faith well enough to know that she wouldn't reach out to him unless absolutely necessary. And even then, it would depend what it was. For the baby, she would. For herself?

"Not likely," he muttered as he took his frustration out on scraping the baked-on barbeque sauce from the chicken wings he'd cooked.

Marcella sidled up beside him. Leaning against the counter, she crossed her arms over her dark blue uniform shirt. She nodded toward the pan Gage was scouring.

"Ryker piss you off again?"

"No. Why?"

"That's usually when you volunteer to clean up as well as cook."

Gage dipped the pan in the soapy water. Then, balancing it on the edge of the sink, continued his assault on the baked-on sauce. Had he been thinking, he'd have lined the pan with tinfoil, but clearly, his mind hadn't been working properly. Maybe it *was* a good thing they hadn't gotten a call. Although he'd never had a problem focusing on his job when he was in action.

"I've just got a lot on my mind." He shrugged. "With Dad and everything."

"Has there been any change?"

"Not when I called on my way in." He'd get Ryker to stop on their way home. Or Roy. Whichever man came to pick him up.

"I know it's not uncommon for a patient to remain in a coma, but your dad's case is weird. There's no medical reason to explain why he's not waking up."

"And no sign of him coming out of it, either." Which was just as troubling.

Finally, scraping off the last of the crust, Gage ran the soapy dishcloth over the pan, rinsed it, and put it in the other sink. Marcella grabbed the towel Gage had left on the counter. She wiped the pan dry and put it away.

With lunch over and only a couple hours left in their shift, the firehouse went quiet as some of the firemen, EMTs, and paramedics spread out in front on the TV, while others stretched out on cots in the dorm room for a nap. Four decided to play a doubles game of Ping-Pong. Apparently, Marcella wasn't inclined to do any of those things as she resumed her spot next to the sink and watched Gage wipe down the counters and long table.

"Your dad has been in the hospital almost two weeks now, and this is the quietest, most distracted I've seen you." Her knowing gaze locked onto Gage's. "This has to do with the woman that hit the ditch, the one you said you knew from high school. My mom said she saw you with a woman at the grocery store yesterday. Was it her?"

"Yeah." Gage rinsed the cloth, hung it to dry on the edge of the sink. "She came for a cookout and ended up staying over after her hag of a grandma kicked her out."

"Why would she do that?"

Though he'd yet to tell his brothers, and he'd told Faith they wouldn't tell anyone about his raising the baby, he could trust Marcella with his secret. Besides, he'd love a woman's advice, and even though Ashley was a mother and Marcella wasn't, he didn't know Dallas's girlfriend well enough to go to her. And he'd never tell a virtual stranger before his family. At least he considered Marcella the sister he'd never had.

Though the TV and the rapid-fire *tap-tap* of the Ping-Pong ball on the table filled the fire hall with noise, Gage didn't trust they wouldn't be overheard. Gesturing Marcella to follow, he led them through the building and out back where the basketball court was. Since they'd just eaten a big meal, nobody was inclined to play. It was the perfect place for a private conversation.

With its trees and picnic table, it was just the right spot. Gage settled on one side, Marcella on the other.

"Faith wasn't coming to visit her grandma like I assumed when we found her the other day. She was coming to see me."

Marcella arched her brow. "She was? I'd have never guessed. It seemed as though she wasn't thrilled to see you."

"Because she hadn't expected to see me then and it caught her off guard. Besides, it wasn't the place to disclose what she'd come to tell."

"Which is?"

He swallowed hard. "She's almost three months pregnant with my child."

"She's…" Marcella clasped her hands on the tabletop. "Wow."

"Yeah," Gage agreed.

"So now what? I mean, she doesn't even live in Last Stand."

"Actually, that's not the biggest hurdle."

"Oh?"

"She's decided she doesn't want to keep the baby. She was looking at adoption."

Marcella's brows arched up her forehead. "She decided all that before talking to you?"

Gage laced his fingers together, gripped them tight. "It's not my body. It's her decision."

"Well, yeah, but…"

"I'm going to raise it."

Marcella gaped. "On your own?"

"I have family. I won't be completely on my own."

"Yeah, but still." She chewed her lip. "It won't be easy. Especially with our schedule."

"Nope, it definitely won't. But I know I can't live every day wondering how my kid is doing. At least, this way, I'll know."

"Aren't there open adoptions for that kind of thing?"

"There are, and it's what Faith had decided to do before she told me about the baby."

"So it's not just about knowing it'll be okay for you?"

"No. It's part of me. Part of Faith." He stared at his hands. "Part of my mom. I know it won't be easy, but there's no way I'm not keeping it."

"Okay," Marcella said. "So now what?"

He hadn't realized until then how much he'd expected his friend to try to talk him out of it. Or tell him he wasn't thinking things through, or any other number of arguments that would have him questioning his decision. He hoped his brothers would be as supportive when he told them.

"I think I should talk to a lawyer."

Marcella nodded. "I agree."

"Well, obviously, I know nothing about how this process works, and I want to make sure I go through all the steps legally. I mean it's mine, but I don't know if I have to adopt it or if she can just sign over her rights."

His heart bled thinking about that. Not only for the baby's sake, but for his, too. Because once she gave the baby to him, it would be the last he ever saw of her.

Though Gage hoped it wouldn't come to that, that he'd convince her between now and the time the baby came that they could be a family, he still needed to ensure the baby would have at least its father in its life.

So he'd call a lawyer and see what needed to be done.

"WHERE THE HELL are you?" Ryker bellowed.

Wincing, Gage moved the phone away from his ear. "Just about to leave town. Why?"

"Your shift was done at two. What's taking you so damn

long?"

Since it was Roy who'd picked him up, and Faith had already told Gage she'd told the ranch hand about the baby, Gage had gotten the man to stop by the law office. He'd thought he'd just make an appointment, since he hadn't had a minute alone since his and Marcella's talk outside the fire hall to call the attorney. But it ended up the lawyer had time, so he'd seen Gage right then.

Not something he was going to tell Ryker. So he lied and said he'd stopped in to see their dad. It wasn't as though Joe could bust him. Although, at this point, that would be a good thing.

"I had Roy stop at the hospital. Why?"

"Why? Because your girlfriend showed up early."

Gage's stomach leapt. "Faith is there already?"

"Yes, genius, that's what I just said."

Gage hurried down the sidewalk away from the law office. Roy was leaning against the passenger door of the ranch truck. When Gage signaled for him to get in, the man wasted no time.

"Well, stall her. Don't let her leave." Gage hopped in the driver's side, slammed the door, and buckled up.

"I'm not. Under the pretense of a test drive," he said, grievance dripping off every word, "I'm currently sitting about a mile down the road talking to you. So, get your ass home so I can quit babysitting."

Ryker ended the call before Gage could get in another word. Tossing his phone in the cup holder, Gage pulled onto the street and, as fast as he could with tourists crossing the streets at every intersection taking their sweet time, made a beeline for home. A little while later, he spotted Ryker in Faith's car. He was pulled into the approach that accessed their hayfield.

His brother must have been keeping an eye on his rear-view mirror because seconds after Gage recognized the car, it pulled out into the gravel road. Staying far enough behind that he wasn't eating Ryker's dust, Gage followed his brother the rest of the way home.

Gage would have to pay for the favors Ryker had done for him, but when he drove up the driveway and saw Faith standing by the porch in a lavender T-shirt and jean capris, the copper highlights shining in her dark brown hair… Whatever the price was, it would be worth it.

Just to have her there.

She moved forward as he pulled in next to her car and put the truck in park. For a moment, he envisioned her walking toward him, a smile on her face and their baby on her hip. The vision was so real, so incredibly perfect, it gutted him when, instead of walking toward him as he figured she would, she aimed for Ryker instead.

It's still possible. Don't give up.

With that pep talk, he cut the engine and got out of the truck.

"So it's good?" she asked before his brother had a chance to do more than open the door.

"Yep," Ryker said as he unfolded himself from the car. "It sounds good, and with the wheel alignment I gave it, it's running straight."

Gage frowned when her shoulders sagged with relief. Was being around him really that bad?

"Will you take a check? Or can I pay with a credit card?"

His brother gestured toward the garage. "Either. We can settle up in there."

Finally acknowledging Gage was there, she looked at him. "I'll, um, be right back."

He nodded. "Okay."

Looking over her head, Ryker gave Gage a pointed look before heading off toward his garage. Knowing he didn't have a big window of time, Gage loped up the walk, took the porch steps in one long stride, and went inside to change out of his uniform.

He tossed his work clothes onto the bed, pulled on a pair of Wranglers and a baby blue T-shirt. In the mudroom, he tugged on his favorite boots and lifted his Stetson off the rack. He stepped onto the porch as Faith walked out the roll-up door of Ryker's garage.

Their gazes met across the yard, the impact snapping like a bullwhip. She'd felt it, too, because her mouth suddenly opened, and her hands coiled at her sides before she wiped them down the sides of her thighs. Perfect. Since he wasn't above using any advantage he could get, he added a little extra swagger to his step as he walked toward her.

She wiped her hands again as they met in the middle of the yard.

"You all set?" he asked.

"Yes, finally. Thanks for letting me use your Jeep. I know it was an inconvenience, but I fueled it up."

He took her hand. "It was no inconvenience."

She pierced him with a knowing look. "Why do I suddenly get the feeling you're the reason I had to come back?"

He let the grin spread. "I've no idea."

"Yeah, right," she scoffed. She stared down at their joined hands. "I should get going."

Not ready to let her go, he kept their fingers entwined as they walked to her car. Then he brought their joined hands to his chest and stepped forward until he closed her between the vehicle and him.

"I wouldn't mind if you didn't go back at all."

She sucked in an audible breath. "I have a job, Gage. And my life is in San Antonio."

He leaned in, hovering his lips over hers. "It doesn't have to be," he said.

Then he captured her mouth with his. Having thought of little else but that all day, the kiss went straight to scorching. Hot. Open mouth. Tongues tangling. Against the back of his hand, her breast was soft. Beneath it, he felt the staccato of her heartbeat. The same beat pounded in his chest and ears.

His other hand took a handful of her hair and tugged her head back so he could take the kiss deeper. Hotter. She latched onto his waist, and the bite of her short nails through his T-shirt made him harder. God, he wanted her. Needing her to know how much, he arched his hips forward, then groaned when she reciprocated.

A weird humming sound penetrated the haze of lust engulfing him. Gage eased back. Faith's cheeks were flushed. Her hazel eyes were the perfect shade of sexy. Hoping that look could lead to other things, he dipped his head again.

"Gage," she said, holding him back with one hand. "That's my phone."

"Ignore it," he said as he went in for another kiss.

But when she pushed a little firmer on his chest, he reluctantly released her hand and stepped back. He leaned against her car, arms crossed, as she checked the call display. He watched, very satisfied with himself, as she ran one hand over her hair, cleared her throat, and put a smile on her face before answering.

"Hey, Soraya. What's up?"

His satisfaction quickly turned to alarm when her mouth gaped, and she gasped. "No! When? How bad?"

Her face drained of color. "But it can't. I was just there a few hours ago." Tears filled her eyes.

He steadied her when her knees buckled and she stumbled back into her car.

"I can't believe this. I—No, I can't even—" She pressed her fingers to her forehead. "I know. Okay. Me, too." She nodded. "I will. Keep me posted."

She continued to hold the phone in her limp hand long after she'd ended the call. Finally, Gage grabbed it before it slipped from her fingers.

"What's wrong? What happened?"

Faith's stunned gaze met his. "That was my best friend. The restaurant I work at is engulfed in flames. She says she doesn't think they'll be able to save it." Her chin quivered. "Looks like I'm out of a job."

IT WAS SUPPOSED to be that good things came in threes. Not bad things. But here she was, strike three, and she was officially out. First, she'd lost her apartment—or would by the end of next month. Second, she'd discovered she was pregnant. And now her job was gone.

"Come here," Gage said.

He wrapped her in a hug, his chin resting on her head. His strong hands rubbed up and down her spine. He made her feel safe. As though everything was going to be okay. But it wouldn't be. How could it?

"What am I going to do?" she muttered. "I've been looking for another apartment since Soraya got engaged, but it's hard to find a decent roommate, and the few I found that looked promising suddenly filled the openings when I told them I was pregnant. It didn't matter that I was giving up the baby; they still declined me. A prospective new employer isn't going to feel any different.

"And even if I found one that did, I've worked my way up from hostess to waitress to supervisor. That came with a raise. Chances are, anywhere else will start me at minimum wage."

She squeezed her eyes closed. She couldn't afford to live on minimum wage. Not with the medical bills a pregnancy accrued. Not without dipping into her college fund. Though she had her own insurance, the restaurant had offered a minimal policy to its supervisors and management team, which had added to her own. Now that would be gone, too.

Make that four strikes.

Faith choked on a sob.

"Hey." Gage gently drew back. He gave her a reassuring smile. "Maybe this was a good thing."

"How do you figure that?"

"Because now you have no reason to go back to San Antonio. You can look for work in Last Stand. And you can stay here."

He kept talking, but Faith stopped listening. It was her worst nightmare come to life. She'd prided herself on being independent. On taking care of herself and never again being a burden to anyone. Never imposing herself on anyone who didn't want her. Yet, here she was, jobless and soon to be homeless. Pregnant. And forced to lean on the one person she never wanted to be indebted to. Because she didn't want to give him reason to resent her. To wish she'd never come into his life.

It wasn't enough she was going to give him a baby he hadn't planned on? Now he'd have to endure the pregnancy, too, and all the appointments and hormones that came with it. But what else could she do? She was out of options.

She leaned back against her car, deflated.

"I guess I don't have much choice."

DAMN. HE'D KNOWN he'd have an uphill battle to convince Faith he wasn't just interested in her because of the baby. But now? How the hell was he supposed to persuade her he was glad she was going to stay there and that it had nothing to do with the child, the loss of her home, or her job?

She was ornery enough not to believe him no matter what he said or did.

He took a deep breath. *Mama, if you're up there, I sure could use some help.*

"Why don't we go inside?" he suggested. "We can have some iced tea while we talk about what comes next."

But she dug in her heels, literally. "I'll only stay temporarily. Until I find a job and another place to live."

Not if he could help it, but he figured she had enough to deal with at the moment without adding more to it. He was careful, however, not to agree.

"What else?" he asked.

"Chores. If I'm going to be eating and sleeping here, I want to do something to repay you for the hospitality."

"You're here as a guest, Faith. There's nothing to repay."

"There is. And until I find a job, I'll do what needs doing. And after that, I'll pay rent."

Gage's back went up. "The hell you will. You're carrying my—"

He stopped himself but it was too late. He saw the hurt in her eyes, knew he'd said the exact wrong thing.

"Faith—"

She raised her chin. "I'll pay rent, Gage. Either here or somewhere else. Your choice."

Goddammit, she was stubborn! But if she thought he'd let her pay a cent to live there, she was in for a surprise.

"Whatever," he said vaguely. "For now, let's just figure out when we can get your stuff from San Antonio."

"I don't have that much. It's mostly Soraya's furniture. All I have is my bed, dresser, and clothes. I can rent one of those small hauling trailers."

"No. I'll borrow Ryker's truck. Or Cam's. He's due back from the rodeo anytime." He was supposed to be back Sunday night, but he'd sent a vague text that he was delayed.

In Cam's world, that meant he'd hooked up with someone. "Either way, we'll get your things moved here."

Her eyes narrowed. "Then I'll pay you the same I would to rent a trailer."

He bit down on his temper. He understood why it was so hard for her to accept help, but damn, just once, couldn't she appreciate that someone wanted to do something nice for her?

Her attention suddenly shifted over his shoulder about the same time he heard the rumbling sound of an approaching vehicle.

"Looks like you have company."

Not now. Ready to tell whoever it was to come back another time, Gage turned. Recognizing the fancy truck and new stock trailer it was pulling, he said, "That's just Cam."

Before he had a chance to take her hand to lead her somewhere private where they could finish talking, Ryker's shouting drew his attention toward the garage.

"Gage!" Ryker came running. "Gage!"

Annoyed, he glared at his brother. "What now?"

Ryker held up his cell phone. "That was Sean Highwater."

Gage sucked in a sharp breath as Ryker kept running forward. Sean was a detective with the LSPD.

"Was it about Dad?"

"Yeah." Ryker huffed as he neared. "They found his car."

Chapter Twelve

RYKER GAVE CAM time to unhitch the trailer and that was about it. Roy, who'd come out of the bunkhouse when he'd heard Ryker shouting, was tasked with looking after Cam's horses, despite Cam's protests. Since it was only midafternoon and he didn't trust Faith to wait for him to get her stuff, Gage had taken Roy aside and given him specific instructions to keep Faith there. And *not*, he'd added with a scowl, to let her do chores.

Now here he was, in the leather back seat of Cam's fancy truck, bumping along some back county road that, far as Gage could see, led nowhere his dad would have reason to go.

Gage dug out a little container from his pocket, shook three orange Tic Tacs into his palm.

"I don't get it," he said over the Blake Shelton song that was drumming through the speakers. "Why would Dad even be out here?" He popped the candy in his mouth then shoved the container back into his pocket.

Ryker reached over and turned the radio down. "No clue," he answered. "It's not like there's anything here other than ranches and farms."

"You're sure this is the right road?" Cam asked.

"I'm sure," Ryker answered.

When silence filled the cab again, other than the rocks pinging the undercarriage of the truck, Cam turned the radio back up. Though Cam was only two years older than he was, Gage figured his hearing must be going to need the music that loud.

Three miles and nothing but fields, rocks, hills, barns, and grazing animals later, Cam slowed the truck and lowered the volume.

"There it is," he said.

Gage shifted to look between the bucket seats. Sure enough, parked in some grass-overgrown access road leading to nothing as far as Gage could see, sat the dusty sedan. Considering where it sat, and the fact Joe usually drove his ranch truck and not the old car they only kept around because it was worthless to sell, it was clear his dad hadn't wanted to be recognized.

On the road, pulled to side, was a police cruiser. Sean Highwater leaned against his car, arms crossed. Gage and Ryker stepped out of the truck as soon as Cam stopped it. Cam wasn't far behind.

Ryker reached the detective first. They shook hands.

"Sean."

"Ryker." He then shook both Cam's and Gage's hands. His ice blue eyes took them in. "I appreciate you coming so quick."

"I got them moving as fast as I could," Cam said, gesturing between his brothers.

Ignoring him, Ryker gestured toward the car and asked, "So you want us to have a look inside?"

"Yeah. But first, have a look at this."

Leading the way, he stopped where the approach met the road. He pointed down at the tracks. Gage didn't really notice the other set until Sean pointed them out.

"Someone else was definitely here, the treads are different. Now, it's possible they just happened by and, seeing the car, thought they'd see if there was anything inside worth stealing."

Gage looked up from the tracks. "But you don't think so?"

"There's also some footprints. Here, I'll show you."

They followed him up the approach, stopped when he did. "It rained the day before your dad was brought in, so the ground was soft. It's hard to see clearly with all the grass growing, but if you look..." He bent his tall frame and parted the grass. "See it? Looks like a sneaker."

Gage and his brothers squatted. Gage didn't care if it was a sneaker, a boot, or a flip-flop. What struck him right away was the size.

"Looks like a woman's size to me."

Cam whipped his gaze to Gage's. "So he *was* with a woman," his brother said.

Ryker scowled. "Not necessarily. Like Sean said, it could've just been a female passerby."

"Who just happened by when he was having a heart attack?" Gage questioned.

"We don't even know if they were here at the same time," Ryker argued.

"I believe they were," the detective said.

Though it took Sean to point it out, there were definitely signs of smaller footprints next to his dad's. But what really rocked Gage was when he saw the blurred footprints that led away from his dad's car to where, Sean suspected, her car had been parked behind his dad's.

"Looks like he was struggling, and she helped him get into her car." He indicated where her foot had sunk deeper as though she was carrying extra weight.

"But this doesn't tell us more than we already knew or suspected," Gage said as he stood. "We already knew he was brought in by a woman who, for whatever reason, doesn't want us to know who she is."

"And we knew by the blood work and the examination he's had that there weren't any drugs or alcohol in his system, nor any bruising." Ryker looked at Sean. "You've already ruled out foul play."

Cam scowled under the brim of his Stetson. "So, he met some woman and while they were standing here, he had a heart attack. She then helped him into her car, drove him to the hospital and, under the guise of having to go the bathroom, slipped out before anyone could question her."

Gage heaved a frustrated breath. "I get that this helps confirm what we suspected, but I wish we had new information. Like what they were doing here in the first place."

"Maybe they were having sex."

"Cam!" Ryker growled. "For fuck's sake."

"What? Isn't it possible?"

Sean shook his head. "If they did, it wasn't here. From the tracks, it appears she got out of her car, walked to your dad's. I assume they talked and, at some point, your dad must have felt off or something. By the tracks, I can tell you he was at least semiconscious when she helped him into the

185

car, because there would be signs on his body and clothes that he'd been dragged.

"Besides that, it would take a pretty strong woman to lift a man like Joe off the ground into the car. Hell, even some men would have struggled with his weight.

"Since she did tell the nurses she performed CPR, then I'd say she did it in the car," Sean stated.

He looked at Gage. "So, really, we do know more than we did before."

"Yeah, except what they were talking about and who the hell she is."

"There's more," Sean said. He turned to Ryker. "You bring the spare set like I asked?"

Ryker fished in his pocket, tossed Sean the keys.

"What are you thinking?" Gage asked. He stood behind the detective as the man pressed the fob and the doors unlocked with a loud click.

Sean snapped on a pair of latex gloves.

"The keys weren't with your dad, and I doubt he'd have thought to lock his car given what he was going through. I suspect," Sean said as he opened the driver's door and started looking through the console, "that maybe she pushed the lock button on the door before tossing the keys inside and driving away."

"You think she'd do that?" Cam asked.

Sean pulled his dad's wallet from the console. When he opened it, Gage saw the bills inside.

"Holy shit!" Gage exclaimed when Sean thumbed through the bills. "There has to a couple thousand there."

"And more here."

He pulled a thick envelope from the console. There had to be another couple thousand there.

"What was Dad doing with that kind of cash on him?"

"I think it's pretty clear she wasn't interested in stealing anything. If she did keep the keys, she could've been back since and rifled through his car. It's not as though anyone else knew where it was."

"Maybe she didn't know he had that kind of money on him. Or she didn't want to get caught," Ryker muttered.

Sean handed Gage the wallet and envelope. "That's a possibility."

He pulled down the visor. "But given the fact she met him in this remote location, helped him to the hospital, and then fled before anyone could talk to her, I'm more inclined to believe she didn't really want anything to do with your dad."

"Then why come here at all?" Cam asked.

"And who is she?" Gage asked. Because, really, that was the question that haunted him the most. He wanted to know if this woman was Joe's mistress—or worse, his daughter.

Sean, who'd all but gotten on his knees to look under the front seat, stood.

"I can't answer the first question," he said before turning around. Hooked on the tip of his finger was a set of keys. "But if she has a record, these may help track her down."

Gage's heart kicked up. "You mean fingerprints?"

Sean's mouth tipped into a grin. "Exactly."

THEY WERE HALFWAY home before any of them spoke. Despite his usual penchant for loud music, the radio in Cam's truck remained so low it couldn't be heard over the engine's noise and that of tires crunching gravel.

"You think they'll get anything with her fingerprints?" Cam asked.

"I doubt it," Ryker said. "Like Sean said, it hardly appears she's a criminal."

"Or she is," Cam countered, "and that's why she fled."

"Doesn't make sense. Even if she was a criminal, it doesn't seem as though she's done anything wrong. So she'd have no excuse to run." Ryker turned his head toward the passing fields. "And the chances she is, and they get a clear fingerprint that happens to be in the system? I don't think our luck is that good."

Gage took a breath, opened and closed his fists. The timing wasn't ideal, but if Faith was moving in—in the next few days if he could swing it—then he couldn't delay telling his brothers. Since Dallas wasn't there, he'd have to call him later.

"Speaking of luck," Gage began. "There's something I have to tell you."

Since he hadn't ever told them he'd had a crush on Faith back in high school, he started there, then explained about the weekend with his friends in San Antonio that resulted in the best night of his life back in his hotel room. Well, he didn't exactly tell them that much. Only that he'd taken Faith up to his room, and she'd been gone the next morning. And that he hadn't seen her again until Friday when he'd found her and her car in the ditch.

Then, with his hands sweating, he told them they were going to be uncles.

Cam slammed on the brakes. Gravel went flying. The truck fishtailed before it jerked to a stop. Luckily, they weren't yet off the quiet country back road so the truck sitting diagonally across the road wasn't going to block anyone or get them hit by oncoming traffic.

Cam twisted in his seat. "Are you serious?" he asked.

"Yeah," Ryker added as he, too, turned around, "because I always figured if anyone was going to get a woman pregnant outside of marriage, it was going to be Cam."

Cam flipped him off before focusing on Gage. "So now what?"

"Well, just before Ryker came running out of the garage to tell us about Sean finding Dad's car, Faith got a call from a friend of hers. The restaurant she works at was on fire, and it was looking like a total loss."

"That's rough," Cam said.

"Yeah. And her roommate got engaged the day Faith and I hooked up in San Antonio. That's why they were at the bar; they were celebrating. Anyway, the roommate's fiancé will be moving in, so Faith has been looking for a place to live."

Ryker studied Gage. "You want her to move in?"

Gage dried his hands down the thighs of his Wranglers. "I've already asked her to." At Ryker's scowl, he hurried to add, "I know I should have discussed it with you both first, but she'd just gotten the call and looked completely defeated."

"I can understand that. What I don't understand is you

offering up our house as though you're the only one who lives there."

Ryker turned back and glared out the windshield. As though it felt the strength of his brother's stare, one of the grazing cows in the field they were facing lifted its big head and swung its gaze over.

"Look, we'll make it work," Gage said. "Maybe Roy can have my room, and her and I can have the bunkhouse. Or she can keep my room, and I'll stay with Roy in the bunkhouse."

"Or you both stay in your room and the sound of your frequent sex can remind Ryker what's been missing," Cam said.

He laughed when Ryker told him where he could shove his ideas. Then, turning to face the front once more, Cam put the truck in gear and resumed driving.

"Quit rearranging the damn living arrangements," Ryker swore. "It's not just your house."

"I know," Gage admitted. "I'm just trying to figure this all out. It's not like any of this was planned."

"Whose fault is that?" Ryker asked, scowling at Gage through the mirror on the visor.

"Condoms break, Ryker. But maybe you actually need to have sex to realize that."

The moment he said, it Gage regretted the words. Not because his brother's eyes narrowed, but because sniping at each other wasn't the way to rebuild a relationship.

"I realize this is an inconvenience." He again met Ryker's gaze through the mirror. "And I know it's asking a lot of you." Since Dallas only stayed overnight once a week, and

Hudson wouldn't be home for at least another month, and Cam was away as much as he was home, if not more, Faith moving in really only affected Ryker.

"She's carrying my baby. I want to be there for both of them. I don't want to miss out on any part of this. I can't do that if she lives somewhere else. And if I can get through her stubbornness and fear, I'm hoping it'll be temporary."

"Meaning?" Ryker asked.

"Ideally, I'd like to take my allotted parcel and build a house on it. So, really, it would be short-term, and if I hustle my ass, I'm hoping we could move in before the baby comes."

Assuming his sons would one day take over the ranch, Joe had set aside five equal parcels of land on the Diamond G. Though Gage wasn't privy to any changes in the will, it was rumored Dallas had been cut out when he'd moved to San Antonio.

"So you're that serious about her?" Ryker asked.

"I am." Gage hadn't put a label on his feelings yet. But serious fit, so for now, he'd go with that.

"Well, that fixes her housing issue. What about her job?" Cam asked.

"I assume she'll look for something in Last Stand." Though Gage was okay with supporting her, he knew she'd never go for that.

"I have an idea," Cam said.

"That's never a good thing," Ryker grumbled.

Cam grinned. "You'll like this one." He angled his head and, speaking over his shoulder, said, "We could use a housekeeper."

"A housekeeper?"

"Yeah, and a cook. Then we wouldn't have to keep living on takeout and frozen pizzas."

Gage arched a brow. He did a hell of a lot better than that when it was his turn to cook.

"At least the nights supper is up to me, Ryker, or Dallas," Cam added. "And it would save me money on clothes if she could do laundry that actually got the stains out of my shirts." He said this with a pointed look in Ryker's direction.

Ryker scowled. "What is it with you and Gage and your bitching about the laundry?"

Now that he thought about it, it would be nice not to always have mountains of laundry stacked on the machines. And not have to go around the house half naked looking for clean clothes.

"I can ask," Gage said. "But I'm not sure I want her schlepping baskets up and down the stairs as she gets further along. Not to mention scrubbing floors. I don't want her overdoing it."

"If she's willing to cook and wash clothes," Cam said, "I volunteer to carry the laundry. Besides," he added, "house-work wouldn't be twenty-four-seven. She could rest as she needed, and some days, other than cooking, she'd likely have little else to do."

Gage frowned. Not likely. Knowing her, she'd find something to do in the barn. But he could have Roy keep an eye on her for that.

Staring at the jet stream that crossed the blue sky, Gage had to admit, it wasn't a bad solution. Ryker was usually around so, along with Roy, they'd be close by if Faith needed anything. And since she was adamant about earning her keep, this was a way to help both her and his home situation.

Besides, it wasn't like they were slobs or needed a woman to do the domestic stuff. Maybe they weren't great at it, but they'd kept the house relatively clean and had kept themselves fed since their mom had gotten sick.

He blew out a breath. Brought his gaze back around. Two pairs of eyes, one blue and one green, looked at him through the visor mirrors.

"I can ask her about the job," he said as he looked from one mirror to another. "Does that mean you're okay with her living at the ranch?"

"If you do decide to share your room, keep the sex noise down," Ryker muttered. "Your room butts against mine, and there are things I don't want to hear."

Like Faith's moans and her pleas for me to go harder and faster, Gage remembered with a rush of heat. Not that he and Faith had even discussed sleeping arrangements. He'd just assumed they'd each have their own rooms.

It didn't stop him, however, from wanting to hear those throaty words from her again.

He squirmed as he shifted to get comfortable in his suddenly very tight jeans.

"YOU LOOK EXHAUSTED," Soraya said.

"I feel it," Faith confirmed.

She was slouched onto the couch in what had been her living room since moving from Last Stand. In the only place she had ever truly felt she belonged. And one that, once Gage arrived with the truck, would no longer be her home.

She looked by the door to the stacks of boxes, her bed, and dresser that were ready to make the journey to Last Stand. Tears clogged up her throat.

She looked at her best friend. "I'm going to miss you so much."

That she'd even found Soraya in the first place had been a stroke of luck. A furnished apartment she'd only have to supply her bedroom furniture and personal effects? It would allow her to save for college.

Her enthusiasm had faded when Soraya had opened the door. The woman's dark brown eyes had been guarded, and though Faith wouldn't have called her rude, she'd definitely been on the reserved side. Almost as though she expected showing the apartment to Faith would be a waste of time. But she had, and though it hadn't taken long, by the end, Faith had been even more excited than she'd been before.

Since she hadn't given the woman much notice, there was no way the apartment could have been cleaned so spotlessly in such a short amount of time. But the counters had gleamed. There weren't any water splotches on the bathroom mirror and the shower had sparkled. Which meant the woman was also a neat freak. Since Faith ran the same way, the place had immediately felt comfortable.

Of course, the woman's taste in decorating had also helped make the place special. What the plain eggshell-colored walls lacked in individuality and personality, she'd made up for with colorful rugs, throw pillows, and eclectic art scattered throughout.

"I'll take it," Faith had said the moment they'd returned from the short tour of the bedroom.

Soraya's dark brows had arched up her forehead. "You will?" she'd asked, her voice thick with doubt as though she couldn't fathom such a thing.

"Of course. Why wouldn't I? It's perfect."

"Because." She'd gestured to herself from her bright pink painted toenails to the top of her head where her box braids were pulled back in a thick band.

Faith had frowned. "And?"

Soraya had rolled her eyes. "I've shown this place a half dozen times now and, over the phone, they were all kinds of excited and enthusiastic. Until they saw me. Then suddenly the place was too far from their work. Or the rent was too much." She'd pursed her lips, planted a hand on her curvy hip. "I'm not stupid. I know exactly why they'd changed their minds. They didn't want to room with a black woman."

"But that's ridiculous. The place is perfect. You've got a talent for decorating and it's spotless. What is that smell, by the way? It makes me think of the ocean."

Soraya's wide smile had lit her face. "Lemongrass. I have a small reed diffuser in the corner."

"I love it. And I love the apartment." She'd grinned then. "And I have no problem living with a gorgeous black woman who has exceptional taste if you have no problem living with a white one who has no real talent other than being organized and tidy."

They'd struck a deal and a friendship that day that had lasted six years, one boyfriend for Faith and two for Soraya, until she'd met Darius, and more bottles of wine shared between them than either was willing to admit.

Soraya reached her hand over and squeezed Faith's. Though the color of their skin couldn't be more opposite, Soraya was the sister Faith never had, and she truly couldn't imagine not seeing her every day.

"I'm going to miss you, too, girl. But you won't be that far away."

"And it'll be temporary," Faith hurried to add as she blinked away her tears. "I'm still planning on moving back to San Antonio once the baby is born."

Soraya settled back into the ocean blue and lime green pillows. She studied Faith with serious eyes. "Honey, I know you said he's just being nice to you out of obligation and because that's just the kind of man he is, but I have to tell you, it doesn't look that way from where I'm sitting."

"You only met him for five minutes yesterday when he dropped me off and helped haul up the moving boxes."

Though he'd offered to help pack, Faith had wanted a night with Soraya before the move.

"And you don't think that was enough to notice how he kept looking at you? Not to mention the way he made me promise I wouldn't let you lift anything heavy."

"You just proved my point. He's worried about the baby and doesn't want me to overdo it."

Soraya's white teeth gleamed as she smiled. "I'm pretty sure he wasn't thinking about no baby when he was looking at your butt when you bent over."

"That's just sex."

"So you've slept with him again?"

"No."

"Ah," her friend said, holding up a finger that was painted with the same nail polish as her toes. "Then how can it be about sex if you only slept with him the once, three months ago?"

"Because he's a guy and he remembers."

"So he just wants to get laid again? Is that it?"

She'd never known her friend to hold her punches. But that didn't mean a well-aimed one didn't sting. Especially when it was the truth.

Soraya shook her head. The dangly silver earrings she wore swung from her lobes. "I hate what your mother and grandmother did to you. And I hate that, after six years of me telling you, you don't believe it any more now than you did when you first told me about them and I told you how wrong they were. You're not a burden. You're worth every good thing life has in store for you, if you just give it a chance.

"Any man would be lucky to have you. And I think Gage sees that. I really do. And I hate that you can't even entertain the idea that he is interested in you, *for you*. Not as his baby mama. Not as a convenient, warm body. But because you're a good person. Because you're pretty and kind. Because you have an open mind and an equally open heart."

A hot ball of emotion pressed against Faith's chest. There was another reason she found her grandmother and her mother's words and actions so easy to believe. One she'd never told anyone. Because it cut too deep. Because it brought her back to the one time she'd dared think maybe she *was* good enough. Maybe someone *could* love her.

She crossed her arms, tucked her fists tight against her chest. She swallowed the pain and humiliation. Fought the urge to hang on to her secret with both hands so nobody else would know her shame.

"He already rejected me once," she whispered.

Soraya frowned. "At the hotel?" she asked.

Faith shook her head. "At the end of high school."

"High school?"

"Yeah." Faith looked down, toyed with the teal binding that edged the throw pillow. "He took me to prom."

"When you said you hooked up with a guy from high school in that bar, you never said he was your prom date!"

"He wasn't. Not really. We both knew he only asked me because I had no other friends."

"Faith—"

"No, it's true. And because, by then, I had the biggest crush on him, I accepted. I told myself friendship was enough. I'd rather have him as my friend than nothing at all. But he said some things that night that suggested his feelings for me ran deeper than friendship."

Soraya leaned forward, her ponytail of braids falling over one shoulder. "And?" she prodded.

"And the whole night was special. We mostly only danced with each other, though I really had nobody else to dance with anyway," she added. "He kept me close, held my hand when we took a break from dancing to sit at a table and talk."

She took a trembling breath. "He'd made me feel so special, that I was different than any other girl. And so, when he walked me to the door later, I pulled him into the shadows of the porch."

God, her heart beat as fast now as it had that night. Only, this time, she knew how it ended. Not for the first time, as she saw the scene in her head, she wished she could yell at her former self not to do it.

"Girl, don't make me drag it out of you."

"I leaned in to kiss him." Faith pulled the pillow into her chest, much as she had when she'd raced up to her room after having her heart shattered into a million jagged pieces. "But he stepped back."

The memory poured into her, as clear as if she was watching a scene from a movie on the big flat screen TV that hung on the opposite wall. How handsome he'd been in his suit. How his blonde hair had been a bit more tousled by the end of the evening than it had been when he'd picked her up. He'd been smiling when he'd helped her from his car.

He hadn't been smiling when she'd tried to kiss him.

In fact, his eyes had looked haunted. Like she'd just run over his dog.

She'd laughed it off until she'd closed the door behind her that night, and she'd managed to get through the last few days of school as though nothing had happened. As though her heart wasn't still an open, bleeding mess.

"Did he ever say why?" her friend asked.

"No, and I never asked him."

"Faith—" she began.

"I was mortified enough by the rejection, Soraya. Having him tell me he wasn't attracted or that I wasn't his type wouldn't have made me feel any better about it."

"But maybe it was something else entirely. You don't

know. Besides, the fact he took you back to his hotel room three months ago clearly proves he *is* attracted to you. And before you claim being tipsy was the reason, let me remind you he's kissed you since." She dropped her chin, looked pointedly at Faith. "When you were both stone-cold sober."

"Because he wants the baby," Faith reminder her.

Soraya rolled her brown eyes. "He doesn't need to kiss you for that." The silver rings adorning her fingers tinkled as she took Faith's hand.

"All I'm saying is give him a chance. Don't be so quick to brush everything off because of the baby. Because he'd be lucky to have you, and if he's smart enough to realize that, then you owe it to both of you to give it a try."

It all sounded so simple. But years of being told she wasn't enough for her own family made it hard to trust. After all, if they couldn't love her, how could anyone else?

The buzzer sounded then, the abrasive sound startling Faith. Realizing it meant Gage was back to pick her up, a weird slurry of emotions pressed against her chest. Excitement and nervousness even though it had only been a night since she'd seen him. Sadness because no matter if she'd keep in touch in Soraya, she still felt as though she was losing her.

Unfolding her long legs, Soraya moved from the couch to let Gage in past the lobby. In a matter of minutes, he'd be at the door. Faith's heart squeezed painfully. *This is it.*

Feeling weighted down, she followed her friend to the entrance. Soraya turned from the wall-mounted buzzer. She looked as crestfallen and miserable as Faith felt. Wordlessly, they came together in a tight hug. Faith inhaled her friend's perfume, knowing the smell of Chanel would always make her think of the woman who, other than Gage back in high school, had been her best friend.

"I'm going to miss you so much," Faith said, her voice wet with tears.

Soraya sniffled. "Me, too, girlfriend. Me, too."

They both sighed when the inevitable knock on the door sounded. Drawing back, they wiped their tears, took a moment to collect themselves. Then, despite Faith wishing they could hold back time, her friend opened the door.

Faith was surprised Gage wasn't alone.

Gage jutted his thumb toward Dallas. "I recruited extra manpower."

He introduced Soraya to Dallas. "Since he lives in San Antonio, I asked him to help."

Dallas grinned. "Paid in full with a thick steak."

They started with the bed, mattress, then dresser. As expected, Gage wouldn't hear of her lifting anything, and since Dallas scowled and relieved her of even a small box when she tried to help, she knew Gage had told his brother about the baby. Which meant they likely all knew by now.

It made her feel a bit nauseous. She'd known it couldn't stay a secret forever. Already, she couldn't fasten the button on her jeans. But she couldn't help wondering what his brothers thought of the situation.

And what they thought of her.

"Stop worrying," Soraya said.

Gage and Dallas had gone back down with another load. That only left one box in the entryway.

"I can't imagine what they must think of me."

"If Dallas is any indication, I'd say none of it is bad.

Faith," she took her shoulders, "nobody has ever thought worse about you than you have about yourself. I love you. Darius adored you right away," she said. "And Gage seems to be very fond of you. Now, before they get back up here, I want you to promise me you'll stop seeing yourself through your mother's and grandmother's jaded lenses. Just be yourself. They'll all love you, same as I do."

She hoped so. Because she couldn't imagine the agony of moving into another house where every day, she felt scorn and judgment. Although, to be fair, she hadn't felt any of that in the Granger house. But that was before she moved in. Before they knew about the baby. It might be different now.

"Thanks," Faith said.

"Anytime. Now, there's one more thing you need to promise me."

"What's that?" Faith asked, looking into her friend's eyes.

"You tell Gage about prom. And you tell him your feelings toward him have never changed."

Faith's stomach lurched. "I can't do that."

"Yes, you can. Because your happiness is worth the risk."

Faith was starting to realize no matter which way she went happiness wasn't in her future. Either she had the college education she'd dreamed about and worked tirelessly for, or she had Gage and the baby. A baby, Faith was still convinced, would have a better life without her in it. Telling Gage how she felt wouldn't change any of that so what was the point in telling him?

Before she had a change to tell Soraya any of that, Gage walked back through the door.

"Okay, we're all set. Dallas said to say goodbye. He's gone back home, but he'll be back at the ranch tomorrow with Ashley."

Soraya squeezed Faith's shoulders, leveled a gaze at her that spoke loudly without her having to actually say a thing. Then she brought Faith in close for another hug.

"I'll just grab this last box and meet you at the truck," Gage said.

"No, it's fine. I'm ready."

Faith clutched Soraya tightly, then kissed her cheek. She stepped back before she collapsed into a puddle of tears. It was best all-around if they didn't drag out the goodbye. Faith grabbed her purse, the one thing Gage actually let her carry. She stopped in the hall, looked back one last time.

Her friend's dark eyes shone with tears. Faith's own blurred with them. But not before she saw Soraya's mouth moving silently. Faith blinked her eyes clear to see what her friend was trying to tell her.

"Tell him."

Chapter Thirteen

I T WAS SUPPERTIME by the time Gage and Faith returned to Last Stand. Having texted Ryker and Cam about his plan before leaving San Antonio, he'd stopped in town at Valencia's for Mexican takeout. And had been tempted by the mouthwatering smell of tamales the whole way back to the Diamond G.

Equally as satisfying as knowing he was about to eat delicious food was knowing the smell would linger in Cam's fancy truck for a day or so. He hadn't readily handed Gage the keys when he'd asked to borrow it. Instead, Cam had given him grief about using Ryker's instead, or even the ranch truck. But Ryker had needed his, and Roy had errands to do with the ranch one.

Gage hadn't known what the big deal was. So it was new and had cost a fortune. It wasn't like Gage was a reckless driver. Besides, he'd left Cam his Jeep, so it wasn't as though his brother was without wheels.

Not that that had made any difference to Cam. He'd bitched about it being a girly vehicle. Which was why, Gage thought with a smirk, his brother deserved to have his truck smell like something other than leather for a few days.

Bumping into the yard, Gage backed the truck so the trailer was positioned facing the house for easy unloading.

He shut off the engine, but neither he nor Faith made a move to get out.

Faith, who'd kept her arms wrapped around her purse the entire way, worried her bottom lip. She'd been quiet on the drive, and he hadn't pressed to make conversation. He couldn't imagine the changes she'd had to face in so short an amount of time, and he'd felt painfully inadequate sitting next to her, not knowing how to make her feel better. Any words that had come to mind sounded patronizing and hollow.

He couldn't promise everything would be all right, even if he had every intention of ensuring it would be.

"Let's go eat," he said. "We'll deal with the boxes and furniture after supper."

She said as little over the meal as she had on the drive. Unfortunately, none of the Granger men were known for being chatty, which normally didn't bother Gage. But tonight, knowing Faith was already tense, the silence was even heavier than normal. He'd never been more aware of every scrape of fork or gulp of water. Or more grateful when a meal was over.

When Faith pushed away her empty plate, Gage quickly finished the last of his beans and slid back his chair.

"Come on," he said. "Let's get you settled."

Outside, he opened the back of the trailer. His brothers were going to help once they were done eating, but Gage could start on the boxes without them.

"I really don't like kicking you out of your room," she said again.

She'd expressed her displeasure about that when he'd

first told her where she'd be sleeping.

"It makes the most sense. You know Cam and Ryker better than Roy. And with Hudson due back in just over a month, if you took his room, you'd just have to move again when he got back." He grabbed a box. "This way, you can settle in and make yourself comfortable.

"Besides, you're generous enough to let me take your bed and dresser into one of the spare rooms in the bunkhouse to use. So it's no big deal. I'll really only be in there to sleep."

And she'd be in his bed. Warm and soft and...

He shut down that train of thought before it gained too much momentum. He could dwell upon it later when he was in the bunkhouse and nobody was around to see the reaction such thoughts generated. For now, he just wanted her to rest. And the sooner they got the boxes upstairs, the better.

He let her carry the small suitcase, but otherwise he, Cam, Ryker, and Roy did the rest. Which didn't take them more than three trips each. So it hardly warranted the profuse thanks she gave them. Ryker and Roy just nodded and left. Cam, being Cam, tipped his hat and said, "I'm just down the hall. You call now if you need anything."

Gage shoved him out into the hall. "Maybe you should go outside and check on your truck. Make sure that scratch doesn't show too bad."

Cam's blue eyes darkened to the color of a thunderhead cloud. His charming grin twisted into a scowl. "You better be kidding," he growled before he spun on his heel and marched down the hall.

Faith looked alarmed. "Did you really scratch his truck? Because if you did, I can pay for—"

Gage held up a finger, waited for the quick thud of Cam's footsteps to finish stomping down the stairs. He lowered his hand, chuckled. "I didn't. But looking for it will keep him busy for a while."

Faith's lips twitched. "That's mean."

He shrugged. "He deserved it." Then, with his gaze locked on hers, he stepped closer.

He liked how her eyes widened. How her breath caught. He stopped when the toes of his boots met those of her sneakers. Reaching out, he brushed his thumb across her cheek.

"I didn't like how he was flirting with you."

"I wouldn't worry about that. It's harmless." She shrugged. "You get used to it when you're a waitress."

He moved his thumb to the corner of her mouth. He didn't want her indifferent. Not to him. For him, he very much wanted her affected. He lowered his gaze to her mouth, to the natural pink of her lips.

"I still didn't like it."

For a moment, she swayed. Not a lot, but enough to give him hope he was slowly chiseling his way through the wall she insisted on keeping between them.

But then she stepped out of his reach. Her gaze narrowed. "I know what you're doing."

All innocence, he asked, "And what's that?"

"You're trying to, for lack of a better word, woo me."

He grinned. "Woo you?"

"You know what I mean. And it isn't going to work, Gage. You're not going to convince me to play happy family. There's no such thing when it's built out of obligation."

She wasn't the only one who knew what the other was up to. He closed the distance again. If she backed up any more, her legs would be up against his bed. Not a bad place to end up, he figured.

"You're under the misunderstanding that I feel obligated. I feel a lot of things right now," he drawled, "but obligation isn't even in the mix."

Fear clouded her eyes. "I can't be a mother, Gage. It's not in my genetics to be a good one."

"We have months to worry about that. How about, for now, we just concentrate on us?"

"There wouldn't even be an us if there wasn't the baby," she argued.

"Only because you made it impossible to find you. Otherwise, I'd have tracked you down the very next morning in San Antonio."

"Right," she scoffed.

"What's that supposed to mean?"

She shook her head. "Never mind. I'm just tired."

"No, no. There was more to that comment than exhaustion. It was loaded. So how about you tell me what it really meant?"

"It meant nothing. I just really want to start unpacking."

She sidestepped him to do just that, but he caught her wrist, pulled her back.

"I'm not leaving until you tell me what you meant."

"Fine." She huffed even as a blush crept into her cheeks. "You already had a chance at 'us', but you didn't want it."

His thumb rubbed the inside of her wrist where her pulse pounded. "You're talking about prom night?"

Her brows arched. "I didn't think you remembered."

"I never forgot it. I can't tell you how many times I'd wished I'd have done it differently. That I'd just kissed you the way I wanted to."

She shook her head. "You never wanted to."

"I did," he stated. "More than you know."

"Then why didn't you?"

He lowered his fingers from her wrist and intertwined them with hers. "Because all you talked about in high school was leaving. How you couldn't wait to get out of here. I wasn't going to be the man that held you back. Not when I knew my life was here."

Her eyes searched his. "You still could've kissed me."

He shook his head. "No, I couldn't. Because I knew I wanted all of you, and a piece, a moment, no matter how incredible, would never be enough."

But, God, it had killed him to step back from the invitation of claiming her mouth, of finally tasting her sweetness.

He brought their hands to his mouth. "That day haunted me. So many times, I wished I could go back in time and do it different. Because, it ends up, not tasting you at all was just as much torture.

"Then, there you were, six years later, in a San Antonio bar, and I thought, 'not this time.' This time, I wasn't going to let you go. And it was more than a kiss and, *damn*, any fantasy I'd ever had was eclipsed by how you felt in my arms that night.

"But then, the morning after, once again, you were gone. And I swore if I ever found you again, I wouldn't let you go." He grinned at her shocked expression. "So, Miss Stone, my interest in you has nothing to do with the baby."

Drawing his hand free, he slid it around her waist, pulled her close. "Now, are we about done talking?" he asked, his voice a low timbre that reflected the need and desire coursing through his blood.

HER HEAD REELING from his words, Faith clung to Gage as his lips claimed hers, as the world around her disappeared. Possessive and hot, the kiss stole her breath. More, it stole her doubts. It was impossible to feel anything but desired when his mouth took hers with such passion. When he held her tightly against him, drawing her even closer when her tongue flicked against his.

There, in the circle of his arms, with his scent enveloping her, with the feel of his silky hair clutched within her fingers, and the feel of his heart pounding against hers, she believed him. Believed he'd liked her all those years ago. Believed his feelings toward her were genuine. Believed she was enough.

When a cackling voice that sounded suspiciously like her grandmother's shoved its way into her thoughts, trying to diminish what Gage had said, Faith pressed herself a little closer, clung a little tighter. She elbowed the doubt aside and instead focused on Gage and how he smelled of the outdoors. How his kiss left no part of her mouth unclaimed. How she could feel the solid wall of his chest pressed against her aching breasts. The hot length of his arousal cradled between her thighs.

Faith's lower belly clutched. Her breasts went hot and

heavy. She'd always wanted Gage. And after that night in San Antonio, once she'd known how good it really was with him, she'd wanted him even more. Being in his arms now, with his erection poised where she was wet and throbbing, her desire turned to need. There was a queen-size bed mere feet from them, and Faith craved to pull him further into the room, slam the door, and ride him until they were both spent.

But Gage burst her sexual bubble when he ended the kiss.

In tandem, they sighed heavily.

Faith looked into his eyes. They were heavy-lidded and full of desire.

The corner of his glistening lips tilted upward. "That'll keep me up tonight," he said, clearly meaning the double entendre.

Heat rose to her ears and she shifted her gaze. She wished she felt as confident when they weren't kissing as she did when they were. But the moment she wasn't in his arms, wasn't lost in his embrace, the world intruded again and with it all the old insecurities. All the reasons a relationship between them was impossible.

As though he knew where her thoughts had shifted, he wrapped an arm around her shoulders and squeezed. "Come on," he said. "Let's start on these boxes."

Again without letting her lift, he set two down on his bed. She was touched he'd already emptied his dresser for her, and there were more than enough hangers in his closet for her to use. By no means was she a shoe addict, but she was glad to see a space had been cleared on the closet floor for the few pairs of heels, boots, and strappy sandals she owned. The more serviceable everyday footwear, she set aside to take down to the mudroom later.

As she emptied boxes, Gage replaced them with full ones, flattened the empty ones, and carried the cardboard away. It felt weird putting her few cherished ornaments and personal effects on his dresser and nightstand, but she had to admit, once she did, it helped her feel more comfortable.

Like she wasn't just visiting but was truly home.

Faith gnawed on her lip. He said they'd take it a day at a time, and they'd focus on them for the time being, but the reality was it wasn't just the two of them. Ignoring the boxes sitting on the bed, Faith sat heavily beside them. She bowed her head, clasped her hands between her knees.

Gage came back into the room. He lifted the box by her hip to the floor then took his place beside her. The mattress dipped with his weight. His broad hand covered her knee.

"I know it's a lot right now. Try not to worry."

"I'm not sure I can just take it one day at a time, Gage. The end result is still the same. You want the baby; I can't keep it. Right away, that means there's no future between us."

He took her chin, turned her toward him. His green gaze was sharp, and it locked onto hers. "Do you realize what you just said?"

"Yes," she answered.

"I don't think you do," he said.

He shifted his hand from her chin to cup her cheek. He might be a full-time EMT, but his hands bore callouses from ranch work. The roughness wasn't unpleasant on her skin.

"You said you *can't* keep it." He tilted his head. "You didn't say you don't want to."

Tears blurred her eyes before she could hide them.

"Hey," he crooned. "It's okay."

But Faith's heart was breaking, and none of this was okay. "No, it's not." She moved his hand from her face, then stood, walking as far away from him as the bedroom allowed. It meant literally standing in a corner next to the window with the paneled navy-and-white striped blackout drapes.

"From the first moment I suspected I was pregnant, I wanted this baby." She placed her hands over the swell that wasn't noticeable to anyone else but one she felt all the same.

"But I also know that would be selfish. And I promised myself from a very young age I would never be as selfish as my mother and grandmother. In this case, that means putting what's best for this child before what I want."

Suddenly, Roy's words shoved their way through her doubts. If she made a conscious decision every day to ensure her child was happy, then wouldn't it be? Wasn't that, right there, more than either her mother or grandmother had ever done?

Her throat clenched tight. Her next breath was more wheeze than anything. Gage leapt to his feet. She held up a hand, indicating she was fine, and managed to suck in air until she no longer sounded like she was dying.

Then, despite the bud of hope that burst in her chest, she shook her head, mentally yanked the shoot out by the roots. It couldn't be that easy. Because if it was, surely her mother and grandmother would have done it.

"I have to give this baby up," she said. "You already

know why. I can't keep going over the reasons." She couldn't. Every time she did, it ripped her heart wide open.

Though he'd stopped his approach when she'd signaled, he hadn't gone back to sit on the bed. He walked across the hardwood toward her now, his boot heels loud in the otherwise silent room. Actually, now that she listened, she realized the whole house had gone quiet. Since she doubted Ryker, Cam, and Roy were at the top of the stairs eavesdropping, she assumed they'd all gone outside.

"You don't have to," he promised. "I heard you loud and clear."

She narrowed her gaze. "Why do I hear a 'but' in there somewhere?"

He laughed. A low, gravelly sound that went straight to her heart.

"Because you're a smart woman. And you happen to be right. There is a 'but' in there."

"I already know what it is. Just as I know it's a waste of time. You want to change my mind, but it won't work."

He crossed his arms over his T-shirt. "It's not so much changing anything I'm after. It's more showing you a different possibility. If you're willing to look at it."

She, too, crossed her arms. "And you think you can do that in six months' time?"

His smile spread slowly, but it was even more lethal for the time it took to form.

His green eyes glittered with certainly. "Darlin'," he drawled. "I can do it in a hell of a lot less than that."

LIVING ON A working ranch meant getting up at what Faith liked to call the butt crack of dawn. It wasn't her favorite time by any means, and she felt sluggish getting dressed, but there was no way she was going to keep sleeping while everyone else went to work.

On the way from San Antonio the night before, Gage had brought up the suggestion of her working at the ranch. Not—he was clear—in the barns, but cooking and cleaning since he admitted they were dismal at it. Despite his telling her she didn't need to give an answer right away, Faith had agreed on the spot. She wanted to earn her room and board.

When she found a job in Last Stand, it would mean planning meals in advance so all the guys would have to do was reheat things, but it was doable. First, though, she needed to tackle breakfast.

In the pale dawn light that spilled from the bedroom curtains she'd opened, Faith pulled on a pair of yoga pants and a T-shirt then made her way downstairs. She squinted as she walked into the kitchen. It seemed every light was on, and they all blasted her still-awakening retinas.

Gage turned from the stove. Nobody should look that good first thing in the morning. Since he wasn't expected at work until that afternoon, he was in what she'd begun to consider his second uniform, jeans and a T-shirt.

His hair was still shiny from his shower, and his green eyes were bright. He looked good enough to eat.

Holding a loaf of bread in his hands, his brow creased. "Why are you up so early?"

She padded closer, took the bread from his hand. "I thought it was my job to cook." She looked into the bowl sitting by the stove then shifted her gaze to the skillet. "French toast?"

He reclaimed the loaf. "Yes, and I'm cooking this morning."

"That's my job now, remember?"

"I never said anything about breakfast."

"You said meals. Breakfast is a meal."

"Yes, but usually, we just eat cereal and toast, maybe fry up some eggs. Even Cam and Ryker can handle that."

"Yet, here you are, making French toast."

His gaze dipped to her toes then slowly climbed up her body. He smiled the smile that never failed to warm her insides.

"I had a craving for something sweet, and since you were still sleeping…"

Her stomach dipped right along with his voice. Then dipped again when he leaned in and kissed her softly. He tasted like mint, smelled like an ocean breeze, and felt like heaven. Oh, man, she was in over her head.

"I've got this. You can set the table if you want."

Ryker, Cam, and Roy came in shortly after the table was set. Other than Roy, who was as fresh and alert as Gage, the other two apparently weren't morning people. They kept their comments to nods and mumbles and otherwise seemed to prefer to eat in quiet.

That was fine by Faith as she watched and made mental notes of who liked what and ate where, other than Roy, who took his plate and left. If she was going to cook for them, she needed to know their likes and dislikes.

But no matter how much she tried to focus on the trivial

things, nothing kept her thoughts from veering to Gage and their kiss last night. And, judging by the gleam in his eye when he caught her staring, what she'd already guessed was inevitable. There was far too much chemistry between them not to have sex again.

And with her wild hormones of late, it was coming—no pun intended—very soon.

But she really needed to stop thinking like that when surrounded by his brothers. Shoving her chair back, Faith began to clear the table. The other two offered their thanks then shuffled off, but Gage lingered.

Of course he did. He had warned her it wouldn't take long to change her mind. Apparently, he was wasting no time getting started.

Sighing, Faith ran the water in the kitchen sink. When it turned hot, she set in the stopper and squeezed blue soap into the stream. "Shouldn't you be getting to your chores?" she asked.

"Soon."

Coming from behind, he wrapped his arms around her and pulled her against him. Something shifted inside her when he settled his hand over her stomach. It was the first time he'd touched her belly and the first time since learning she was pregnant that she *felt* pregnant. That she could actually envision him holding a baby. *Their* baby.

Faith pinched her eyes closed as a stab of longing pierced through her heart, so sharp it stole her breath.

"Can't you see it?" he asked, his breath warm against her ear. If he realized how still she'd gone, he made no comment.

Trying to ignore the weight of his hand on her belly,

Faith opened her eyes and looked out the window. She didn't think he meant his, hers, and Cam's vehicles parked side by side in front of the porch. There wasn't anything special about the bunkhouse, and even though it was a nice barn, it wasn't as though she hadn't seen it before, either.

"You mean the horses?" she asked as four of them suddenly appeared from the back of the barn and galloped through the corral, tails fanned out behind them in the fading morning mist.

"I mean us. Can't you see us standing together every morning, starting our day like this?"

She wanted to deny being able to see any such thing, but the lie wouldn't come. Because, yes, she could see it. But she could watch fairy tales on TV, as well; that didn't make them real, either.

He pressed a kiss to her temple, then reached over and shut off the taps before the bubbles overflowed the sink. "I'll see you later."

He left without waiting for her reply, which was just as well since she didn't have one. It wasn't until he disappeared into the barn that she lowered her hand to where his had rested.

And allowed the tears she'd been holding back to fall.

Chapter Fourteen

F AITH HAD ALWAYS been the sort who liked to see instant results. Like cutting the grass at her grandmother's once she'd been deemed responsible enough to run the mower. With just the first pass, the fruits of her labor were obvious and satisfying.

So seeing the mountain of laundry dwindle throughout the morning gave her a sense of accomplishment. As did polishing the taps and bathroom mirrors until they were no longer speckled with water spots or toothpaste spray.

Feeding off the satisfaction, Faith charged from room to room, the smell of lemon furniture polish following her throughout the house. Except in the kitchen. There, the spicy smell of chili she had simmering on the stove competed for supremacy with the yeasty smell of biscuits she'd just taken out of the oven.

Faith had worked in a restaurant for six years, and despite having served thousands of customers in that time, nothing gave her more satisfaction than seeing the men dig into the food she'd prepared. Than knowing it was appreciated. At work, good food was expected and rarely praised beyond anything more than "good" or "fine". And though she didn't need glowing praise, her cheeks, nonetheless, went hot and pride swelled in her chest when Ryker set aside his empty bowl, his second helping, and proclaimed it to be the best chili he'd ever had.

With a belly full of food, Faith's energy waned. She yawned through the dishes, and by the time Gage left for work and she'd pulled the vacuum out of the cupboard and hauled it down the hallway to his father's office, she was dragging her feet. She looked at the small mantle clock perched on the desk and whimpered when she saw it was only two thirty.

Physically drained, Faith dropped into the high-backed, leather office chair. She'd take a minute, rest, then get on with the floors.

She jerked awake, startled and disoriented a while later, when a woman's chuckle pulled her from the dream she'd been having. It took a few seconds to remember where she was, what she'd been doing, and who she was looking at. And what time it must be. Horrified, she pushed to her feet as she glanced at the clock. It was three thirty.

Dear God, her small rest had turned into an hour. No wonder her neck was stiff.

"Ashley," she said, addressing the blonde. "I'm sorry. I didn't touch anything," she hurried to say as she gestured to the neat stacks of papers. Well, mostly neat stacks. There was also a basket of receipts that looked as though they'd just been tossed in there.

"I swear I only meant to sit for a minute." She shook her head. "That was an hour ago." Faith reached for the vacuum, rolled it away from the desk so the woman could do the bookwork.

"I remember those days," Ashley said on a sigh.

Faith looked over. Ashley had settled herself in the chair Faith had just vacated. The tender look in her honey-gold eyes matched the smile curving her lips.

Though Faith held the handle of the vacuum in her hand, she didn't move. Since learning she was pregnant, she'd felt isolated and alone. While Soraya was a great support and friend, she'd never been pregnant, and so while Faith could share how she felt, it wasn't as though Soraya could offer advice or commiserate with her. And reading a book about pregnancy wasn't the same as talking to someone who'd been through it.

Faith might have only met Ashley, but she'd liked her immediately. And since Faith was living here now, and it sounded as though Dallas and Ashley were serious, they were definitely going to get to know each other better in the next few months. And, really, who else could she go to for advice? It wasn't as though she could ask her mother. And she especially couldn't go to her grandmother.

Leaving the vacuum, Faith walked toward the desk. Considering Ashley's comment, it was clear Dallas had told her she was pregnant.

"I've read, for some women, this tiredness can last the whole pregnancy. Was that your experience?"

Ashley shook her head, her blonde ponytail swaying. "No, it got better after the first trimester."

Faith sat in the only other chair in the room. "Thank God."

Ashley laughed. "It's not all fun, that's for sure. There's stretch marks to look forward to, weird cravings, not being to get comfortable and, if you're like me, wicked heartburn."

All of that, Faith could deal with. Maybe it wouldn't be fun, but she could get through it. What she wasn't sure she'd survive was the turmoil tearing at her. Clasping her hands tightly together, she swallowed the lump that rose in her throat.

"Were you ever scared?"

Ashley snorted. "Only every day after finding out I was pregnant. And most days since."

Faith's gaze searched Ashley's. "Did you ever consider giving her up?"

Ashley shrugged. "Not seriously. I mean, maybe for a few days, I thought it might be easier and better, but—" Her eyes widened. "Are you considering adoption? But you're living here, and you and Gage are a couple—"

"We're not a couple. I'm not really sure what we are anymore, but whatever it is it's not a long-term thing."

Ashley leaned back in the chair. Her dark blonde brows drew together. "I'm confused."

So was Faith, so she told Ashley everything. "We're not telling anyone about Gage raising the baby, though," she said as she finished. "So I hope you won't say anything to Dallas."

"I won't," Ashley promised. "But I'm no less confused now than I was before. In fact, I'm more so. Gage likes you and you like him. You already know he wants this baby, which is more than I had since Brittany's father bailed the moment he heard about her. I know you're worried about your upbringing, but I think you're selling yourself short.

"Just because your mom and grandma weren't great at it doesn't mean you'll be the same. Heck, look at me. My parents disowned their only child and have never known their grandchild because I got pregnant outside of marriage. But you know what? I'm a damn good mom. Not perfect by any means, but I try. I show up every day and do my best.

"Faith, being a parent doesn't come with a manual, and no matter how many books you read—and I read *a ton*—it's a learn-as-you-go kind of thing. Nobody's going to be perfect, and no child is going to be, either. You do the best you can."

"That's what I'm afraid of. What if it's not enough?"

Ashley tipped her head. "But what if it is?"

"You and Gage make it sound so simple."

"Because it is. Not easy," she hurried to explain before Faith could argue, "but simple. You said you moved out right after high school, right?"

"Yes."

"And you went to another city and managed to make a life there, didn't you?"

"Yeah."

"Exactly. Because you *wanted* to. And because you wanted to, you found a way to make it work. It's the same with me. I wanted my baby. And I wanted to make a good life for her. She may not have the latest and greatest where clothes and electronics are concerned, but I know she's well-adjusted and as happy as most sixteen-year-olds can be," she added with a grin. "Look, if I can raise a child on my own and make that work, you and Gage can easily do it together."

Though Faith didn't move, inside, she was a trembling wreck. Her heart galloped with hope and possibilities. But fear, that ever-present shadow, crowded in, filling her head.

"I know he's says it's not the reason, but I keep thinking he wouldn't be pushing so hard to have a relationship with me if I wasn't pregnant."

"Has he given you any reason to believe that?"

"Not really. But he's adamant about me not lifting heavy things, about not working too hard, and this morning, he put his hand over my stomach." Faith chewed on her lip. "It's hard to believe it has nothing to do with the baby when he's always doing things that prove he's thinking about it."

"The truth is, you *are* carrying his child, and it is a part of things, not to mention it's clear he's happy about it. But that isn't exclusive to you. It doesn't mean he only wants you because of the baby. He can want you, too."

God, how she wanted to believe it wasn't just about the baby. Even though he'd told her it wasn't, she was struggling to accept it. Just as she was struggling to accept the future he'd painted in the kitchen that morning was a possibility. She still didn't see how she could be a mom and go to college. And she really, really wanted to go to school.

"I'm trying to believe it's possible," she admitted. "But it's hard."

Ashley's smile was full of understanding. "Oh, I get that. There's still times I wonder how a man who looks like Dallas could be interested in a single mother who shops at thrift stores."

"What do you do when that happens?"

"I trust in him. That's the key. It doesn't have to make sense to be real."

Ashley leaned across the desk. "Your name is Faith. Maybe it's time you live up to your name and have a little of your own."

ONCE THEIR STRETCHER was clear of the elderly woman they'd brought in after she'd fallen and broken her hip, Gage took a moment to do his usual rounds. Though lunchtime was over, the lingering smells of hospital food mixed with that of antiseptic cleaner as he strolled down the corridor. He couldn't say either was very appealing.

He poked his head in to check on his favorite patient. Though her TV was on and tuned to what appeared to be a soap opera, the older woman was sound asleep, mouth open, and snoring loud enough to drown out the voices on the television.

Gage backtracked to the desk, borrowed paper and pen, and jotted down a quick note for her, which he left under the pitcher of water sitting on her table.

Since all his other patients had been discharged, he headed for his dad's room. Unlike the older woman, his dad slept quietly. Other than the rise and fall of his chest and the spikes and dips of the waves on the heart rate monitor, nothing else moved. And it was silent as a damn tomb, which Gage hated.

At the bedside, Gage did his own quick examination. His dad's color was good. Pulse was steady at eight-two beats per minute. Arterial oxygen was also good at ninety-six millimeters of mercury.

"Come on, Dad," Gage murmured. "Everything looks good. Why aren't you waking up?"

But as usual, his dad remained asleep and unresponsive. And since Gage had another stop before heading home, he didn't linger too long. Just promised he'd be back the next day.

Marcella was waiting for him in the ambulance. "Any change?" she asked as she started the engine.

"None," Gage sighed.

They drove back to the fire hall in silence and, together, cleaned and ensured the ambulance was once again ready to go. By then, their shift was over.

"Any plans for the rest of the day?" Marcella asked.

"I texted Faith earlier. Asked her to come with me to San Antonio. I want to take her to meet Josh."

Marcella's brows arched. "Your little brother?" she asked, referring to the boy from the Big Brothers program Gage participated in. "Why?"

"Because I'm trying to convince her we can be together and raise the baby as a family. But she's fighting me on it, so I thought I'd show her."

"And so, what? You'll all go out for ice cream, and you think that'll convince her?"

"Of course not, but it's a piece I want her to see. Besides, ice cream isn't until after the game."

"I don't know," Marcella shook her head. "I'm not sure coaching Little League and taking the kid for ice cream is enough."

"I just want to show her she won't be alone in this. That if she does this with me, I'll be a hands-on dad."

"And if it doesn't work?"

Gage grabbed his backpack from his locker, swung it

over his shoulder. "That's why I met with a lawyer."

FAITH LOOKED AT the navy golf shirt with the Little League logo and team name scrolled across the front and knew immediately where Gage was taking her. Though he'd never mentioned he coached ball, she wasn't surprised he did. And she was glad now that she'd opted to wear a long, sleeveless tunic over stretchy capris as opposed to the sundress she'd contemplated when he'd texted her earlier telling her to dress casual as they were going into the city that evening.

What did surprise her was when he stopped at a nondescript brick apartment building.

"I'll be right back," he said.

As he walked up the sidewalk toward the front doors, Faith couldn't help but appreciate the view. Along with the uniform golf shirt that accentuated his biceps and shoulders, he wore khaki shorts that showed off the muscles in his tanned legs. Not to mention how his ass looked in them.

Yearning clenched low in her belly. She actually swiped at her mouth in case she was drooling. But, Lord, he was hot. Firm and toned and, she remembered with another punch of lust, thick and hard in all the right places. Places that wept for him at the moment. Places that throbbed in need.

Glad he'd left the Jeep running, Faith cranked the AC and directed all the vents her way. Of course, it did nothing to alleviate the ache in her breasts, nor the pounding between her legs. But it did help cool her heated cheeks. Damn those pregnancy hormones!

She'd just started to cool off when Gage emerged from the building, his hand on the shoulder of the cutest tow-headed boy she'd ever seen. The bottom fell out of her stomach.

Though they didn't look at all alike, and he'd never mentioned the boy before, she immediately wondered if he was Gage's son. All heat drained from her as jealousy ripped through her like a tornado. Though it made no sense given her decision, she hated the idea of Gage having a child with another woman. Of him having another woman in his life, even if it was clear they weren't together.

Her head spun as a dozen different thoughts whirled through her head. Who was the woman? Judging the boy to be around eight, Gage would have had to have gotten her pregnant in high school. Which, surely, she'd have heard about given the size of Last Stand and the fact they'd been friends at the time.

But she couldn't deny the way the hand on the shoulder and the warm smile he gave the boy, and the grin the boy returned, spoke of a close relationship. Watching them approach the Jeep, her hand dropped to her belly. She might resent the fact he'd fathered a child with someone else, but at least she knew he'd be a good dad.

Which made the ache in her heart hard to explain.

Since they'd reached the vehicle and weren't making any attempt to get inside, Faith set the troubling thought aside and stepped out into the late afternoon heat.

Gage's hand remained on the white uniformed shoulder of the boy. "Faith, I'd like you to meet my little brother, Josh. Josh, Faith is a real good friend of mine."

Little brother? But Gage was the youngest of the Granger boys. Guessing her confusion, Gage went on to explain that he was Josh's big brother through the Big Brothers organization.

Faith's smile bloomed as relief spread through her. He winked at her, as though he knew what she'd been thinking.

His fingers flexed on the boy's shoulder. "What do you do when you meet someone?" he prodded.

Though the boy's face went as pink as the inside of a grapefruit, he extended his hand, looked her squarely in the eye. "Pleasure to meet you, ma'am," he said.

Charmed, Faith took his little hand, shook it. "And you."

She looked up at Gage. His eyes shone with pride.

"Hop in," he said.

Ball glove held tightly in his hand, Josh hopped in the back and buckled up. She happily listened as Gage asked him questions about school and homework and how he'd done on his math exam. It was clear Gage took his role as Big Brother seriously.

Just as, she witnessed later once she was settled in the stands, he took his role as coach seriously. He always offered praise first, then helpful pointers, and both in the same easy tone with a warm smile on his face as he patted them on the back.

Faith wasn't much into sports but, sitting amid the parents, she soon found herself cheering and standing as balls were struck and players raced around the diamond, sliding into the bases. It broke her heart when Josh raced for home plate only to get there a second too late. He was tagged out before his little cleat hit home plate. He bowed his head as the umpire shouted, "Out!"

But Faith remained standing after the others had sat and shouted, "Nice try, Josh! You almost made it!"

He stopped short, turned and stared. Then, recognizing her, his frown flipped into a smile. Faith's heart about burst when he waved excitedly at her before running to join his teammates.

After the game, one they lost six to four, Gage took her and Josh out for ice cream. She enjoyed listening to Josh talk excitedly about the game and was happy to sit back and let Gage focus on the boy, who lapped up the attention. She, on the other hand, focused on Gage as she slowly worked her way through her chocolate fudge sundae.

What struck her most was how real he was. He never spoke down to Josh. He treated him with respect and a soft, guiding hand when the boy needed a little reminding. Like when he corrected his grammar or reminded him not to talk with his mouth full.

But he didn't just listen and guide. Gage also told him about his day, shared what was going on at the ranch and how Josh would need to come see the kittens before they got too big.

When they dropped Josh off at the apartment, Faith stepped out, too. Again, she shook his hand.

"I'll see you again soon," she said, because if she was going to stay for the next while, she planned on coming to more games.

His brown eyes went wide. "Maybe the next game?" he asked hopefully.

Her heart turned over. "If I can," she promised.

She waited in the Jeep as Gage walked the boy inside, again watching as he strode toward the building. Only this time, it wasn't just her body that heated and expanded at the sight of him. It was her heart. And for once, it agreed with her head.

Both claimed she was head over heels in love with Gage Granger.

Chapter Fifteen

I F THEY WERE back in high school, it would be a simple matter of telling Gage her feelings. But they weren't, and as much as she thought life had been complicated back then, it was infinitely more so now.

There was another person involved, even if that person wasn't born yet. But that wasn't the only reason she was keeping her feelings to herself.

She had baggage she'd been schlepping around for as long as she could remember. Her upbringing had shaped her, and she couldn't change that, but she'd come to realize it was up to her to decide if she was going to let it continue to dictate her life.

She admired the hell out of Ashley for what she'd accomplished on her own. And Roy, who'd remained sober and was building his life again. Faith hoped, in time, that would include his children again, but at least for now he was moving ahead.

It was what she wanted, too. She wanted to move forward. To stop feeling caught in the same loop of believing she couldn't do something. Couldn't be who she wanted to be. She'd moved to San Antonio and made a life for herself. Maybe it wasn't glamorous, and she wasn't super successful, but she hadn't fallen on her face and failed, either.

She'd found a job and a roommate and supported herself. Why? Because she'd needed to. Because she'd wanted to. So maybe it wasn't a big splash, but at least she'd kept afloat.

And she was proud of that. Proud she hadn't had to come back home, hadn't had to ask for help, though there was no shame in that. In most families, at least. In hers, there would have been. Her grandmother would have made sure of it, just as she'd belittled and undermined Faith her whole life. If she ever doubted that, it had been made clear the other day when she'd all but called Faith a slut right there in her front yard.

The same yard Faith stood in now.

Her grandmother had a tidy little house. The lawn was kept up. Not a dandelion or weed dared mar her grandma's deep green grass. The hedges were clipped ruler straight, and the flowers in the pots bloomed. It was as though nothing dared go against Alice Stone. Likely because nothing ever had. Other than her own daughter. But she hadn't gone up against Alice as much as just walked away. Faith doubted Linda had ever truly stood up to her mother. She'd ignored her, mostly. Just as she'd done with her daughter.

Faith was prepared to walk away from Alice, too, this time for good, if that was what was needed to stay healthy. But she hoped it didn't come to that.

"Guess I'm about to find out," she mumbled.

Knowing the reception she was sure to get, given what had been said the last time she was there, Faith drew several steadying breaths before moving up the walk.

Since she didn't want to have the conversation she had in mind on the porch, and she doubted her grandmother would invite her in if she were to knock first, Faith let herself in. Figuring Alice's routine hadn't changed much in the six years Faith had been gone, she'd deliberately come just after lunch and before her grandma's afternoon nap.

Despite it having just been lunchtime, the only scent that greeted her was that of the lavender air spray her grandmother favored. Wrinkling her nose at the heavy hand Alice had with it, Faith closed the door. Though she hadn't wanted to give her grandma a chance to refuse her entry, she didn't want to give the woman a heart attack, either. As she slipped off her sandals, she called out, "Grandma, it's just me."

Alice was waiting for her at the entryway to the living room when Faith stepped into the kitchen. The house might have smelled of lavender, but the pucker on her grandma's lips suggested the woman had just eaten a handful of lemons. And despite the soft floral dress her grandma wore, there was nothing soft about her. She stood straight and stiff as though she were made of steel.

"What are you doing here?" Alice jutted her pointy chin. "I think you said more than enough the other day."

"So did you," Faith pointed out. "In fact, you've said more than enough my whole life."

Ignoring her grandmother's gasp and the hand that went to her narrow throat, Faith pulled a chair out from the table for Alice then one for herself. She sat, folded her hands on the table, and looked at her grandmother.

"I have a lot to say. It might be more comfortable if you sat."

Insult flashed through Alice's pale blue eyes. "You will not talk to me in that tone. Especially not in my own home."

A younger Faith would have apologized. Would have done anything to try to gain her grandmother's favor. Would have bent over backward to prove she was worthy of love. But Faith knew now there wasn't any point. She'd tried being the good girl, the respectful, quiet girl. She'd listened, obeyed, toed the line. It hadn't gotten her anywhere.

With nothing to lose, she answered, "What tone would you prefer? Because none that I've tried in the past ever made a difference."

"Well, I can see there's no point to this discussion." Her grandma turned on her orthopedic heel.

"Actually, there is a point," Faith said as she rose to her feet, prepared to follow Alice anywhere until they got this settled. "The point is, you've never liked me. If you resented me that much, if you never wanted me to begin with, why didn't you just put me up for adoption or into foster care when Mom left me with you?"

Her grandmother turned back around. She looked as though she'd been slapped.

"Why would I give you up to strangers? You're family."

Faith couldn't believe her ears. "I'm family?" She gaped. "Family doesn't treat each other the way you've treated me. Or it's not supposed to."

Alice clasped her hands together at her slim waist. "I gave you a home, an education. You always had clothes on your back and food in your belly."

"An orphanage or a foster home would have done the same!"

Her grandma scowled. "I won't be yelled at in my own home."

Faith threw up her hands. "This isn't a home, Grandma. It's a house. And there's a big difference between the two. A home has laughter and love. A home is a place where you feel safe. Where you seek refuge. This place has never been anything but a house. A cold, empty house."

Alice's already thin lips disappeared into a straight, hard line. "Then why are you here if everything I've ever done for you is so awful?"

"Because I want to know *why*. Why didn't you ever love me? Why didn't you ever do anything but criticize and assume the worst in me? Even the other day, you said I was no better than my mother and suggested I didn't know the father of my own baby." Faith's blood surged hotly through her veins. "For the record, it's Gage."

Her grandma merely stared at her. No apology. No hint of warmth. No sign of softening. She didn't even deny that she'd never loved her only grandchild.

Angry tears burned Faith's eyes. "I got good grades. I respected your curfew. I did all the chores you ever asked of me and never got into trouble. None of it was ever good enough. *I* was never good enough, and you made sure I knew it every day."

Finally, some emotion flitted through Alice's eyes, shook in her voice. "I didn't treat you any different than I treated your mother. Than how I was treated myself."

Faith's shoulders fell. Well, didn't it all make sense now?

"Didn't you ever, as a young girl, wish for more?"

Her grandmother's chin tipped up. "I was taught to be thankful. And if I ever forgot, I was quickly reminded."

Alice didn't have to say the words. Faith could see by the

haunted look on her grandmother's face what "reminded" meant.

"Your parents abused you?"

Alice sniffed. Though Faith didn't think it possible, her spine went a little straighter. "I was *disciplined*," she corrected. "And at least I spared both you and your mother that."

"Yes, you did," Faith acknowledged. She softened her voice. "Thank you for that. And I can see now that you raised me and Mom the only way you knew how. But it didn't make it right, Grandma. Surely, you can see that. It's the reason Mom has a new boyfriend every other week. She's craving love and attention. And me…"

Faith broke off. She curled her fingers and toes to keep herself together.

"I was so afraid when I found out I was pregnant. I was scared I'd be the kind of parent you were, or worse, the kind my mom was. I didn't want to leave my kid with the same scars I had, so I'd convinced myself to give it up."

Alice's hands dropped to her side. Her porcelain skin went even paler. "You're giving up your child?"

Faith sniffled. "I'd convinced myself it was the only way to ensure my baby would be happy. That it would never feel resented and unloved."

She wiped the tears she couldn't contain anymore as they trailed hotly down her cheeks. "But now I see it's a cycle. And you broke part of it when you refused to raise a hand to me."

Her grandmother's chin trembled. "I wasn't ever going to have you afraid of me the way I was of my father."

"And you did that," Faith acknowledged. "I was never

scared of you." She smiled at her grandma. "You broke that cycle because it was important to you to do that. And now I know I can break the rest of it."

She pressed a hand to her belly. Love so bright, so pure, filled her heart. Oh, God, she was going to be a mother! She smiled through her tears. She was going to be the best damn mother!

She could see it, now. Her, Gage and—

Her stomach fell. Shit. Shit. What about college? What was she going to do about school? Dammit, she wanted a career, too. An education. She shook her head. She'd think about that later. Like Ashley had reminder her, she'd made a life for herself in San Antonio because she'd wanted to, because there hadn't been another option. Surely, she could figure out a way to have her baby and a career. But she wasn't talking about college now. She was talking about breaking a cycle.

"This child will know it's loved every day," she vowed. "By me. By its father. But," she continued, "I won't bring it here, ever, if you treat it the way I was treated. If you can't love it unconditionally, be kind and supportive, then you'll never know your great-grandbaby."

Alice jerked as though struck. Faith steeled herself. While she understood her grandmother more now, it didn't make how she treated Faith any better. Alice could do better. She just had to choose to.

Wanting to lead by example, Faith stepped closer, kissed her grandma on her smooth cheek. It was the first time in her life she'd ever done it, and Alice's face couldn't have looked more stunned. Faith bit back a grin. That got the pucker off her grandma's mouth!

"You have my number. I'm staying at the Granger Ranch for now. If you want a real relationship with me, you just have to call. But for the health of me and my baby, I can't be around the kind of toxicity that lives in this house. So, if you're willing to change, you only have to call."

Faith stopped at the entry to the porch. She turned, faced the woman who'd raised her. "I do love you. And you did provide for me. Thank you."

Then, figuring she'd given the woman enough shocks for one day, Faith let herself out.

FAITH COULDN'T WAIT to tell Gage. Fired up and giddy with excitement over her newfound clarity and the decisions she'd made, she wanted nothing more than to run and tell him everything. But though he should have been on days off, he'd taken on an extra shift when he'd been called at breakfast that morning.

Since she had no intention of telling him her life-changing news in the middle of a fire hall, she had to wait until he got back.

There was no shortage of things to do, thank goodness. She went back to the Diamond G, stripped beds and washed sheets while she prepared a stew to put in the slow cooker for supper. Then, with Ryker's permission, she hooked up her laptop to the office printer and printed off her current resume.

With lunch done and supper cooking, she headed back

into Last Stand. There, she handed out resumes at the local restaurants and bars, such as the Last Stand Saloon and the Dragonfly. And though she had no experience in retail, she also left some at the Yippee Ki Yay Western Store and Nailed It, the local hardware store.

She stopped at the grocery store to get the few things that were on the list before once again returning to the ranch. With things in the house running smoothly, Faith went to the barn. Roy scowled at her.

"It's hotter than hell out here. You should be inside. Besides," he added with stern look as he wiped a drop of sweat trickling down his temple, "you know Gage doesn't want you doing physical work."

Faith laughed at that, because men never seemed to realize just how physical running a house could be.

"I'm not here to do chores. I thought I'd check on the kittens."

His face softened. "Well, that, I can accommodate."

He left her to them. Dust tickled her nose as she settled into the straw next to the mama cat and her babies. She smiled as she saw the saucer of milk nearby. She'd bet money Gage had set it there.

Relaxed and a little tired, Faith soon nodded off right there in the corner of a stall. She jerked awake when a tractor chugged into the yard. Embarrassed, she wiped the straw from her butt, pulled a few strands from her hair, and hurried outside.

She waved at Ryker, who waved back from inside the cab of the orange tractor. Feeling guilty for having fallen asleep, Faith baked cookies and homemade buns.

After supper, she folded laundry and put it away while Ryker and Cam did the dishes. She was dragging her butt by eight o'clock when she trudged into the living room. Two recliners flanked the couch. Ryker was tipped back in one of them, Cam in the other. They were watching some shoot-'em-up action movie.

They both dropped their footrests and stood when she entered.

"No, I'm okay. I'm happy to take the couch."

She'd have been even happier to lay on it but settled for an end instead. She set her glass of water on the coffee table on her right.

"You know that's a recliner, as well?" Cam said as he paused the movie.

"Really?" While she hadn't wanted to chase them from their seats, she'd definitely been ready to put her feet up. Reaching between the small table and the couch, Faith found the lever. She sighed as she leaned back, sinking into the cushions.

"You okay?" Cam asked.

Though it was Cam who asked, Faith felt Ryker's gaze, as well. She looked at both with a reassuring smile. "I am. It's normal to feel tired."

"You did a lot today," Ryker said. "We don't want you overdoing it."

It wasn't until he said it that she realized she'd seen a lot of them during the day. If it wasn't Roy in the barn, either Cam or Ryker had come into the house every hour or so. She hadn't put it together until now because they'd always seemed to have a reason for being there. They needed a drink or a snack. They'd forgotten something in the office or the mudroom.

"I'm fine. And you don't need to check up on me. You have your own work to do, and it's not as though I'm fragile."

"Until my niece or nephew is born you are," Cam stated.

Faith bit her lip. She stared at the paused actors on the screen. She'd had superficial conversations with Gage's brothers and clearly, they'd agreed to let her stay, but she really didn't know how they felt about any of it—her living there or the baby.

"I know having me here has got to be an inconvenience."

"Yeah," Ryker snorted. "I hate having home-cooked meals and clean clothes I didn't have to wash. It really sucks."

"I was more thinking you don't know me, really. And I'm living here. And in six months, you'll be uncles, whether you want to be or not. It's got to throw a hitch in your lives."

"Not a big one," Ryker said. "Sure, it's a bit different having a woman in the house. I promise to try to remember to put the seat down. As for the baby," he shrugged. "Might be cool to have a kid around here."

"So, just like that?" Faith asked.

"Pretty much," Ryker answered before taking a pull on the beer he'd had sitting next to him.

"You're part of the family now," Cam said. "Just like Ashley and Brittany."

"Even though Dallas has only been dating her for a short time?"

"If you knew Dallas," Cam said, "you'd know she's it for

him." He looked at his brother. "I guess that already kind of makes us uncles, doesn't it?"

"Yeah," Ryker agreed with a nod. "Guess it does."

Cam pressed play on the movie. The actors resumed their shooting and fighting, and a car lifted off the ground in a ball of flames as it exploded. Faith could only marvel at how easy it was with Gage's brothers. No rants, no judgment. No belittling or making her feel either guilty or a burden. They'd just accepted.

After years with her grandmother, it was a shock to Faith's system. Sure, she understood better after her talk with her grandma earlier, but it didn't change the fact she hadn't been raised that way. Alice had yet to say anything more about the baby than what she already had when she'd accused Faith of not knowing the father.

And she'd been raised by Alice. By a woman who knew her. And yet, her grandmother hadn't had an ounce of the acceptance she'd been shown by the Grangers, despite the fact she was practically a stranger to them.

It was a great comfort to know men like this were going to be part of her baby's life.

"Thank you," she said.

Though back engrossed in their movie, Cam managed a thumbs-up and Ryker, a nod. She was happy they were no longer focused on her as she'd gotten a little misty at their words. She really wasn't in this alone, and not only was she determined to do better than had been done to her, there'd also be others there to help guide and nurture. To be there without judgment.

Between having to look for another place to live, then

finding out she was pregnant and needing to find another job because of the fire, hope and faith had indeed been hard to come by. It had felt, at every turn, for every step she'd tried to move forward, she was getting knocked back two.

But now…

Now she had at least one family that was going to stand with her. She had a home and a job—hopefully more than one if her resumes panned out—and best of all, a man who wanted her. And not—she firmly told the little voice in her head that wanted to argue—just because she was having his baby. But because of who she was.

With Gage and his brothers around to help, maybe college could be a possibility after all.

She couldn't wait for Gage to get off shift. Not only to tell him everything that had happened that day and the revelations she'd come to, but because of just how she planned on celebrating.

She smiled to herself as she snuggled deeper into the couch. Those lusty hormones were finally going to get put to use.

GAGE WAS EXHAUSTED. They'd been run off their feet the last twenty-four hours. They'd had two calls back-to-back, and after the second, when he'd tried to climb into one of the bunks in the dorm room for some much-needed shut-eye, the sirens had gone off again. It didn't happen often, thank God, when they had nights like the previous one, but when they hit, they hit hard. And despite knowing he had the next twenty-four hours off, Gage couldn't wait until that evening to sleep.

He caught up with Ryker in his brother's garage. He must have looked as exhausted as he felt, because he didn't even have to explain. Ryker popped his head from the open hood of his own truck, took one look at Gage, and said, "Go. We've got things under control."

Gage didn't know what Cam and Roy were busy doing, and he couldn't have cared at that moment, but he did want to see Faith. Even if it was for only a minute before he crashed.

"Faith in the house?" he asked.

Ryker, who'd resumed his tinkering, once again lifted his head from his truck. "You must be some tired if you didn't notice her car wasn't here."

Gage took off his sunglasses, rubbed his gritty eyes. "Did she say where she was going?"

"I sent her on a few errands. She should be back soon."

Yawning, Gage spun on his heel and trudged toward the bunkhouse. Much as he'd missed Faith, he needed sleep. He was so beat, he even considered not showering, but the thought of washing off the last twenty-four hours was a siren call he couldn't resist, no matter his exhaustion.

He made it quick, though, because otherwise, he was liable to fall asleep standing up, and he really didn't want his crew finding him naked and hurt in the bottom of his shower because he'd passed out from exhaustion. The hot water blasted his tired shoulders. Feeling limp, Gage toweled himself dry.

One of the first things he'd done when he'd given Faith

his bedroom in the house and moved to the bunkhouse was change the curtains. He drew the black-out curtains closed, dropped the damp towel on the floor, and crawled into bed. His whole body sighed. After being on his feet for an entire day, it was blissful to be horizontal. Closing his gritty, tired eyes, Gage drifted off.

He was startled out of a dead sleep when the bed dipped and his covers lifted. Groggy, he pushed onto an elbow as he blinked and tried to orient himself. And jerked when a hand slid under the covers and grazed his waist.

The hell!

"It's just me."

It took a second for the voice to penetrate through the fog clouding his brain. That was a woman's voice. It was Faith's voice. His brows drew together. Faith was there? In his bed? He shook his head to clear the sleep from his head. Why would she—

The bed dipped again, and this time, it wasn't only her hand he felt. Oh, he didn't miss it sliding up his chest, but what caught his attention, what cleared the fog from his brain, was the bare skin brushing his side. His *entire* side.

Even though he could see her now in the dimness of the room, he was almost afraid he was still dreaming. Gage reached for her. He found warm, silky skin. Nothing but skin. His mouth curved as his fingers splayed over her naked hip. He could get used to this kind of wake-up call.

"If this is a dream, don't wake me up."

"Well," she purred as she slid a leg over his as her head lowered toward his, "I do need you awake for what I have in mind."

Hot blood rushed through his veins. He was instantly hard. Instantly hungry.

"Oh, I'm awake now."

He wove his fingers through her hair, pulled her closer, and when even that seemed to take too long, he lifted his head, his mouth desperate for hers.

Their lips met in a hot, wet, hungry kiss. Need slammed through him. His tongue swept her mouth, claimed her, then went back for more. He lay down, the glorious weight of her settling over him. He felt the hard peaks of her nipples on his chest, the heat of her sex as she straddled his thigh.

Hooking a leg over her hip, he rolled over her. Settling himself within her thighs, Gage cupped a full breast in his palm. His thumb stroked her nipple while his mouth continued to make love to hers.

Moaning, she arched her body toward his. Not just her breast, but her hips, too. He ached to take her, to slip inside and feel the rightness of it, the way he'd felt it in San Antonio. But despite his body's demands, he held back.

He gave her another kiss, softer this time, then looked down into her face. Even in the dimness of the room he saw the desire in her hazel eyes. Her lips remained parted, an invitation he struggled to decline. But before they went any further, he needed to know this wasn't going to be another one-night stand. Because he was long past that.

Moving his hand from her breast, he brushed a few tangled strands of her hair from her cheek. His heart squeezed at how right she looked just then. Her hair spread over his pillow. Her body molding to his. Her pretty eyes looking into his.

"I don't want another one-night stand, Faith. If we're going to do this again, then it has to be because we have a relationship—a real one."

He braced himself for her to shove him away. To say that wasn't possible. That this was the best she could do. So it took a minute to recognize what the smile on her face meant. His heart stumbled. Could she finally be ready?

"I want that, too," she stated.

"You do?"

"I know it's taken me a while, but I've been doing a lot of soul searching." Her lips twitched. "I even went and hashed it out with my grandma today."

"You did?"

"I did. It's up to her if we have a relationship moving forward, but I spoke my piece, and I understand her a little better now." Some of the happiness dimmed from her face. "She wasn't treated well growing up, so part of it was her perpetuating a cycle. It was all she'd known."

He frowned. "I know people say that, and I'm not disputing the validity of it, but I've known so many who've stopped it, too."

"Yeah. And I've decided to be one of those."

His heart gave a hard kick, and hope bloomed in his chest. Was she saying what he thought she was?

"I was scared. I *am* scared," she corrected. "But I don't want being afraid to keep me from what I want most. And that's you. And our baby."

Choking up, he needed a moment before he trusted his voice. "You're sure? Because I don't think I could take it if you—"

She pressed a finger to his lips. "I won't change my mind. But I may need you to reassure me now and again that I'm not the worst parent ever. And I still really want to go to college, so I'll need your help to make that happen."

He took her hand, kissed it. "Anything. You've got it. And as for being a mother? You'll be a great mom." Then he released her hand so he could place his over her belly. He froze. "Are you—"

Her smile lit up the dim room. "I'm starting to show."

Excitement bubbled up his chest. Suddenly, everything was so real. He was going to be a dad. He could see the proof. Feel the reality of it. His cheeks stretched along with his heart, which suddenly felt too big to be contained.

Looking into her eyes, he leaned down, and just before his lips met hers, he whispered, "I love you."

Her palm pressed against his chest, holding him back. "I love you, too," she said.

He'd feared he'd never hear those words from her, but they poured over him like a warm July rain. Putting his heart into the kiss, he showed her with every sweep of his tongue, every caress of his lips, that she meant the world to him. That she *was* his world.

Last time they'd made love, he'd had alcohol clouding his system. Not that he hadn't been aware what he'd been doing, because he sure as hell had, but he'd always felt as though his senses had been dulled somewhat. That he hadn't been able to enjoy being with Faith as much as he could have.

He intended to make up for that now.

He started with her mouth, taking languorous sips of her

soft lips. He moved to her neck and the sensitive skin there that smelled of rose petals. He grazed his teeth over her collarbone before pressing an open-mouth kiss over the plumpness of her right breast.

Gasping, Faith arched into his touch. He filled his hand with her left breast. Then, noticing something, lifted his head. They hadn't spilled from his hand before.

"My stomach isn't the only thing growing," she said.

"I'm not complaining," he said before lowering his mouth to her nipple. He ran the flat of his tongue over the sensitive peak.

Her hands dug into his hair, held him firm as he sucked her deep into his mouth. As he rolled the hardened tip across the roof of his mouth.

Clinging to his head, she rocked her hips.

Not willing to be rushed despite the throbbing in his erection, he moved to the other breast. She trembled underneath him. God, she was responsive. Her throaty moans and desperate begging were a hell of a turn-on.

Slowly, he moved his mouth down her body. He remembered she'd hesitated when he'd parted her thighs to do this in San Antonio. But this time, she just sighed and spread her legs for him. God, she was gorgeous. Naked and open for him. Wanting him.

Moisture spilled from his sex. His balls were tight and hard. He wanted to plunge inside her, rock them both until they exploded. Instead, he bit down on his lust and focused on her pleasure. Not that it wouldn't also be his, because it would be.

With his palms on the insides of her thighs, Gage settled

his shoulders between her legs. He touched her first, his fingers brushing over her. She was erotically wet.

"More."

She bent her legs. Planting her feet into the mattress, she lifted her hips. Fighting to control his lust, Gage dipped two fingers inside. She was so hot. He spread the moisture that coated his fingers over her clit.

"Gage, please."

Who was he to deny her? But instead of his fingers, he dipped his head and, with his tongue, tasted her intimately, giving her a kiss that pushed her over the edge.

He held her as her muscles convulsed, as her body broke then went limp. Easing from between her legs, Gage slid up her body, kissed her mouth. And did some rocking of his own when she wrapped her hand tightly around his arousal.

But he didn't want to come in her hand. He wanted to be inside her.

"I haven't been with anyone since you," he said. "And there wasn't anyone for a long while before you. I can run to the house and get condoms if—"

"You're not going anywhere," she said.

He smiled against her mouth. "I was hoping you'd say that."

He took her hands, because it mattered to him that she knew this wasn't just about sex. With his fingers intertwined with hers, he positioned himself between her thighs and, this time, when she opened for him, it was his erection he slid inside.

It was beautiful and perfect. *She* was beautiful and perfect. He'd always thought so. From high school to the night in the hotel and every day since. She was made for him.

He whispered it all as he made love to her, as he gave his heart fully. It had been a long time since Gage felt he had a real family. He'd have that with Faith. He'd ensure it. Releasing her hands, Gage wrapped his arms around her, pulling her close and relishing the feel of her in his arms. Back in his life.

But his heart wasn't the only thing about to burst. Kissing her, he slid a hand between them, cupped her breast.

"Yes." She gasped.

She clasped his ass, her nails little bites on his skin. Knowing her need matched his, he increased his speed. She wrapped her legs around him and raised her hips, met him thrust for thrust. *Oh, God.* Bracing on one hand, toying with her beaded nipple with the other, Gage drove hard.

Flesh slapped against flesh. When he was afraid anyone who happened to be in the yard would hear her, he caught her screams with his kiss as he brought them both to the brink. And, choking back a triumphant scream of his own, leapt over the edge with her.

Chapter Sixteen

WITH HAPPY FEELINGS fluttering in her chest, Faith stepped from the bunkhouse into the sunshine. Raising her face to the warmth of it, she breathed deeply. Embraced this new reality she'd never in her wildest dreams dared hope for. Gage Granger loved her. They were having a baby. They were going to raise it together.

Her stomach squeezed at that, the old fears resurfacing. For once, she refused to let them take hold. She already loved the baby and its father. And, like Ashley had said, just because she was scared didn't mean she couldn't do it, and do a good job of it, as well. Ashley was proof being scared didn't mean she'd screw it up.

Besides, she reminded herself, she wouldn't be alone. Gage would be there. So would his brothers. In this case, it wasn't going to take a village to raise a child, but it might take a whole ranch.

"Bunkhouse wasn't too dirty, I take it?"

Faith lowered her gaze, met Cam's amused one. He stood hip-shot, arms crossed, his lips curved into a cheeky grin.

"Sorry?"

He nodded toward the bucket and cleaning supplies she'd brought along with her earlier. In case anyone had seen her going into the bunkhouse, she hadn't wanted it to look like what it had been—a booty call.

She flushed because she had the awful feeling Cam knew exactly what she'd been up to and that it had little to do with cleaning.

"Uh, no." She forced a smile, though it was fake as the reason she carried a bucket. "Roy and Gage keep it pretty tidy."

Cam rocked back on his heels. "That's Gage, all right. Tidy."

Oh, God, he knew she was lying. Mortified, though not sorry because her body was still humming from Gage's lovemaking, Faith excused herself. She scrunched up her face as she heard Cam chuckling behind her.

Four hours later, she'd mopped the upstairs, had chicken marinating in the fridge, and was taking a much-needed break with a glass of iced tea when the house phone rang. It was the first time it had rung since Faith had started staying at the Diamond G, so she wasn't sure what to do. Did Ryker have an extension in his garage that he could pick up? Or was there one in the barn? Assuming, of course, there was someone in either place to answer it.

She didn't feel right answering, but when it rang for the third time and she didn't see an answering machine near the phone, Faith went ahead and lifted the receiver.

"Hello?"

"Hello. I'm looking for Gage Granger," a man answered.

"Oh, um, he's sleeping at the moment. Can I take a message?"

Since the phone was sitting on a built-in desk in the corner of the kitchen, Faith tucked the phone between her shoulder and ear as she grabbed a pen and pad of paper.

"Sure. Can you tell him Douglas Henderson from Hickory Creek Law Office called? The papers he had me draw up are ready for his signature. He'd asked that I call him on his cell but, you know, for the life of me, I couldn't find it. I thought I'd just track him down at the ranch instead."

The pen fell from Faith's fingers. Her blood chilled. "Where did you say you were calling from?"

"Hickory Creek Law Office, here in Last Stand. He's expecting my call. If you can let him know, that would be great. I know he was anxious for me to finish."

"Can I—" Faith swallowed hard. Not only because she was afraid of the answer, but also because her mouth had gone bone dry. This couldn't be happening.

"Can I ask when Gage was in?" she queried.

"Tuesday."

Faith was going to throw up. Tuesday was the day the restaurant had burned. That was the night he'd held her outside, made her feel safe. As though she could lean on him. And all the while…

"I'll pass on the message," she answered, though she made no move to pick up the pen.

Numbly, she disconnected the call, dropped the receiver onto the desk. Her ears started to ring. Her legs started to tremble. While she certainly wasn't privy to all of Gage's business, dread churned in her gut. She had a sick feeling she knew what this was about. And if she was right, then it meant she was a fool.

A fool for trusting in him. A fool for believing his wanting her wasn't only because of the baby. She spread her hands on the desk, bowed her head, and pinched her eyes closed.

So it wasn't about her after all. And telling herself that her grandmother had just continued a cycle, that it had more to do with her grandma's upbringing than anything about Faith, was just more bullshit she'd allowed herself to believe. Because, clearly, she wasn't worth anyone's effort.

Pain lanced through her chest. It spread hot and fast, like a grassfire out of control. It consumed her, robbing her of breath. Faith struggled to do more than wheeze. The desperate sound filled the otherwise quiet kitchen.

You're getting ahead of yourself. You don't even know for sure what the papers are about.

No, no she didn't. Forcing herself to take slow breaths, Faith focused on that. She didn't know for sure what papers the lawyer was talking about. Maybe it was something ranch related. With his dad in a coma, it was possible there were legal things that needed to be taken care of like living wills or power of attorneys.

The muscles in her chest relaxed enough for her to breathe. But she still felt nauseous. When she'd left Gage in the bunkhouse, she'd never been happier. For once, she'd felt as though life were going her way. As though all the crap she'd had to go through growing up had been for a reason. That it had all been leading to her having a good man in her life. One she could build a real family with.

She'd let herself believe it was possible. She'd opened herself completely to him. Gave him her heart and soul. Given him her faith and trust.

"It can't have been for nothing." She prayed. "It can't."

"What can't?"

Faith spun. Gage stood in the kitchen, hair disheveled from his nap. He wore a black T-shirt with Outlaw Tequila's logo stamped in the middle of it. His jeans were snug in all the right places—places, a handful of hours ago, Faith had known intimately.

Raising her gaze to his, she studied him closely. His green eyes were intent on hers. He seemed genuinely interested. Angling his head to the side he asked, "Did something happen?"

Oh, Lord, she hoped not. She hoped he hadn't done what she feared he had. Because if he had…

"I just took a message for you," she said.

His brows drew together in question. "But I have my cell," he said as he tapped the back pocket of his jeans. "It didn't ring."

"He didn't call it. He called the house because he said he'd lost your cell number."

"Okay. So who was it?"

"Douglas Henderson from Hickory Creek Law Office."

The last of the sleepiness cleared from his eyes. There was no missing the "oh, shit" look that took its place. Or the "oh, damn" feeling that settled in the pit of her stomach. Steeling herself for what was to come, Faith grasped the back of a chair.

"He said the papers you were waiting for are ready to be picked up." She dug her nails into the wood of the chair and locked her knees. "Please tell me those papers are about the ranch. Please tell me they don't have anything to do with the baby."

His chest expanded as he inhaled. He blew out a long breath. "I can't, because they are about the baby. But that was—"

She cut him off before he could start rattling off excuses like her grandmother had. "The other day, in this very room, you held me, placed your hands over my belly, and said you could see us standing like that every day."

"Because I can—"

"I spoke to Ashley about being afraid, about not trusting that you cared about me as much as the baby."

His green eyes sparked. "I do love you. I've told you that."

"She told me you could love us both. And I believed her. And then you took me to meet Josh. I was so touched by how you were with him. I knew why you'd done it and, despite that, it worked. That night was the night I finally admitted to myself I loved you."

He took another step toward her, palms open before him. "Faith, listen to me."

She shook her head even as her heart begged her to do as he asked. "Despite my fears, despite my head telling me there was no way you'd want me, I listened to my heart. I took a leap, Gage, a huge one for me. And the whole time I'd convinced myself you did love me…you did want me—" Her voice cracked. But it wasn't the only thing. Her heart was breaking, too.

"And the whole time," she said as tears burned her eyes and turned her words wobbly, "the whole time you'd already gotten a lawyer to draw up papers."

"Yes, I had a lawyer draw up papers. But you yourself said that was a few days ago. Faith, you'd told me you were giving the baby to me. I figured there were legal things to that. That it wasn't as simple as you handing it over. It was always my hope to convince you to stay with me, to make a family with me, but in case you didn't change your mind—"

"You wanted to ensure, no matter what, you got the baby." She swiped at her tears. "Why didn't you tell me about the lawyer?"

If he had, if he'd explained before, or asked her to go along, then maybe she'd believe him. But it all felt so underhanded, so sneaky.

He shook his head, blew out another breath. "Because I knew you would take it exactly as you are now."

"Well, there aren't too many ways to take it, are there? You claim to love me, want a family with me, and yet, you went behind my back to draw up documents."

"I explained why!"

"And I'm not buying your lies anymore!" she shouted back.

His green eyes narrowed. "I have never lied to you. It's not who I am, and you should know that by now. I never lied to you in high school. I haven't lied to you since. I want you. I want us. I've shown you in every way I can think of, and now I'm telling you in the most direct, no-bullshit words I can. I can't make it any clearer than that. I can't make you believe it. Only you can do that, Faith. Only you can put aside your fears and your past and trust what's before you. What's between us. It has to come from you, Faith. I wish to hell I could do it for you, but I can't."

Her eyes burned. "And I thought I could. Until this. If you'd told me, Gage. If you'd come to me, if we'd gone there together. I told you everything about me. You know it all. I *did* trust you. That's the problem. But clearly, you don't feel the same."

He scowled. His face went red. "Where are you going?" he asked as she marched past him.

Fueled by hurt, betrayal, and anger at herself for believing Gage could love a woman like her, Faith answered, "To town. Hopefully, there's a vacant apartment somewhere."

It would mean dipping into her college fund, but she wasn't staying at the Diamond G, in Gage's room, another night.

"I'll come back for my things when I have a place," she said.

In the mudroom, she grabbed her purse, slipped on her sandals. She didn't turn around to look at Gage, but he was behind her. His gaze bore into her back. She waited for him to say something else, to make another plea, to tell her he did trust her, but he said nothing.

Which, really, said it all.

GAGE STOOD AS he was until he heard the car door slam and her tires spin on the gravel as she drove away. Though the sound of her leaving faded, his emotions did the opposite. Hot and bubbling, they surged through him. Anger, frustration, denial, insult.

They rose faster and wilder than the Pedernales River in

a flash flood. And churned up a shit ton of mud and debris he hadn't even realized had been lying beneath the surface the whole time.

And like that flash flood, they swamped him whether he was ready or not.

He wasn't.

How the hell had things gotten so fucked up? He'd woken up during his nap to find Faith in his bed, and after the best sex of his life, she'd finally told him everything he'd been waiting to hear. She loved him. They'd make a family together. God, he'd fallen asleep blissfully happy and it had nothing—or little—to do with the two orgasms he'd had.

It had all been because of the woman he wanted to spend the rest of his life with. The one who'd finally realized his feelings for her were real. The one who'd finally admitted she loved him back. The one who'd put her fears and insecurities aside and put her trust in herself. And in him.

And now, less than five hours later, it had gone to shit. And while it pissed him off that she'd regressed back to her fears, what really had him seeing red was the fact she'd called him a liar. She'd told him *he* was the one with trust issues.

"My ass." He snarled as he slammed open the screen door on the mudroom and stalked outside.

There was a section of fence Ryker had been bitching about lately. It was still standing, but the posts were starting to rot and lean, and he'd been after them to change them out. With Gage's current mood, taking a sledgehammer to the posts felt like a damn good idea.

He hadn't seen either hide nor hair of Roy, Cam, and Ryker when he'd stepped from the bunkhouse twenty minutes ago. He'd hoped it would stay that way. He really wasn't in the mood to talk to anybody. But he'd no sooner loaded the new posts into the back of the utility side by side when the three of them rode in on horseback.

Gage cursed his shitty luck.

They reined in next to the ATV. Ryker jutted his chin toward the posts.

"You going to fix that fence?"

"Doesn't it look like it?" Gage growled.

Ryker's brows arched, disappearing beneath the brim of his Stetson. "Maybe you needed a longer nap if you're still bitchy," he said before jumping to the ground.

Something in Gage snapped. He tossed his leather gloves on the seat of the side by side, glared at his older brother. "Maybe I wouldn't be so bitchy if you cared for anything else half as much as you do the damn ranch."

Though his gaze stayed fixed on Ryker, from the corner of his eye, he saw Cam dismount and hand both his reins and Ryker's up to Roy. The ranch hand rode toward the barn with the other two horses plodding behind.

"What's that supposed to mean?" Ryker asked.

"It means all you give a shit about is this ranch. About the only time you talk to any of us is when you're asking us to do something."

Ryker's green eyes were the same color as Gage's. He imagined his had the same flinty look in them at the moment that his brother's had. Just as his mouth was set in the same hard line.

"That's bullshit."

"Is it?" Gage tipped up the brim of his hat. "When was

the last time you talked to me about anything besides crops, fences, horses, or cattle?"

"We talked the other night when we watched the game."

"Yeah, about baseball."

"He's right," Cam added. "I was there."

"Don't even," Gage said with a sideways look at Cam. "You're no better."

Cam looked at Ryker. "You're right. He is bitchy."

Gage shoved Cam in the chest.

"Hey! I was just stating a fact."

Gage spun to face Ryker.

"You touch my face, and I swear I won't be the only one with a busted nose around here," he growled.

He was referring to the break Dallas had given him. The one that still had a hint of yellow on the skin underneath his eyes.

"I don't want to bust your stupid nose. I just want us to have real conversations. Is it really so much to ask? I live with the both of you, but it was Dallas who came riding with me last week when he knew I was upset. Dallas, of all people, the one I've seen the least of in the last twelve years."

He glared at the brothers standing before him. "Neither one of you asked or gave a rat's ass. I could've just been diagnosed with cancer and you didn't care enough to see what was wrong."

Ryker's face paled. "Don't fucking joke about that."

"I'm not joking. I'm stating a fact. We live together, but we're the next best thing to strangers. We've lost Mom. We don't know when, or if, Dad will wake up. We lost Dallas for over a decade. God dammit, how many more do we have to lose before we wake up? Before we act as though we actually like each other?"

When neither Cam nor Ryker said anything, when they simply stared at him, looking a little shell-shocked, Gage snarled. "Of course. Why should you two be any different? Dad checked out of the family for years. Dallas left. Hudson took off. Cam, you're only home when we're your last resort, and you…" he said, addressing Ryker. "You're so withdrawn I feel like I know Roy better than I know you."

"That's as much your fault as mine," Ryker answered. "You talk about Dallas following you out. Okay, maybe we could have, too. Or, you could have just said what was on your mind, and we could have helped you with whatever the problem was. You're not a kid anymore, Gage. If you need us, you can ask. You called Dallas when Dad had the heart attack and he came. You can call on us, too."

Cam nodded.

It was Gage's turn to stand there, speechless. Not because he didn't believe Ryker, because he did. And not because his brother's words totally surprised him, because they didn't.

But because they illuminated something that Gage hadn't seen until now. And he stood there, the bright light of realization blinding him to what he hadn't seen until now.

He was afraid. As a kid, he'd lost so much. He'd prayed his mom would live. She hadn't. He'd wished his dad would give him a hug, some encouraging words. Some love. And he hadn't. He'd watched three of his brothers walk away, even if Cam did wander back from time to time. Ryker had withdrawn into himself, and Gage was left alone.

He'd learned not to ask for what he wanted most because

he'd learned he couldn't be disappointed if he didn't put his faith in others. He wanted his family back together, but he'd been as responsible as the others for keeping it broken. He might have become an EMT to save others as he hadn't been able to save his mom, but it sure as hell hadn't helped him bring his family together.

Because he hadn't had faith in them.

Faith.

He blew out a breath. Holy shit. Faith. He hadn't trusted her, either. He'd accused her of not believing in him, but the truth was he hadn't believed in her, either. Yes, getting legal counsel was a good idea, especially when she'd first said she was giving up the baby. But he could have done it with her. Instead, he'd done it alone.

He could argue he'd only intended to make the appointment that day he'd stopped at the lawyers, and it wasn't his fault the lawyer had free time and had taken him into his office instead. But the truth was, he hadn't been thinking of including Faith when he'd stopped to make the appointment, and when he'd been taken in right away, hadn't even considered rescheduling until she could come.

Because he was used to doing things alone. He'd learned to look after himself when nobody else had seemed to care. So instead of reaching out to her and doing it together, he hadn't even mentioned it to her. Same as, instead of talking about his problems that night with his brothers, he'd ridden off alone. Yes, he'd hoped he wouldn't end up that way, that someone would care enough to follow, but he hadn't asked.

Just as he hadn't asked Faith.

Well, shit. Revelations were a bitch. Especially when they

were right.

Humble pie had never been his favorite, but Ryker had a point. Gage could have said something. Could have asked for help. The fact they were still standing there despite his outburst showed his brothers could be counted on.

He just had to trust them.

Wiping his damn palms down the thighs of his jeans, Gage screwed up his courage. "I messed up with Faith. She left here earlier. I have some groveling and explaining to do. I'm still hoping she'll take me back, but whether she does or she doesn't, we've still got a baby on the way that's going to need his uncles."

"We'll be here," Cam said.

It was as serious as he'd ever seen Cam.

Gage looked into Ryker's eyes.

His brother nodded. "Whatever you need."

Chapter Seventeen

G AGE HADN'T REALLY expected Faith to be at her grandmother's, so it was no surprise when he drove by the tidy house and Faith's car wasn't there. There was a chance she'd gone back to her friend's apartment in San Antonio, but before he went all the way over there, he wanted to be sure she wasn't licking her wounds somewhere in Last Stand.

He drove down Wisteria Lane, past the hospital and fire department. Turned onto Main Street. Though he was going slowly, he slowed even more as he passed the Carriage House on one side and August Wolf's wine tasting room, *Verflucht*, on the other. There'd been a bad accident there last year that had claimed the lives of two young people and left a small child orphaned.

He still remembered the chaos of that afternoon. The sight of the truck on fire, and that of the tour bus crashed through the window of *Verflucht*. Driving past it, he swore he could still smell the smoke in the air, hear the wailing of sirens.

Passing the site only reinforced his decision to find Faith. Life was short. He didn't want to waste any more of it.

But he didn't see her car anywhere. Not at the park, not at any of the restaurants, not even at church. He wracked his brain for places that were special to her, but he couldn't think of any. Other than her grandma's and the ranch, the only other place they'd been together was San Antonio and—

He breathed a sigh of relief. It made sense she'd go there seeing as how that was where she'd told him about the baby. Checking his rearview mirror for traffic, Gage pulled a U-turn in the middle of Honeysuckle Drive. Luckily, none of Shane Hightower's deputies were currently patrolling that street.

He turned left on Laurel, drove over Hickory Creek, then onto Hickory Creek Spur until he came to one of the turnouts. Slowing down, he signaled. He recognized her car the moment he turned onto the dirt road. She was sitting on the picnic table, her feet on the bench below her. Her hands were folded under her chin as she gazed straight ahead.

Over the tops of the willows, he saw the elementary and middle schools, as well as their park and sports area. Parking the Jeep behind her car, Gage got out of his vehicle. He stood for a moment, his hand on top of the open door, and watched her. She looked especially alone sitting there, and it made him feel even worse.

She'd been alone her whole life, and when she'd been brave enough to trust in him—after he'd promised her she could—he'd hurt her. It didn't matter that it wasn't intentional. The point was he'd wanted her to feel safe with him, to know she could depend on him, and instead, he'd failed her.

With a sigh, he closed the door.

When she didn't turn around, he had to assume she

knew it was him. Maybe she'd seen his Jeep drive by the school. There weren't that many blue Jeeps in Last Stand, after all.

He approached the picnic table. "I'm glad you're here. I was looking for you."

She continued to stare ahead. "I'm keeping the baby."

His heart gave a hard kick. While he was relieved to hear his child would have its mother in its life, he wondered where that left him.

Since she wasn't running away, he lifted himself up beside her. "You were right," he stated.

She turned. Surprise registered in her hazel eyes. "I was?"

"When you accused me of not trusting you. I didn't see it at first. I was sure you were wrong." He grimaced. "I might have gotten a little defensive."

She arched a brow. "A little?"

He shook his head. "I never saw it. Would have sworn on my mom's grave, if anyone ever asked, that I was a pretty trusting guy."

He scoffed. "After you left, I got all righteous. Told myself you were wrong. Then Cam and Ryker rode into the yard, and I took my anger out on them. Blamed them for us not being close, for them not knowing anything about me. It took Ryker to point out that most streets run both ways. That if I wanted to be close to them, I had to put in effort, too."

He blew out a labored breath. "That's when I realized that not only hadn't I had faith in them, I hadn't had any in you, either."

He reached over and took her hand. A little calm settled

over him when she didn't pull away.

"I might have never been treated the way you were, Faith, but our family wasn't close, either, after mom got sick. As the youngest, I always felt a little abandoned. A little lost. I grew to not expect too much because, that way, I couldn't be disappointed."

He squeezed her hand, brought it to his heart. "You're right. I didn't trust you. But that's not a reflection on you. It's a reflection on me. I told you earlier that I couldn't make you believe me. That only you had the power to believe and accept what I was saying. But the same goes with me. Nobody can make me trust. Only I can do that."

There was a reason he'd never really talked about his feelings before now. It was damn uncomfortable, and the words wanted to stay hidden where they'd been safe and protected for years. He dragged them out whether they wanted to be or not.

"It scares me, Faith, to give all of myself. To know that I haven't left any part of me protected, but I know I have to for you. For us."

His heart missed a beat when her eyes filled with tears. Was he too late? Was it not enough? But, Lord, he had no idea what more he could do.

"Tell me I haven't damaged this beyond repair," he pleaded.

FAITH COULD SEE it wasn't easy for Gage for open up in such a way. And that, more than anything, swayed her. As long as she'd known Gage, he'd seemed so easygoing.

When they'd bumped into each other that night in San Antonio, he'd just grinned and taken her in his arms. Then when she'd told him about the baby and that she was going to give it up for adoption, he'd just accepted that, too. Offered, so simply, to take it and raise it. Maybe that was why she'd found it easy to doubt him. He'd just been too easy about it all. Like he wasn't invested.

But she saw now that he was. That this wasn't easy for him. That he, too, struggled with his past, with doing what was right.

That he cared as much as she did.

It made everything a little less scary. Because while things could go wrong, at least they were both committed to making it work. Knowing that gave her the courage to reach for him.

With one of her hands held against his warm chest, she placed her other on his thigh, looked into his worried green eyes. And smiled.

"Of all the things you could have said to me, that was exactly right."

His muscles twitched beneath her hand. "Yeah?"

"Yeah. My mom wanders in and out of my life when it's convenient for her. As though it's perfectly normal to treat a child that way. And even after talking to my grandma, she still defended herself. Never acknowledged how her behavior hurt me."

She shook her head to clear her eyes. "All I ever wanted was for them to recognize the hurt they caused and say they were sorry." She squeezed his leg. "You did that. You took responsibility for what you did, and you apologized. You swallowed your pride and your fears, and I saw how hard that was for you."

She scooted closer until their knees touched. "I know we're going to have fights and disagreements along the way, but if we keep talking to each other, keep being honest, we have a chance."

All the worry faded from Gage's eyes. His whole posture changed. The rigidity faded from his shoulders, the lines marring his forehead smoothed. The mouth that had looked so serious before softened. God, she loved his mouth.

"I'd do anything for you," he said. "I hope you know that."

She brought their joined hands to her chest. "I do."

"And you know it's not just because of the baby?"

"I do."

His sigh floated on the breeze. He tipped his forehead to hers. "I love you, Faith."

She let the words fill her, lift her. It had been a weird, winding road to get where they were, but it had all been worth it. Because it had led to this moment.

"I love you, too."

Still holding her right hand, he moved his left around the back of her neck. Shivers danced down her spine as butterflies went wild in her belly. She smelled the clean scent of his soap, felt the heat of him pressing against her when he moved closer, when he lowered his mouth to hers.

It was beautiful and perfect. There in the Texas sunshine, the birds twittering in the trees, the only man she'd ever loved held her tight, kissed her as though she were the only thing that mattered.

With his mouth claiming hers, he slid their joined hands down her chest to her belly. There, he repositioned her hand so her palm was open over her stomach. He covered hers with his.

It didn't bother her that he was there for the baby. Because it was true. He always would be. But she also knew he was there for her. For them. For the family they were going to have together.

LATER THAT NIGHT, swaying on the swing on the front porch, the cicadas and frogs singing in chorus, Faith nestled into Gage's shoulder.

"Have you thought of any names?" he asked.

"Not really. You?"

"My mom's name was Abigail. If it's not your favorite, I'm okay with it being a middle name, if it's a girl, that is. But I would like it in there somewhere."

Faith hugged him close. He really was the sweetest man. "I like Abby."

He kissed her head. "Thank you."

"What if it's a boy?" she asked.

"How about you pick that one?"

She didn't have any role models or father figures she could name a son after. And she'd never been partial to the whole junior thing. She thought of characters in books, in movies. Actors and singers. And came up with the best.

Bracing a hand on his chest, she looked into his eyes.

"How about Luke?"

He tipped his head. "I like it. Is it after anybody in your life?"

She laughed. "Nope. Well, in a roundabout way. But nobody I've met. Though, I wouldn't be opposed to meeting him."

"Are you going to tell me who it is or not?" he teased.

"That night in San Antonio. Do you remember the first song we danced to?"

His eyes widened. "You want to name our son after Luke Bryan?"

"Why not? It's a nice name. He seems to be a genuine, nice man. And when I hear his music, I think of you."

Gage kissed her softly. "It's perfect."

So was he. Or at least, he was for her. Melting into him, she deepened the kiss. With her tongue sliding along his, she moved her hand slowly up his thigh. Even without him doing anything but cupping her cheek, Faith's breasts became heavy. Between her legs, she became wet and needy.

Before her hand reached any higher, her phone trilled.

"Ignore it," she said when Gage paused.

He pulled back. "It could be important."

"The only thing that's important is right in front of me. And," she added with a nip at his bottom lip, "will hopefully be on top of me soon."

Even in the shadows on the porch, she saw his eyes heat. Felt the grip on her hip tighten.

"Answer it," he said. "The sooner you do, the sooner I'll take you to bed."

"Deal."

Laughing, she yanked the phone off the small side table next to the swing, then did a double take when she saw who was calling.

"Who is it?" Gage asked.

"It's my grandmother."

"Answer it," he said when she just looked at the screen.

She accepted the call. "Hello?"

"Faith. It's your grandmother. I was hoping if you had some time tomorrow, you could come for tea. I've thought a lot about what you said, and while I know I can't change the past, I would like to change the future. If you don't want to, I'll—"

"No! I'll be there. What time?"

Once they'd agreed on the time, Faith ended the call. She set the phone down on the table, still a little dazed.

"What did she want?" Gage asked.

She dragged her gaze from the phone to his face. "She said she wants to move forward, change the future."

He brushed his thumb across her cheek. "That's a good thing, right?"

"Yeah. I'm just a little shocked."

"I'm not. The thought of losing you forever scared me into some much-needed soul searching. Obviously, it did the same for her."

Happy tears clouded her eyes. "Life's going to be so much better from now on."

He kissed her long and hot. "You got that right."

The End

If you enjoyed this book, please leave a review at your favorite online retailer! Even if it's just a sentence or two it makes all the difference.

Thanks for reading *Cowboy True* by Michelle Beattie!

Discover your next romance at TulePublishing.com.

TULE
PUBLISHING

If you enjoyed *Cowboy True*, you'll love the next book in….

The Tangled Up in Texas series

Book 1: *Cowboy Up*

Book 2: *Cowboy True*

Book 3: *Coming May 2020!*

Book 4: *Coming September 2020!*

More books by Michelle Beattie

The Frontier Montana series

Small town, Montana. There is no shortage of gumption and grit in these hard-working folks and one thing rings true for them all: they love big as the Montana sky. Strolling the boardwalk between the false-fronted businesses, locals are likely to meet ranchers, cowboys, lawmen, gamblers, saloon owners, and a woman veterinarian to name a few. Welcome to Marietta, Montana.

Book 1: *A Rancher's Surrender*

Book 2: *A Cowboy's Temptation*

Book 3: *A Sheriff's Passion*

Book 4: *A Gambler's Pleasure*

Book 5: *A Marshal's Promise*

About the Author

Award-winning author Michelle Beattie began writing in 1995,
almost immediately after returning from her honeymoon. It took
12 long years but she achieved her dream of seeing her name on
the cover of a book when she sold her novel, What A Pirate
Desires, in 2007. Since then she's written and published several
more historical novels as well a contemporary. Her pirate books
have sold in several languages, been reviewed in Publisher's
Weekly and Romantic Times. Two of her independent self-
published works went on to win the Reader's Choice Silken Sands
Self-Published Star Contest.

When Michelle isn't writing she enjoys playing golf, reading,
walking her dog, travelling and sitting outside enjoying the peace
of country life. Michelle comes from a large family and treasures
her brothers and sister as well as the dozens of aunts, uncles and
cousins she's proud to call family. She lives outside a tiny town in
east-central Alberta, Canada with her husband, two teenage
daughters and their dog, Ty.

Thank you for reading

Cowboy True

If you enjoyed this book, you can find more from all our great authors at TulePublishing.com, or from your favorite online retailer.

Made in the USA
Middletown, DE
13 July 2020

12560004R00170